"Say something

"Are you okay?" he asked. Mike leaned forward and put both hands on her knees. He could feel her warmth through the blanket draped over her legs. He wanted to keep her warm. And safe.

"I'm as fine as I can be. I'm not sick. I'm just... pregnant."

"I was afraid something was terribly wrong," he said.

"Well," Hadley replied with a short, humorless laugh, "this isn't exactly right."

A moment of incredible clarity flashed over Mike. He could make this right. He was good at fixing things. All he had to do was ask one important question and everything would fall into place. Without hesitating, he knelt in front of her and took both her hands. His knee still smarted from his fall on the ice, but he ignored it. This was the most consequential decision of his life so far. Betty sat up, alert to a change in the atmosphere of the room, and she wagged her tail expectantly, but Mike ignored the dog. He kept his focus on Hadley's face. Her lovely, familiar face.

"Will you marry me?"

Dear Reader,

It always seems like time flies from one Christmas to the next, but a lot can happen in the span of a year. *A Merry Little Christmas* is the third book in the Return to Christmas Island series, and it proves that choices during one Christmas can lead to a big surprise by the next one. Longtime friends Hadley Pierce and Mike Martin share a birthday and a silly marriage pact made years earlier. Soon they'll share something else—a little bundle of joy that will be under their tree by Christmas!

Christmas Island is in the Great Lakes region of the United States. Just off the Michigan shoreline, it has warm summers and snowy winters. It's a beautiful area with clear water, trees and rocky shores. Several hundred people live on the island all year, but Christmas Island really comes alive for the summer tourist crowd and the holidays. Day visitors travel aboard the ferry to the island, where they bike, rent golf carts, shop in downtown boutiques, enjoy the scenery and buy souvenirs of their excursion.

I hope you'll love your visit to Christmas Island and come back for the rest of the series!

Happy reading,

Amie Denman

HEARTWARMING

A Merry Little Christmas

—

Amie Denman

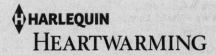

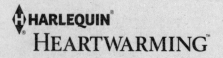

HARLEQUIN®
HEARTWARMING™

ISBN-13: 978-1-335-58484-7

Recycling programs for this product may not exist in your area.

A Merry Little Christmas

Copyright © 2023 by Amie Denman

For questions and comments about the quality of this book, please contact us at CustomerService@Harlequin.com.

Harlequin Enterprises ULC
22 Adelaide St. West, 41st Floor
Toronto, Ontario M5H 4E3, Canada
www.Harlequin.com

Printed in U.S.A.

Amie Denman is the author of fifty contemporary romances full of humor and heart. A devoted traveler whose parents always kept a suitcase packed, she loves reading and writing books you could take on vacation. Amie believes everything is fun, especially wedding cake, roller coasters and falling in love.

Books by Amie Denman

Harlequin Heartwarming

Starlight Point Stories

Under the Boardwalk
Carousel Nights
Meet Me on the Midway
Until the Ride Stops
Back to the Lake Breeze Hotel

Cape Pursuit Firefighters

In Love with the Firefighter
The Firefighter's Vow
A Home for the Firefighter

Return to Christmas Island

I'll Be Home for Christmas
Home for the Holidays

Visit the Author Profile page
at Harlequin.com for more titles.

This book is dedicated to my aunt Charlotte, aunt Kathy and aunt Carol, who always get an advance copy of my books when they have "girl time" with my mom. Thank you for your love, support and enthusiasm for my writing.

With love,
Amie

CHAPTER ONE

HADLEY PIERCE PRIDED herself on being a practical woman. She bought the heavy-duty garbage bags, changed her furnace filters and brushed her teeth after every meal. Proactive, practical and very seldom surprised by anything or anyone. So, as she stared down at the white stick in her hand as if it were a living thing, she didn't have the experience necessary to process the shock waves rolling through her stomach.

She sat on the closed toilet lid in her neat bathroom where the towels were lined up on the rack and the soap dispenser was never empty. An extra roll of bath tissue padded her head as she leaned back and focused on the shower curtain depicting a peaceful beach at sunset. Maybe she should get on a plane and go to that beach where she could hide from everything except herself and the mistake she had made after the island Christmas party.

Surviving almost thirty years on the planet without being a fool for love doesn't come with a prize, especially if the one time you throw caution to the wind erases all those other years of sensible living. Hadley sat up straight and held the stick up in the morning light. There was no mistaking the little pink lines that confirmed the message her body had been whispering to her for a month.

Motherhood.

Her phone rang, startling her into dropping the stick on the white tile floor, where it clattered into the vent of the electric baseboard heater.

"Oh, no," she said, kneeling in front of the heater. "No, no, no, you'll melt in there and it won't turn out well." She grabbed her toothbrush and used the handle to pry out the pregnancy test, and then she threw both the toothbrush and the test stick in the trash can under the sink. Her phone had gone to voice mail, and she leaned back against the bathtub rim, exhausted and half-nauseous from the events of the last five minutes.

"I can't be a mother," she said. She hated surprises and anything she couldn't neatly manage. Even her job as a bartender and server at the Holiday Hotel on Christmas Island had the same beauty and order as her house and her life. The bottles and glasses were always clean and always in exactly the same order. On her days off, her bosses, Griffin and Maddox May, filled in at the bar, and they knew the drill. When she returned to work, her tools and supplies were just as she liked them.

Babies were one surprise after another, a fact she knew from her sister's kids. And the older they got, the bigger the surprises. She swallowed, and as she steadied her breathing, her phone perched on the edge of the sink chirped to remind her of the voice mail. Hadley got up, reached into a bathroom drawer and withdrew a new toothbrush, unpackaged it and put it in the holder. The simple act felt like a victory over chaos.

She picked up her phone and checked her voice mail, just like any ordinary Thursday, and not the day she received confirmation of the wildly unexpected turn her life's road had taken.

Griffin May's voice greeted her. "Hey, Hadley, sorry about this, I know this is your day off, but Maddox's son is sick and I've got six couples checking in for the Valentine's Day weekend. That romance package was way more successful than I thought it would be and I'm wondering if you might be able to come in and help me out at the bar tonight for a few hours. Rebecca's playing the piano, so it will be a happy crowd. I'll understand either way but call me if you can. Thanks. Bye."

She'd never been happier to get called in to work and have something to occupy her mind. Not trusting her voice, she texted Griffin and said she'd be in at four o'clock. She'd walk to work, like usual. On winter nights, Christmas Island was quiet. Snow blanketed the downtown streets and made the lesser-traveled island roads difficult to navigate with anything other than a snowmobile or four-wheel-drive truck.

That convenient location a short walk from downtown had been one of the reasons she and Mike Martin had gone back to her place after the island Christmas party. And the snow-covered roads were one of the reasons he'd stayed. What else happened that night had nothing to do with safety, wisdom, forethought or practicality.

It wasn't even lunchtime yet, leaving her

plenty of time to eat something light, curl up with one of the dozen crocheted blankets her grandmother had given her and nap until it was time to walk to work. If she was very lucky, the bar would be filled with strangers who wouldn't notice anything was amiss with the lady dispensing neatly poured drinks and practical advice on things to do on the island.

She sure as heck knew what not to do, just in case any tourists wanted advice about having a fling with a lifelong friend just because they were both facing down the age of thirty, single and living on an island where it was always Christmas but there weren't a lot of opportunities in the dating department. And because they'd watched everyone else leave the party with someone and they found each other's company comfortable.

Apparently, too comfortable.

Grabbing a bath towel, Hadley opened the door that led to the back porch and yard. "Come in, Betty," she called. An eighty-pound black Labrador retriever bounded obediently toward the door where she stopped on the rug and held up her paws, one at a time, for Hadley to wipe off the snow. Hadley gave Betty a good rubdown with the towel and hugged her. "A lot has changed since you went outside twenty minutes ago," she said. "I'm going to need your help."

Betty licked Hadley's cheek, and, for a moment, everything seemed like it was going to be okay. She'd gotten Betty as a tiny puppy and done just fine training and loving her. That had to be a sign of at least some kind of fitness for motherhood.

Hadley made a turkey and Swiss sandwich on wheat bread and ate it in tiny careful bites as she watched the February snowflakes drift through the air outside her kitchen window. Next February, she would have a baby. How old would it be? She held out both hands. Forty weeks, a fact she knew well from following her sister's pregnancies and cheering her on as each week passed. Hadley counted the months on her fingers. October. When the autumn leaves flew and pumpkins decorated the storefronts of Christmas Island, she'd be sharing her life with another person. A tiny person.

Suddenly, tears filled her eyes, and she gripped the edge of the sink. Her life had seldom seemed lonely, but the idea of having another human tied to her, filling her days and nights, needing her… She felt a rush of warmth. Motherhood was more than just that stick that had clattered into the heater vent.

She would have someone to love. Someone of her own. Hers. She couldn't think about Mike's role in this. Not yet. She needed time for herself to process the thought of her baby first.

The unmistakable squeak of her front door opening roused her from her thoughts. There were only two people on the island who would come in without knocking, and her grandmother better not be out in the snow.

"Hello," her sister Wendy called. "I hope you're not busy, because I have the afternoon free for girl time. For once."

Betty rushed to the door and delayed Wendy's entrance into the kitchen for fifteen seconds by demanding attention and petting, so Hadley had a moment to pull herself together. She grabbed a paper towel from the rack by the sink and hastily dried her face. She looked at her reflection in the microwave door. Not good enough. She turned on the faucet and splashed her face with cold water as Wendy came into the kitchen.

"Are you okay?" she asked.

"Something in my eye," Hadley said. "Just a sec."

She used the dish towel to wipe off her wet face and forced a smile for her sister. "I was cleaning and must have gotten some dust in there. It's fine now."

Wendy tilted her head and gave Hadley a long look. "Are you sure?"

Hadley nodded vigorously, almost making herself dizzy with the effort, but it seemed to do the trick. Wendy opened her fridge and peered in. "Half a bottle of wine. That should do it."

"It's only noon," Hadley said.

"But it's a special occasion. Justin is off work this afternoon, and I have three hours away from any parenthood responsibilities. Plus, his parents are coming for the weekend, and I'm persona non grata when Grandma's around, which is fine with me." Wendy pulled the bottle from the fridge and got two wine glasses from the cabinet over the toaster. Hadley knew her way around Wendy's kitchen, too. Having her sister and best friend on the island was wonderful even though Wendy hadn't had much sister time since having three children in less than five years.

"None for me," Hadley said. "It's technically my day off, but Griffin asked me to come in because Maddox's son is sick and there's a group checking in for the Valentine's weekend."

"That's lousy," Wendy said. "What time do you have to be there?"

"I told him I'd come in around four."

"Good enough," Wendy said, pouring one glass. "Time for a movie. I just want to sit down and watch a girl movie without being interrupted and without listening for the baby monitor. I tell you, kids are a blessing and all that, but momma needs some time off. You have no idea how lucky you are to be in control of your life."

Hadley swallowed her relief. She could lay the entire story at her sister's feet. The timing was right. She needed someone to confide in, and they had the entire afternoon to talk it through. No one would understand like Wendy would. It was serendipitous having Wendy show up out of the blue just when she needed her.

"I can't handle one more second of drama," Wendy said as she headed for the comfortable couch across from the television in Hadley's living room, "And you're the only person who never stresses me out or drives me crazy."

Hadley poured a glass of water and grabbed a sleeve of crackers and a tray of cheese cuts. "You get to pick the movie," she said. "Anything you want, even if we have to pay for it."

"I haven't had time to watch an entire movie in about five years," Wendy said, "So I'm sure there's something on one of your subscription services I haven't seen. Ooh, snacks," she said, eyeing the tray in Hadley's hands. "You're the best."

Hadley sat next to her sister and propped her feet on the coffee table. Losing herself in a movie for the afternoon might be just what the doctor ordered. That thought stole her breath for a moment. A doctor. Her sister had an obstetrician on the mainland where she'd delivered all her kids before she and her husband moved back to the island a year ago. Wendy would give her the contact information. She'd get to that. Soon. Right now, a drama-free afternoon wasn't such a bad idea.

"Nothing with children," Wendy said, flipping through the movie selections. "I want romance without the complications."

Too late for that, Hadley thought, as her

dog flopped down on the living room carpet and all three of them settled in for an afternoon movie.

MIKE MARTIN WASN'T in the mood to go home for the night. His bicycle rental was wall-to-wall busy throughout the Northern Michigan summer, which included lucky warm days in May and all of June through September. Plus, there were October days that brought tourists to Christmas Island if the lake was calm and the sun was out. He made his money renting bikes half the year and spent the other half getting ready for the next summer.

With the snow falling outside, it was hard to imagine hundreds of bicycles zipping down Holly Street, carrying tourists looking for an island escape. The snow blanketed everything and made Christmas Island quiet. Too quiet. Even after a day of bicycle repair and maintenance, something he took seriously and did himself instead of delegating the job to someone else, he should be tired and ready to climb the steps to his apartment above the bike rental.

Lately, though, a restlessness he'd never known before had crept into the silences of his bike shop and the solitude of his home. Was it his thirtieth birthday that was coming at him like fog rolling across the lake, unmissable but obscuring everything that came after it? Or was it the irredeemable mess he'd made of his longstanding friendship with Hadley Pierce? If he could go back to the island Christmas party and say a friendly goodnight to her upon leaving the Holiday Hotel instead of…

Well, instead of what had happened. If he could have a do-over, would he?

Probably, he admitted to himself. If only to have his easy friendship back. He and Hadley hadn't spoken of that night. In fact, they'd hardly spoken at all except to exchange a pleasant hello or chat within a group. He'd taken to stopping by the Holiday Hotel on Wednesdays or Thursdays because he knew those were her days off and he could have dinner with some buddies without having to face the awkward silences between him and one of his oldest friends.

But he missed her. Being shut out had been like having the door to the family home slammed in his face. Hadley was his rock, a great listener, a steady force in his life and one of the few people who truly understood him. Unfortunately, she also had a perfect memory and a knack for organization, and he had no idea how long it was going to take for her to either forget Christmas or file it away somewhere.

The lobby of the Holiday Hotel was bright and cheerful, a fire burning in the massive fireplace and the stairwell gleaming with a fresh coat of polish. Piano music drifted out from the archway leading to the bar and restaurant. His friends Griffin and Maddox May had poured themselves into the aging hotel and given it new life, and they were making a go of it year-round with overnight guests, tour groups, and the bar and restaurant. Good food, a warm atmosphere and excellent piano music courtesy of Rebecca Browne had earned the hotel a welcoming reputation.

Life on the island wasn't easy, a fact he knew from long days running his own business, and winter days like this should be a reprieve from the influx of tourists over the summer and the weeks around Christmas. But those tourists kept the beautiful island on the map, and Mike appreciated everyone who stepped off the ferry—especially if they wanted to rent a bike. Having good friends like Griffin and Maddox and Hadley made the winter months cheerful, but Hadley hadn't thrown much cheer his way in about six weeks.

Mike peeled off his coat as he passed through the lobby and nodded to Griffin who was at the desk talking with some guests Mike didn't recognize. As soon as he entered the restaurant, he took a swift glance toward the bar, expecting to see Maddox May there because it was a Thursday. Instead, Hadley's gaze met his until she swiftly turned and zipped through the swinging kitchen door.

Rats. He couldn't just leave. Especially when every part of him wanted to sit at the bar and talk to Hadley just as they always had. Why had they made the fateful mistake of changing everything, and was it possible to reclaim their old friendship? The cowardly thing to do would be to either walk out or take a table far away from the bar. If only there were someone he knew sitting at a table, where he could pull up a chair and join that conversation.

But the only people there were three different couples, people who weren't locals. Taking a deep breath, he strode directly to the center of the bar and parked himself on a stool. Maybe this was what they needed. Get everything out in the open, maybe even laugh about it, and then go back to being best friends.

Almost immediately—had she been watching?—Hadley swung through the kitchen door and began arranging the glasses and bottles behind the bar. Her movements were slow and measured, much like whatever mellow piece Rebecca was playing on the baby grand in the center of the room.

"Usual?" Hadley asked without looking at him.

"I wish."

That got her attention. She looked up and tilted her head, mouth slightly open, waiting for an explanation.

"I mean that nothing is like it usually is. Not between us," he said.

Color flooded her cheeks and Mike thought she was going to scurry back into the kitchen, but then a hotel guest took a seat at the end of the bar, and she retreated to take his order. She was slow and thorough, and when she finally came back toward him, she gave him a small smile.

"Cold out there tonight," she said. "The special is pot roast."

"That sounds good, thanks."

"Draft beer?"

He nodded, and she poured him a draft before going back to the kitchen. In just moments, she reappeared with a steaming plate of roast and vegetables with a thick slice of bread on the side.

"Have you eaten?" he asked as he unrolled the napkin around his fork and knife.

"I'm at work," she said.

"I know, but it's your day off, so I'm guessing you got called in. And you look a bit…"

He wanted to say pale or tired. Where was her usual vibrancy? But he was afraid both those assessments might sound like an insult. "You look a bit hungry," he said.

She gave him a long look and he had the impression she didn't like him making any judgment about her and wasn't interested in his concern, no matter how well-intentioned it was.

"I'll eat something when it slows down," she said.

Mike glanced pointedly around the elegant bar and restaurant where candlelight glimmered on tables illuminating precisely eight people, all of whom appeared content. He'd seen plenty of busy days here, and this certainly wasn't one of them.

"We should talk about it," Mike said. "What happened at Christmas."

Hadley shook her head and put both hands on the edge of the bar as if she needed something solid to hold onto.

"I'm sorry," Mike said. "I shouldn't have stayed for that drink. I shouldn't have…well… done anything. You've been a good friend to me since we were barely old enough to know each other's names, and I don't want anything to change that."

"Anything," she repeated as if she wanted to roll that word around in her mind and examine it.

"Unless you decide to honor our marriage pact this summer," Mike said, jokingly. They had laughed about their silly high school marriage pact so many times over the years, that they would get married if they were both still single on their shared thirtieth birthday. Neither of them took it seriously, and he thought mentioning it might break the ice between them now. Where was her smile and the light that always gleamed in her eyes?

"I'm not going to marry you," Hadley said. "No matter what."

"Hey," Mike said gently, putting one hand over hers. "I'm kidding. We used to laugh about the impending doom of our lonely thirtieth birthdays all the time. Can't we go back to that place where we were friends through thick and thin? I miss you."

Hadley didn't pull her hand away, which Mike considered a good sign. It would be a better sign if touching her didn't evoke any reaction. But it did. What happened between them after the island Christmas party hadn't come out of nowhere. At least not for him. Maybe Hadley didn't—probably she didn't—feel the same way, and she was afraid he'd gotten the wrong idea about them.

"Friends," she said. "Just like the last few decades?"

He nodded. "I'd like that."

"That's all you want from me?"

"Absolutely," he said, convinced that it was the one thing that would salvage their relationship—to acknowledge there wasn't anything more special than a childhood friendship there.

"Okay," she said, nodding slowly. "Okay."

Soft piano music flowed over them, filling in the blanks in their conversation, but Mike had the impression he wasn't hitting exactly the right note. Still, this was their longest conversation since Christmas, so he had to be on the right track. He hoped.

"We have cherry pie tonight," Hadley said. "I'll set aside a piece for you."

It was his favorite, a fact he knew Hadley knew very well. This was a start, and as Mike tucked into his pot roast, he believed they were on their way back to their easy friendship. It was best that way.

CHAPTER TWO

SHE HAD SUSPECTED for a month and known definitively for a week. Seven days hadn't dulled the shock of discovering, for certain, that she would be a mother in the fall. But one thing she did know was that she couldn't keep the secret to herself forever. People were going to find out, and she wanted to control the rollout of information, just as she liked to keep everything else neat in her life. When people asked her what she'd like for a Christmas or birthday gift, she always gave them concrete suggestions. When someone asked where she'd like to eat, she chose the restaurant.

You're a lot more sure of getting what you want if you ask for it. That logic had worked pretty well for her, until it hadn't. She hadn't asked to be going on thirty, pregnant and unattached. She hadn't planned to dismantle her friendship with Mike Martin and turn it into something that would never be the same.

All she could do now was reach out to her family and friends, a few at a time, letting them digest the information in small bites so it didn't overwhelm her or anyone else. That kind of gossip could be controlled, right? She was going to start with her sister, Wendy.

"Do you want to get out of the house with the kids?" she asked when Wendy picked up the phone on the fourth ring. Was that crying in the background? Pots banging? A children's television show with an incredibly cloying voice singing a song? Hadley pressed a hand to her stomach and silently told her new baby that they wouldn't be watching whatever show that was.

"Desperately," Wendy said. "I'll do anything. Parachuting, ski-jumping, bingo at the fire station. What are you offering?"

"Ice-skating," Hadley said.

"Done. We're picking you up as soon as Janey stops crying, we find the TV remote and I find everyone's ice skates, mittens, snowsuits and lip balm. Should only be an hour or so."

Laughing, Hadley clicked off. Her sister had to be exaggerating. If motherhood was so daunting, why had Wendy gone for rounds two and three? Why not stop at one?

Not that it was always an informed decision, she reminded herself. She hadn't planned round one, and here she was, hoping she could manage ice-skating without vomiting discreetly in the bushes alongside the island inlet where locals met up on sunny days to skate.

In the spirit of taking the day's direction in her own hands, Hadley also called Rebecca Browne and Camille Peterson to invite them. She'd known Camille all her life, though Camille was slightly younger. Of the eleven graduates in Hadley's class, a few of the guys remained on the island, but none of the women had. When Camille brought her college roommate to Christmas Island two summers earlier, Rebecca had quickly become part of the gang. Marrying Griffin and working at the hotel as the piano player and bookkeeper had also helped Rebecca fit in with the year-round residents and their circle of friendship usually included advice, laughter, babysitting, shopping trips to the mainland, and cards and movies throughout the winter.

Sunny days were meant for outdoor activity, and Hadley felt better breathing in the cold clear air. Clarity was something she was craving right now, along with friendship and support.

An hour later, she was in the front seat of her sister's car with her nephew and two nieces strapped into their car seats in the back. Already pink-cheeked, eyes glowing with excitement, the kids bounced their legs and talked all at once. Hadley's dog, Betty, sat in the cargo area, licking windows and loving a ride in the car as always.

"I have pink ice skates!" Janey said.

"I know," Hadley said. "I got them for you for your sixth birthday, remember?"

"When I outgrow them, I'm gonna give them to Macey," she said sagely. At six, Janey took her position of big sister seriously, the wise elder to four-year-old Macey and three-year-old Aaron.

Instead of participating in the conversation, Aaron rubbed his mittened hand over the frosted window and cleared a space so he could watch the scenery. He was the only boy, and he was quieter than his sisters. Given the amount of talking going on from the other two car seats, Hadley assumed he was just biding his time, saving up his conversation.

"I hope it's not too cold for them," Hadley said to her sister.

"They'll be fine. They're probably baking in their snowsuits right now, and it's a good thing we're almost there because Macey will usually throw up in the car if she gets too hot."

Hadley was trying to be brave about the waves of nausea that had started to hit her without warning. Deep breaths, tranquil thoughts and saltines had saved her almost every time. But now she was starting to sympathize with four-year-old Macey in the back seat. Hadley took off her hat and unzipped her coat.

"You're never hot," her sister observed. "I better open some windows or we're going to have a mess in the back seat."

Hadley remembered her sister being squeamish when they were kids. Didn't like the sight of blood, hated even ripping off a Band-Aid, would never clean the cat's litter box. But now, she faced everything with a stoicism that motherhood seemed to have bestowed on her. Did that mean Hadley would gain superpowers like being able to tolerate her house being messy, spaghetti sauce on the kitchen wall, running late for everything?

She doubted it. She was pregnant, not in line for a brain transplant. There had to be a way to have a baby without upending her life and changing who she was. Especially since she wasn't going to have a partner. Over a plate of pot roast, Mike had made it clear that he wanted to forget the inconvenient obstacle that had gotten between them and go straight back to being just friends. If he knew about the baby, or rather when he found out, how could they ever go back to being friends? It would be impossible.

She was going to tell him. Soon. And that information would come with the assurance that she wanted nothing from him in the romance or marriage departments. All she expected was…what, exactly? She hadn't had time to figure it out. Growing up without a dad herself, Hadley didn't have a clear picture of that role. In fact, she had no memory of her dad at all. He'd stayed with her mom for the first year of Hadley's life, but when Hadley's mom told him she was pregnant again, he'd run and he'd taken a big piece of her mother's heart with him.

She and Mike weren't going to have that problem, as neither one of them would leave the island, but, boy, were they going to be two total amateurs going at parenting without a clue. Hadley cleared a patch of window fog with her mitten and looked at the passing pine trees covered with snow. Her nephew, Aaron, had the right idea. It was beautiful, and pristine views like that made living on the island not just worthwhile but magical.

When they got to the outdoor rink, windows rolled down and the girls in the back seat singing a song about snow, the first thing Hadley noticed was that the large group gathered around the ice included far more people than the handful she had invited. Panic seized her. She was going to tell her sister first while she asked Rebecca and Camille to keep an eye on the kids, and then she would tell her friends. And they would all encourage her and tell her it was going to be okay and then they would ice-skate like it was any normal day.

But that plan was out the window. Was the entire island there on this late February day?

"We're here," her sister said, giving Hadley a questioning look when Hadley didn't make a move to take off her seat belt or open her car door. "Are you having second thoughts about how strong that ice is now that we've seen the crowd?"

She couldn't honestly claim that. Not when everyone knew the relatively shallow inlet on the north side of the island froze early in the winter and stayed frozen, providing a safe ice-skating location where no one, to her knowledge, had ever fallen through.

"I…was just thinking it's a bit crowded, that's all."

"The more the merrier," Wendy said. "My children will probably knock people down and thin out the crowd pretty early and then we'll have the rink to ourselves."

"There's something I want to talk to you about," Hadley said, putting a hand on her sister's arm as she reached to unhook her seat belt. "When we have a chance."

"Is everything okay?" Wendy asked, her expression turning serious.

"Yes," Hadley quickly reassured her. Together, they had faced growing up without a father, and then their mother's death from cancer when they were younger. Their grandmother had held them together, too, and the struggle bonded them. But Hadley didn't want to worry her sister. An unplanned pregnancy wasn't like losing someone you loved.

Hadley's eyes filled with tears, something that had been happening to her frequently of late.

"Oh, no," Wendy said. "Something is wrong."

"No," she said. "It's not a bad thing. I'm—"

"Mo-o-om," Macey sang out from the back seat. "I'm really hot and—"

Hadley admired the speed at which her sister burst from the car and got all three kids out of their car seats and into the cool fresh air. *Maybe those mom superpowers are something to look forward to.* Hadley opened the rear hatch, let out her dog and unloaded five pairs of ice skates, a blanket, two folding chairs and a bin of snacks. She balanced both chairs against her legs as she closed the hatch, but it was clearly going to take two trips to the edge of the ice to haul the kids and the cargo.

"Let me help you."

Hadley knew that voice like she knew the smell of her grandmother's kitchen growing up—the kitchen that was her own now that Grandma Penny had moved in with her friend MaryAnna in a snug one-story duplex.

Pushing aside that thought, Hadley turned and faced Mike Martin. He wore his usual genial smile and had already tucked the snack bin under one arm and picked up both folding chairs with the other hand. For a moment, Hadley pictured him with an infant carrier in one hand and a case of diapers in the other.

How on earth was she going to tell him, and what would happen then? She wasn't ready. First, her sister. Then her friends. And then—she mentally chided herself for the order—the baby's father.

She swallowed. "Thanks. It looks like we're not the only ones who thought of ice skating today."

"Not by a long shot. But I'm glad to see you," he said, smiling. He looked relaxed and comfortable, and Hadley assumed it was because of their conversation the previous week, when they'd dismissed any lingering complications from their Christmas entanglement. He was happy to be let off the hook and get back to normal. She felt irrational frustration with him for a moment until she remembered he didn't know what she knew.

How much longer could she wait?

"Ready?" Wendy asked. She had Aaron on

her hip and Macey by the hand with Janey holding Macey's other hand. They were a little human chain vibrating with excitement about getting on the ice. Betty pranced beside them, also eager to join the party on the ice.

"Ready," Hadley said. For ice-skating, anyway. For revealing her pregnancy? Not so much.

MIKE SAT ON a tree stump and laced the hockey skates he'd had since he was seventeen and his feet had finally stopped growing. He wasn't serious about hockey. No one on the island was serious about hockey. They knocked around a puck a few weekends a winter, but there weren't enough interested skaters in an athletic age range to field a team. The frozen inlet hosted people looking for camaraderie, not competition, and Mike liked it that way.

"Got all your bikes ready yet?" Camille Peterson asked as she skated past on her first loop.

"Got all your fudge and candy made?" he replied.

Camille executed a neat spin and skated backward as she replied, "All of it. I'm taking next summer off and counting the seagulls."

Mike laughed. There was no such thing as a summer off, and none of them would want it any different. Owning his own bike rental was his lifelong dream, and it belonged solely to him, the work of his own hands, his own sweat. He stood up, tested the feel of his skates and sat back down to tighten the left one. It was then that he noticed Rebecca and Camille taking Wendy's kids by the hands and skating off with them while Wendy and Hadley stood under the bough of an evergreen in what appeared to be a very serious conversation.

Hadley's back was to him, but he could see Wendy's expression. Was she shocked? Happy? What was Hadley telling her? Oh, man. Did everyone know about his sleepover with Hadley at Christmastime? But if Hadley was going to tell her sister, whom he knew to be her best friend, why would she wait almost two months?

Was something wrong with the Pierce family? The sisters didn't have a father, and they'd already lost their mother. Maybe their grandma Penny was sick? He hoped not. She was a sweet old lady, practically a grandma to everyone on the island along with her friend MaryAnna.

Now Wendy was hugging Hadley. Oh, no. What was up? Should he go over there? Get involved?

He glanced over at Camille and Rebecca. They didn't seem concerned, but they were also busy, distracted by Janey's attempts to spin, and Macey and Aaron's efforts to stay on their feet.

Was Hadley drying her eyes with her knitted gloves? She was crying? He reviewed everything he'd said to her at the restaurant a week ago and at the back hatch of her sister's car a few minutes ago. Nope. Nothing bad. He couldn't be the cause of whatever emotions were driving her talk with her sister. Maybe it was a family matter and none of his business…although he was one of Hadley's oldest friends and he'd been one of the first people she'd told about her mother's illness. He remembered that day like a bad dream and he never wanted to see Hadley suffer like that again.

A commotion from the parking area drew his attention, and he looked over and saw Griffin and Maddox May arriving along with

Violet Brookstone and Jordan Frome. Violet was a fellow merchant who owned a downtown clothing boutique. She was someone with whom Mike shared advertising and promotional coupons along with other merchants like the Petersons with their candy store. Jordan, like many other islanders, worked at the massive Great Island Hotel perched on a bluff above town and visible for miles.

"Hey," Mike said to Griffin May. "Shouldn't you be working?"

Griffin gave him a friendly punch to the shoulder. "It's a Wednesday afternoon in late February, officially the dead zone for tourism. The hotel is empty, and the ferry boats are dry-docked, so nobody's going to miss me if I show beginners like you how to skate."

"Is my brother picking a fight?" Maddox asked as he sat on the tree stump Mike had just vacated and began lacing his skates. "He's difficult like that. I'm the good brother."

"Everyone knows that," Mike said. "Griffin's the smart one."

Maddox laughed and waved to Camille Peterson, who he'd been dating since before Christmas when they'd finally put their past behind them and rediscovered each other after a seven-year gap.

"My son is going to be mad he missed this while he's at school. I'll probably have to bring him back later today before it gets dark and let him take a few laps," Maddox said.

Mike nodded in agreement. "Poor kid. I remember being trapped in that island school on days when I'd have preferred to be outside on my bike."

After Griffin and Maddox tied their skates and put their gloves back on, Mike joined them on the ice and risked a glance over to Hadley and her sister. Whatever they'd been discussing seemed to be over now, and they were arm in arm headed for their friends and Wendy's kids. Maybe he'd read too much into what he thought he saw and there was nothing going on with Hadley and Wendy.

Sun slanted across the ice and a few brave seagulls sat on the frozen lake outside the inlet. On the rink, over a dozen locals skated, all of whom Mike knew like he knew his childhood phone number. It was comforting, familiar, and he never wanted anything to change.

Griffin grabbed Rebecca's hand and skated

with her, and his brother took Camille's hand and did the same. What would Hadley do if he linked arms with her and took her for a spin around the ice? He'd done it the previous winter, and the one before that. It was part of their easy friendship with no tension, no strings. Were they back there yet?

"Hi, Mike," Violet Brookstone said as she passed him and grabbed his hand. "Want to race Maddox and Camille?"

"The question," Mike said loudly, "is if they're brave enough to race us."

"Heard that," Camille said. She and Maddox paused on the far side of the ice and waited for Violet and Mike. All of them took a runner's stance, and Mike gave the countdown. He dug in and took off, still holding Violet's hand, and they got a big lead, but then he made the mistake of looking over at Hadley to see if she was watching. She wasn't. She was again in earnest conversation with her sister while Rebecca and Griffin skated with Wendy's kids.

What on earth was going on?

So Mike didn't see the gouge in the ice because he was looking at Hadley, only felt it with his skate a moment before he went flying headfirst across the ice. He let go of Violet's hand in time to save her, but he accidentally tripped Maddox on the way down and they ended up in a pile.

"Get off," Maddox said from underneath him.

Mike heaved himself off Maddox and flopped onto the ice next to him, but their skate blades were tangled.

"This is pathetic," Griffin said as he kicked their skates apart. "You bring dishonor to the family and the whole island." Griffin leaned down and offered a hand to his brother first and Mike second. "If anything's broken, fake it until you get home so you don't look like amateurs," Griffin added.

"Nothing broken," Mike said. "But I'm going to manfully skate to that tree stump and sit for a minute."

His knee burned and he was going to need a long hot shower to free up the muscle spasm in his shoulder, but he'd live to skate another day. Mike took short cautious strides to the edge of ice. He watched Maddox skate off with Camille, and if he was sore from the crash, he was doing a heck of a job hiding it.

Rebecca skated to a stop in front of him.

"Are you really okay? Griffin said you're almost as tough as he is, whatever that means, but I wanted to see for myself."

Mike smiled. "Almost?"

"That's what he said."

"I'm fine, but thanks for asking." He gestured next to him where a fallen log made a long natural bench. "Join me and pretend we're deep in conversation while I discreetly give my knee a chance to recover."

Rebecca laughed and sat on the log. "Sometimes I think I've landed on some magical island," she said. "I know it all seems normal to you because you grew up here, but for someone like me, from the outside, I still just want to pinch myself."

Mike also knew that Rebecca had grown up without a home, so the family atmosphere of Christmas Island was as new as it was wonderful to her. Marrying into the May family with their newfound inheritance from Flora Winter was a stroke of luck for Rebecca, but even luckier for Griffin and Maddox May who needed Rebecca's brains to manage their assets as they expanded their ferry and hotel businesses.

Rebecca had also become fast friends with

the other women her age on the island. *Like Hadley.* Mike glanced over at Rebecca who was smiling and watching the skaters.

"Does everything seem okay between Hadley and Wendy?" he asked.

"Of course. Those two are so close, best friends. I envy that. They always make me wish I'd had a sister."

"I just thought I noticed them having a serious conversation a while ago and maybe Hadley looked a little…upset."

Rebecca shook her head. "I didn't notice. I was skating with the kids. They're so sweet, I just want to take them home and bake cookies with them."

"I'm sure Wendy would let you. They're a handful."

"Is your knee better?" Rebecca asked. Clearly, she was ready to return to the ice, but Mike wanted her to stay just a minute longer. He needed to put his finger on what was going on with Hadley. Had she told her friends about that night he'd spent at Hadley's house?

"Yes, but I was just wondering if maybe Hadley was telling Wendy about something…"

Rebecca turned and gave him her full attention. She had earned a reputation on the island for being truthful, but kind, and Mike had the sudden feeling that he was going to get some straight talk.

"If you're wondering if Hadley and her sister might be discussing you, I doubt it," she said. "Everyone already knows about your little Christmas…celebration, so there's nothing new to say there. If you want to know if something's bothering Hadley, why not just ask her? You've been friends for sixty-five years, right?"

"Twenty-five," he corrected. "And some change."

"Close enough," Rebecca said. She grinned and skated off, leaving Mike with her good advice.

Hadley was skating alone, and she would pass his seat in just moments. He stood, ignoring the pain in his knee, and stepped onto the ice. As she passed, he reached for her hand, but he didn't have the momentum she did, and he tugged her into a tight circle, whirling her into him.

He had only a moment to react when she turned white and went so limp she would have fallen if he hadn't wrapped her safely in his arms. Stunned, he held her close. "Hadley, are you okay?"

She blinked and some color returned to her face. "Fine, you just took me by surprise and I—"

"Hey, sister," Wendy said, skating up and inserting herself between Mike and Hadley. "That was quite a spin, and I know you said you already had a headache. What if we sit out for a minute or, better yet, go back to my house and bake cookies?"

Wendy's tone sounded like a high school actor in a play. What was going on? Mike didn't have time to think about it. The two sisters skated to the edge of the ice where their shoes were lined up with a dozen other pairs, and they sat down. Wendy rummaged through the shoes and found both hers and Hadley's, and Mike watched as they changed out of their skates. Wendy did some kind of whistle and gesture for her three kids, and they made their way across the ice, escorted by Camille and Maddox.

In no time, Wendy's hatchback was loaded with gear, kids and Hadley's dog, who had been running around the edges of the ice. Mike pulled off his skates, and he didn't waste time donning his shoes. He padded across the snow in his socks and tapped on Hadley's window just as the car started to move.

To his relief, Hadley rolled down the window and gave him a faltering smile.

"I'm sorry," he said. "I didn't mean to upset you or make your headache worse."

"It's fine," she said.

"She's fine," Wendy reiterated, leaning forward and nodding at him.

"I'll call you later," he said.

Hadley pursed her lips as if she was thinking hard about a reply, but she didn't come up with one before her sister drove away, leaving Mike with his socks frozen to the snow and his mind bewildered.

CHAPTER THREE

"I ASKED CAMILLE and Rebecca to come over in a half hour. They can stay with the kids until Justin gets home from work," Wendy said as they drove toward downtown Christmas Island.

"Why?" Hadley asked. She felt as if she were in a snow globe being shaken by outside forces, out of control of her own world.

"Because it's Wednesday, and the island clinic is open. You and I are going there this afternoon."

As much as Hadley wanted to protest, she couldn't argue. It was a good idea. She'd need to see an obstetrician soon, but for now, a quick checkup with the visiting island doctor was the smart thing to do. She sat back and closed her eyes as her sister drove.

"Does Rebecca know?" She'd had a chance to tell Camille but not Rebecca before they retreated.

"Rebecca guessed—you know how smart she is. I hope you don't mind that I confirmed her suspicion. You're going to need friends."

Hadley let out a long breath. "You're right about that." Without opening her eyes, she reached over and touched her sister's arm. "I need you. Thank you for being here for me."

"I'm hungry," Janey said from the back seat. "Are we really baking cookies?"

"In a little while," Wendy said. "Miss Camille and Rebecca are coming over, and they'll help you bake."

"The candy lady," Macey said reverently. Because Camille's family owned the Island Candy and Fudge store downtown, she and her sisters were often called Candy Girls. Now that they were grown, the local kids knew the sisters as the Candy Ladies. Camille had taken over the family business and expanded it into a mail-order business with a branch on the mainland managed by her older sister, Chloe. Cara, the youngest, also worked in the family business, but she preferred the outdoors.

"She's an expert," Wendy confirmed. "She knows special tricks when it comes to baking."

In a whirlwind, they arrived at Wendy's

house, unloaded the car and let Betty into the fenced backyard to run around. Wendy got Hadley a glass of water and some crackers and instructed her to sit on the couch until their friends arrived. Hadley had barely had a sip when Rebecca and Camille pulled in and were soon parked next to her on the couch, offering support.

"Can we be honorary aunts?" Camille asked. "Chloe and Dan haven't had any kids yet, but I still think I should practice."

Hadley laughed and felt tension ease out of her shoulders.

"I'm excited for you," Rebecca said. "You'll have a baby by Halloween."

Camille cocked her head and gave Rebecca a questioning glance.

"I did the math," Rebecca said.

"Of course."

"Clinic time," Wendy said, coming back into the room. "Just a quick checkup, and I called so they already know we're coming. We should be back before the last cookies cool."

"We'll be fine," Camille said. "I know my way around a kitchen."

Wendy drove Hadley to the island clinic

where she'd gone for minor illnesses and injuries her entire life. The red countertops and three plastic chairs in the waiting area were as familiar as the downtown ferry docks. The visiting doctor checked Hadley over, took a set of vitals, asked a lot of questions and confirmed what she already knew before giving her a referral to an obstetrician on the mainland. The kind older woman put a hand on Hadley's knee. "Do you have people supporting you?"

Hadley nodded toward Wendy, who'd come into the examination room with her. "My sister and my friends."

"And what about the father?"

"He doesn't know."

"Does he live on the island?"

Not only did he live on the island, but Hadley knew every shirt in his closet and pair of worn-down sneakers he owned. His kitchen tiles and aging cabinets were as familiar to her as the fixtures in her own pretty house downtown where they'd shared meals and card games, friendship and sympathy. Mike Martin was more than just her baby's other parent.

"He's one of my best friends," Hadley said, forcing the words past the lump in her throat.

"So you'll be telling him soon."

"Yes," she whispered. "I have to. But I don't know what happens then."

The doctor squeezed Hadley's shoulder. "I can tell you what happens then. You two are going to be parents in about seven months, and it's a darn good thing you're already friends because parenting is as hard as it is wonderful. I wish you the best, and I hope to see you next time I'm on the island."

When they left the clinic, Wendy invited Hadley back to her house for cookies and company, but Hadley refused. She wanted to go home and think. With each day, the baby growing inside her became more real to her. She knew that she had friends and family, but she alone would have the role of mother to this child she hadn't expected but now couldn't imagine living without.

"If you'd bring Betty over later and maybe some cookies, that would be great," Hadley said, "I think I'll just go home and take it easy."

"Don't forget to take your wet mittens out

of your pocket and lay them on the radiator," Wendy said.

Hadley laughed. "You are such a mom."

"Just you wait," Wendy said. "And you'll be great at this, trust me."

"I hope so."

True to her word, Wendy dropped off Hadley's dog and a plate of cookies shortly after, and left only once Hadley promised to call if she needed anything. Hadley wandered through the upstairs of her house with its three bedrooms. She vividly remembered the day her grandmother had signed over the two-story house with the blue-gingham curtains to her. Grandma Penny had hugged her and told her someday she would fill it up, but Hadley doubted Grandma Penny had had an unplanned pregnancy in mind. She'd have to visit soon and tell her grandmother before she heard it from anyone else. What would she say? Would she suggest that Hadley marry Mike right away?

She sighed. Her sister and friends had not made that suggestion, but she could guess they were thinking it. She and Mike were good friends. Practically a family already. It wouldn't be an outrageous idea, but the fact that her friends hadn't gone there told her they knew she still needed processing time. Or maybe they did.

Hadley leaned in the door frame of the empty bedroom next to hers. She used the other spare bedroom for an office where she kept her laptop and paid her bills, but this one had only one chair in it that she couldn't find a good place for in her living room. Hadley sat in that chair and looked out the window. The house was on a slight hill behind downtown and faced the lake, so she could see glimpses of bright blue water between the taller rooflines of the downtown buildings.

Would she marry Mike? Certainly not. This was the twenty-first century, and she didn't have to rush into anything. She was perfectly capable of handling this herself. She had a good job and a home of her own. She was happy with her life just as it was, and adding a baby to it…well, she would figure it out. And as for including Mike? She would have to give him his fifty percent of the baby's time. If he wanted it.

Would he want it? The thought chilled her as she sat by the window, looking out at the wintry day. Mike Martin didn't seem like father material…but then, did people see her as mother material? Maybe nobody was parent material until they had to be.

She leaned back and closed her eyes and must have fallen asleep because it was almost dark when the sound of her doorbell and her dog barking awakened her. Hadley looked out the window and saw Mike's truck in her driveway. She took the steps carefully and deliberately, holding onto the banister on the way downstairs, knowing her life and Mike's were about to change irrevocably.

As soon as Hadley opened the door, Mike was sure the story about having a headache was a lie. He'd seen her sister hustle her away from the ice, and then Camille and Rebecca had left immediately afterward. Something was going on, and he cared about Hadley too much to just let it go.

"You said you'd call," Hadley said.

"I wanted to see you and make sure you're okay. I'm sorry I gave you such a spin on the ice today."

"It's fine."

Why did Hadley look so serious?

"Can I come in?" Mike said. "It's cold as heck out here."

Hadley stepped back and he followed her inside. Betty nudged him with her nose, and he petted her with one hand while he put his boots on the boot tray. He hung his coat on a peg next to Hadley's, and she dug her wet balled-up gloves out of the pocket and laid them on the radiator by the door. Mike watched her, knowing something was wrong. Hadley always put things in their place. She never let a mess linger on a counter, didn't have socks under her couch or yesterday's plates and cups on the coffee table. She was behaving out of character. Way out.

"Are you going to tell me what's wrong?" he asked, his voice low and gentle.

Hadley met his eyes and swallowed. "Yes." She turned and led the way to the living room where Mike took his usual spot on the couch and Hadley took hers on the other end. If the tension weren't so thick, Mike could convince himself it was a typical winter evening and they'd order pizza and watch television.

But nothing seemed typical. Betty lay down on the rug with her nose right at Hadley's feet. Hadley pulled a blanket over herself even though the room seemed plenty warm to him. Was she sick?

"I don't know how to say this," she said.

He leaned toward her. "Just say it. Whatever it is, I'm here for you. You know that."

"It's not just about me. It's about us."

Did she want to talk about their relationship? About what happened at Christmas? They'd talked about it a week ago, and he thought it was settled. They'd agreed to move forward as if nothing had changed. That one night was just a blip on the radar in their long friendship. What on earth was going on? Mike swiped a hand through his hair in frustration. It wasn't like Hadley to be mysterious, and he didn't know what to say that wouldn't be the utterly wrong thing. Why couldn't they just put everything back the way it was?

"I'm pregnant," Hadley said.

The words seemed to reverberate in the room as if Mike had fallen down a well. He couldn't breathe. Couldn't form any words that would make sense. Although everything made sense now. Something major had changed between them.

"We're pregnant," Hadley added as if he

must not have understood the entire truth the first time.

That one night, that holiday night upstairs from where they were now sitting. They were going to have a baby. Together. Hadley was an old friend, a dear friend. He cared about her. They shared a birthday and a lifetime of memories. Their thirtieth was coming up… The marriage pact… A dozen thoughts rushed through Mike's mind as he sat in silence, staring at Hadley Pierce.

"Say something," she said.

"Are you okay?" he asked. He leaned forward and put both hands on her knees. He could feel her warmth through the blanket draped over her legs. He wanted to keep her warm. And safe.

"I'm as fine as I can be. I'm not sick. I'm just…pregnant."

"I was afraid something was terribly wrong," he said.

"Well," Hadley said with a short humorless laugh, "this isn't exactly right."

A moment of incredible clarity flashed over Mike. *He could make this right.* He was good at fixing things. All he had to do was ask one important question, and everything would fall into place. Without hesitating, he got up, knelt in front of her and took both her hands. His knee still smarted from his fall on the ice, but he ignored it. This was the most consequential decision of his life so far. Betty sat up, alert to a change in the atmosphere of the room, and she wagged her tail expectantly, but Mike ignored the dog. He kept his focus on Hadley's face. Her lovely, familiar face.

"Will you marry me?"

Hadley's mouth dropped open. Of course, she was surprised. She'd probably expected him to run away or panic or at least ask for time to process the monumental news. But he didn't do any of those things. He did the right thing. He was completely sure, more sure of this than anything in his entire life.

Why wasn't she answering him? This could all be so easy...

"Hadley?" he prompted, giving her hands a gentle squeeze. "What do you say?"

"I say no. Absolutely not."

That well Mike had fallen down just deepened into a cavern and he had no idea how to find his way back to the surface.

"What do you mean?" he asked, incredulous that practical Hadley would turn down his sensible offer.

She pulled her hands back and tucked them under the blanket. "I mean I will not marry you, Mike."

CHAPTER FOUR

NOTHING MADE SENSE. Was he such an unappealing choice for a husband? Mike and Hadley had been friends forever. How different could marriage be?

Mike stood alone in his quiet bike shop where there were no employees and no crowds this time of year, just the peaceful feeling of waiting. Summer tourist season was months away, and he was accustomed to waiting for it every year. He should have been enjoying this calm before the storm, the silence of his bike shop broken only by the sound of his tools as he repaired bikes or assembled new additions to the fleet.

His parents and much older brothers had moved away years earlier, and they'd tried to persuade him to go, too, but he'd steered the course of his own life quite well. He liked the quiet winter, even though he had no income. It had worked out, stretching the summer dollars throughout the year. He lived above the shop, drove a ten-year-old truck and had hardly anything to spend money on in the quiet off-season, anyway. He got by quite happily.

Mike ran his hand over a baby seat attached to the back of the rental bike on which he was currently replacing the chain. He'd always marveled at those parents who somehow hauled their kids and kid-related equipment—quite a lot of it, it seemed to him—to the island. They rented adult bikes, kid bikes, pull-behind bikes and baby seats, and he'd always been amazed when the entire group made it back at the end of the day. How did they do it?

He was going to find out.

"Brought you lunch."

He turned toward the familiar voice at the side door of his bike shop. Tourists used the front door, but his friends and employees ducked down the alley between him and a souvenir shop and came in through the side. Griffin stood in that doorway just as he had a thousand times, but his expression was serious enough that Mike could tell he knew about the baby.

"I could eat lunch," he said. "I hope you brought yours, too."

Griffin nodded. "We've both got meat-loaf sandwiches and baked potatoes."

"Perfect for a cold day," Mike said. "Thanks."

Griffin put the food on the workbench, and Mike cleared more space and then washed his hands. The bike with the baby seat loomed right next to the workbench.

"I suppose you've heard," Mike said.

"Rebecca told me. She said Hadley told her and Camille it was okay since it's hard keeping secrets from people you're involved with."

"Huh," Mike said. "That didn't prevent Hadley from keeping it from me for a while, and I'd say we're pretty involved."

"She was probably trying to process it herself and figure out the best way to tell you."

"Well, she was way ahead of me in the processing department when she finally let me in on the news."

"You know Hadley," Griffin said. "She likes things to be in nice, neat little packages. Maybe she was trying to find the right packaging for the bombshell."

Mike unwrapped his sandwich and took the plastic lid off his baked potato. The food smelled delicious and he hadn't stopped working all morning. He was hungry, but not hungry at the same time. Did Hadley feel the same way? He should ask her about morning sickness. Had anyone made sure she got lunch?

Mike took a bite of sandwich and forced himself to chew and swallow. He got two bottles of water from the small fridge nearby and put them on the table. "What do you think I should do?" he asked his oldest friend.

"What are your choices?" Griffin asked.

Put that way, Mike realized his question didn't make any sense. Nothing did. Bicycles made sense. Chains, sprockets, wheels, handlebars. Seasons and even weather—those things made sense. His current situation did not.

"I asked her to marry me, and she turned me down. Flat out. Said no."

"When did you ask her?"

Mike cocked his head and stared at Griffin. "About one minute after she told me about the…our baby. I'm not going to shirk my responsibility."

Had it been just one minute later? He tried to remember the entire sequence of events that evening a week ago when he'd entered her house to check on an old friend and left fifteen minutes later knowing nothing between them would ever be the same.

"She may need time," Griffin said.

"Did she tell you that?" Mike asked. Hadley had worked for Griffin for several years, ever since he and his brother had bought the Holiday Hotel. They were friends. Maybe he had some insight.

"She hasn't said anything at work, and no one has brought it up." Griffin unwrapped his sandwich. "All in good time."

"We don't have that much time," Mike said. October seemed like forever away, a date lurking clear on the other side of the busy summer season. But the time would fly past like clouds on a windy day and he'd be a dad. He and Hadley would be parents. His eyes fell on the bike with the baby seat. Their baby would grow up on the island just as he and Hadley had. The next generation. He pictured his son or daughter in that baby seat, laughing as he rode around the island. The baby would reach its little hands toward the sunshine and blue sky, point and laugh at a seagull overhead.

Suddenly, that baby seemed so real to him he could almost feel its soft skin and hair brushing his cheek. He was going to be a father, an excellent father who cared about his child and took care of his family, provided for them.

"I have to convince her to marry me," Mike said, all the force of his love for his unborn child behind his words. "It's the best way."

Griffin let silence hang in the workshop as he ate his lunch. A few snowflakes floated past the windows and Mike waited. Didn't Griffin think Mike and Hadley should get married right away? He knew they were friends—heck, all the full-time residents of the island knew nearly everything about each other. If he couldn't persuade his best friend, Griffin, this was the right course, he'd have a tough time persuading anyone else—even Hadley.

"We have the pact," Mike said.

"That get-married-at-thirty-if-nothing-better-comes-along pact?" Griffin asked. He laughed. "You can't be serious."

"I am."

Griffin finished his meat-loaf sandwich and tossed the wrappings in a trash can at the end of the workbench. "Listen, I've never been in your situation, but if I were you, I'd just take a few weeks and remember to breathe. Check in with Hadley, let her know you're thinking of her and plan to be supportive, but don't go rushing over there with a ring and a bouquet of flowers."

"Is that what Rebecca told you to tell me?" Mike asked. Did Griffin have insider knowledge from his fiancée? Rebecca was in Hadley's friend group, after all. Maybe he should go visit Hadley's sister, Wendy. Wendy was his friend, too. They'd also grown up together. She'd be straight with him. There had to be a simple answer, a clear way to make everything all right.

"No," Griffin said. "And I don't think anyone can tell you or Hadley what to do." He paused and took a long breath. "So, we're all going to remember to eat lunch, get ready for tourist season, remain friends and plan a baby shower for September when the island quiets down."

"Baby shower?" The idea of it made Mike's mouth go dry. Diapers and strollers and cute little outfits with impossible snaps and mysterious flaps. What did he know about any of that or being a dad? Babies needed a lot of stuff at the start, and a good home. Not two rooms over a bike shop.

"Rebecca's idea. You and I can go fishing with the guys and skip the shower."

"Babies are expensive, aren't they?" Mike asked.

Griffin laughed. "I don't know from personal experience, but it sure looks that way to me."

"I'm going to need a second job," Mike said. "Something in the winter. I could even start now and save up. Do you have any—"

Griffin held up a hand. "I'll ask around, but you know how slow the winter is here on the island. You might be better off raising the price of your rentals and raking in extra cash in the summer."

Mike glanced around his shop. He owned the only bike rental on the island, which had been a financial boon for him for the last decade. If he raised his prices, all those tourists and families with three kids wouldn't have any other choice. Would they pay higher prices? Should they have to pay higher prices because he'd made a huge impetuous mistake in his personal life?

Not a mistake. He'd never think of his child as that. The only mistake would be failing to provide for him or her.

"You're too much of a stand-up guy to double your prices, but you could add more bikes," Griffin said as if reading his mind. "You're already selling out on summer days. It would be a risk, but it might be worth it."

Mike nodded, considering. Griffin knew all about risk. In addition to his ferryboat, he and his brother, Maddox, had bought a hotel and sunk all their spare time and money into it. They'd committed to adding an extra ferry, but that was before they'd stepped into a surprise inheritance that funded that project and then some.

Mike didn't expect a windfall inheritance, but he was going to step up now. His child deserved everything he had, and one of the first steps was to convince his child's mother that he could devise a financial plan that proved his capacity as a dad and a provider. With that reassurance, Hadley would have to see he was serious about doing his part.

"CLASSIC MARCH," Hadley said as she pulled her bedroom curtain aside. It had been almost fifty degrees and sunny the day before, but she'd heard the wind roaring as she went to bed, and the gray morning light revealed at least five inches of snow. Even though the forecast had warned her, Hadley still felt deflated like a leftover birthday balloon. Did she really have to put on boots and go to work? Griffin would understand if she called in sick. He was a kind boss and a friend. Which were both reasons she would never take advantage of him.

There would be plenty of days coming when she would legitimately need days off work. She was having a baby, which meant time off for herself physically and then when her baby had a fever or cold or needed immunizations. Her heart raced with a familiar panic. How was she going to manage it all? She focused on the upholstered pattern on the chair. Patterns, plans and organization. That was how she would manage. She'd always run her life that way and it worked. She'd given in to an unexpected impulse one time, and now she needed all her logic to put her life on the rails again and keep it there.

She sat in the chair by the window overlooking the driveway and street. "Deep breaths," she whispered to herself. It helped the nausea and the fear. Lots of women handled motherhood on their own. Her own mother had. And she wasn't alone. Her grandmother would love to cuddle a baby and would probably start on a knitting spree as soon as she found out. Hadley chided herself for not telling her grandmother already. She needed to do it soon.

And she'd have her sister, who had navigated infancy and toddlerhood three times. She would understand and help.

And Mike. Of course. He wanted to be part of their child's life. Wanted to marry her to assure his spot. Was that his only reason for wanting to marry her? He'd basically said as much, hadn't he?

As she thought of him, his silver pickup truck came down the street, moving slowly and blending into the fresh snowfall. Why was he out driving when all he had to do was walk downstairs from his apartment to go to work in his bike shop?

Mike's truck slowed even more, its headlights glowing dimly in the snowy daylight, and he parked at the end of her driveway. Hadley pulled her robe closed against the cold as she watched him get out of his truck, reach into the bed for a bright yellow shovel and begin clearing her driveway. He cleared a section and moved his truck off the road, and then continued clearing the driveway, tossing great shovelfuls of fluffy white snow alongside it.

Coffee. She should make some and offer him a cup as a friendly gesture. Wasn't that what he was doing, being friendly? Hadley moved unhurriedly—a wise pace in the early morning, she'd discovered—toward the bathroom, where she hung her pajamas in their place on the back of the bathroom door and then pulled on yoga pants, a T-shirt and a sweatshirt. She brushed her teeth and put her long brown hair into a ponytail.

Downstairs, she checked Mike's progress through the window in the front door and then proceeded to the kitchen where she ground fresh beans and loaded the coffee pot. She got out the blue mug he always used when he stopped by, and then she took the creamer from the fridge. The aroma of brewing coffee filled the kitchen, and the pot's gurgling competed with the rhythmic scraping of Mike's shovel.

Hadley pushed open the front door a few inches and the cold blasted her. She held up Mike's blue coffee cup and he smiled and gave her a thumbs-up and then he held up five fingers.

He'd come inside in five minutes, and she'd be waiting with a hot beverage to thank him. In past years, she was usually out shoveling early. But he'd typically stop anyway and help her finish the job, and she knew he did the same thing for other islanders. He was the resident good guy of Christmas Island.

Today, he'd shouldered the whole burden himself. And she waited inside with coffee instead of pulling on her snow pants and parka. It felt…domestic. As if they were married. During next year's snowstorms, she'd be inside with a baby or outside attempting to shovel with a baby monitor hooked to her winter coat. Mike would come over and take the shovel from her hand or offer to go inside and check on the baby. It would be…different.

She was pouring coffee when she heard him stomp the snow off his boots by the front door. She heard the door open and the soft clunk as he took off the boots and dropped them onto the tray.

"Hey," he said, his voice low and cautious. She could understand why. It had been just a week since she'd refused his marriage proposal, and yet here he was in her kitchen, snow coating his eyebrows from his efforts to dig her out.

"Thank you," Hadley said. "I hadn't gotten out there yet to shovel."

"And you're not going to."

She swallowed her irritation at his tone but tried to lighten the pressure in her chest. "I certainly won't since you've already done it."

"And I'll be back the next time it snows," he said.

Hadley handed him his steaming mug.

"In fact, I was thinking of picking up extra work during the winters. Maybe I could put a plow on my truck and clear roads and driveways for some extra cash."

Hadley didn't ask why he'd need more money. She'd already thought about the delicate balance of picking up extra shifts at her job and paying for childcare. For her, it might be a wash. Unless they teamed up. Marriage was not a requirement for sharing childcare and juggling work schedules.

"It's a thought," Hadley said. She tried to smile. "Diaper money, right?"

They were going to have to talk about these things. Diapers, car seats and playpens. And then, later, birthday parties and school shopping. She'd been thinking of their baby as only a tiny little bundle, but he or she would grow up and ride a bicycle and, one day, drive a car and go to college.

It was too much to process at once, so Hadley got up and opened a cabinet. She put four pieces of toast in the toaster her grandmother had given her along with most of the pots and pans and plates.

"I have peanut butter and honey," she said, knowing that was how Mike liked his toast.

"Whatever you're having," he said, getting up from the chair he'd just settled in. "I can make it."

"I've got it," she said.

Mike sat down again, and Hadley took down two plates, got out two knives and assembled butter, peanut butter and the jar of honey. When the toast popped, she still hadn't turned around to face her guest, and he'd sipped his coffee in silence. She neatly buttered her own toast and doctored his how he liked it, and then she put the plates on the table.

"No peanut butter for you?" he asked.

Hadley closed her eyes. "Can't handle it right now."

Mike's shoulders sank. "I'm sorry," he said.

"It's just peanut butter."

"No, it isn't. I want to make all this easier for you," he said.

"You shoveled my driveway."

"I want to take care of you."

Part of Hadley, a larger part than she cared to admit, wanted to melt. If she let him, he would take her in his arms, hold her tight and assure her that everything was going to be all right. He would make it all right. Mike Martin was her friend and one of the best people she knew.

It would be so easy, but she knew it would break her heart in the long run. If he married her from obligation because he wanted to take care of her and their child, what would happen? What if he would be missing out on the love of his life because he was married to her...or what if the love of her life was out there somewhere, waiting?

Even as she nibbled her toast, she knew

she was half lying to herself. She looked up and found him staring at her, his brown eyes sweet and concerned. Was it the situation? Was it the hormones that were robbing her of her usual neat organization of her life and emotions?

Or was there something else going on that she was afraid to name?

Without asking, Mike stood and got her a glass of water. He put it on a coaster and then plucked two napkins from the rack on the counter and placed them by each of their plates. She'd forgotten the napkins and the coasters.

He had remembered.

It was a little thing. She shouldn't make too much of it. But as she watched him finish his toast and drink his coffee, a question hovered in her mind.

When had she fallen in love with her best friend?

CHAPTER FIVE

HADLEY AND HER sister got to their grandmother's duplex thirty minutes earlier than they needed to be. It was enough time to tell Grandma Penny that she'd be adding another baby picture to the collection on the hall table. And it was about time. Hadley had carefully rehearsed ways to break it to her sweet grandmother so she wouldn't be too shocked, and Wendy had even helped out by role playing in the car on the way to pick up Grandma Penny for the island-wide St. Patrick's Day party. They were ready.

As they stood over their grandmother's chair, however, it was obvious they weren't surprising the older woman.

"I just have to finish this row and then I can put this down and put on my party shoes."

Hadley eyed the blanket her grandmother was knitting. It was mint green, certainly an appropriate shade for the holiday, but it was also pretty obvious that it was a baby blanket from the size. Hadley remembered her grandmother using the same pattern for all three of her sister's children.

"What do you think of this color?" her grandmother asked.

"I love green," Hadley said.

"Of course, I'll make another one when you find out."

Hadley and Wendy exchanged a glance. "Find out what, Grandma?" Wendy asked.

"Whether Hadley is having a boy or a girl."

"You know?" Hadley sputtered.

Her grandmother looked up. "The whole island knows. I was just very glad I wasn't the last person. I got to tell MaryAnna and, if she already knew, she did a wonderful job of acting surprised."

"Sorry," Hadley said. "I should have told you right away."

"As long as I have plenty of time to make a few blankets and help plan the wedding, I don't really mind. You were going to tell me when you were ready."

"I was going to tell you now, that's why we came early."

Her grandmother finished the row and

carefully rolled up her knitting, tucking it into an empty pillowcase next to her chair so her cat wouldn't get into it. Hadley had seen Grandma Penny do the same thing countless times, but now it felt special. That green baby blanket was for her. Almost every day, something happened that reminded Hadley that she was going to be a mother, and all the wonderful things that would go along with her new role. Her life would change dramatically, but it would also expand in so many directions she'd never imagined, like a flower opening in the sunshine.

"Since I already know and you don't have to dance around the news before finally telling me," Grandma Penny said, holding up her hand so Hadley could help pull her up from her chair, "we can head to the party early. I want to get a good seat."

Hadley and Wendy exchanged another glance, and Hadley could guess her sister was as relieved as she was. Grandma Penny had practically been a mother to them since their own mother passed away, and her approval loomed large on both their hearts.

Her grandmother hugged her close. "You'll

be a wonderful mother, Hadley. You're so sweet and organized."

"I'm sweet and organized, too," Wendy said.

Grandma Penny reached out a hand to Wendy. "You're sweet."

They all laughed.

"You're taking this news really well," Hadley said as her grandmother found her lucky green jacket.

The older woman shrugged. "Some of the best marriages started this way. You and Mike will be one of them."

Hadley and Wendy exchanged another glance, this one not so relieved.

"I don't know," Hadley said. "I'm not planning to get married."

"He asked, didn't he?" Grandma Penny zipped her coat and looked as if she would go into battle for her granddaughter if Mike had committed the sin of not asking.

"Yes."

"Good."

"But I said no," Hadley said.

"You have time to change your mind," Grandma Penny said. "In fact, I'd bet on it, and you know how lucky I am."

Indomitable Grandma Penny had always been optimistic, even during the very difficult loss of her daughter. Hadley's mother had only been forty-five. But Hadley remembered her grandmother always insisting their luck was going to change for the better. She was the queen of the island's church bingo, loved a scratch-off ticket and was the most likely person in any group to find a penny on the sidewalk.

Grandma Penny loved the annual St. Patrick's Day event so much that she had a wardrobe for it—her lucky pants, green shoes and zip-up cardigan. Every year since Hadley could remember, her grandmother had put on the ensemble and gone to the party.

Hadley and Wendy bundled their grandmother into Hadley's car. The earlier March snow had melted, and the island was blessed with a cold but clear night for the annual St. Patrick's Day party. Set up in a huge heated tent on the grounds of the Great Island Hotel, the games, food, music and camaraderie drew nearly every resident of Christmas Island. And if the weather was good enough for the ferry and small island plane to run, it brought in visitors for the holiday weekend, too. It was as if they were all awakening after a long winter and it was their first step toward the busy spring season of preparing for an even busier summer.

"Aaron will have a cousin not too far off from his age. It will be nice for him," Grandma Penny said as Hadley turned up the street that led to the Great Island Hotel. "Everyone needs a companion."

Did her grandmother think she needed a companion, too? Was that why she was certain Hadley and Mike would marry? Although her grandmother was almost eighty, Hadley wasn't convinced the older woman's ideas about marriage came from traditional ideas of propriety. Grandma Penny didn't usually worry about what other people thought, and she fiercely guarded her own independence, even choosing the date she'd moved out of her three-bedroom house and into a one-story duplex with her friend MaryAnna. If Grandma Penny's assertion about marriage wasn't from a place of old-fashioned thinking, though, what was behind it? She knew Mike, of course, and probably thought he was Mr. Good Guy. Everyone on the island did.

But did that mean he was a good marriage

prospect? He did everything right, but did that make him Mr. Right?

Hadley parked the car in the Great Island Hotel's lot. Green searchlights outside the tent lit up the night and beckoned everyone from the island. Maddox May was one of the event's organizers this year because he was the vice president of the Island Chamber of Commerce, and Hadley had heard plenty of talk at work about how this year's party was going to be one to remember.

She was certain she was going to remember everything that happened this year. She'd look back on it someday and think, *Oh, yes, I remember that party. That was the year I was pregnant.* Or, *That was the hottest summer, the year I was pregnant.*

Her life had a new starting point and Hadley realized it was forever going to be divided into the before and after. Her before had been pretty darn nice, if she did say so herself. But the after? She imagined herself bringing her son or daughter to island festivities and traditions, walking the shoreline, skipping rocks, throwing snowballs downtown, breathing in the aroma of freshly boiled fudge from the candy store and hearing the island church bells ring out on clear mornings, and she realized that her life was truly about to begin with another hand clutching hers.

She and her sister each took one of their grandmother's arms and guided her over the lawn to the tent. Inside, they found a table with a group of island women her grandmother knew. "Drop me off right here," Grandma Penny said. "And you girls go have fun."

"Are you sure?" Wendy asked.

"Just stop by every now and then to see if we need our plates or cups refilled."

Hadley laughed. "There are waiters for that. You just want us to check in so you can tell us how many hands of cards you've already won."

"That's a bonus," Grandma Penny said.

Hadley and Wendy joined a group of their friends, which included Rebecca, Camille, Violet and Camille's younger sister, Cara.

"We've got a table for ten just far enough away from the speakers that we can hear each other talk," Violet said. "Jordan put a reserved sign on it earlier today for me."

Jordan walked past at that moment and high-fived Violet without either of them even having to look.

"You two are always in tune with each other," Camille said.

Violet shrugged. "That's because we've been friends since kindergarten."

Hadley and Mike had been friends since kindergarten, too. They'd grown up together and shared nearly everything. They'd never tried to high-five each other with their eyes closed, but it didn't matter. They were about to embark on a roller coaster together that there was no getting off. Their lives were as closely linked as it was possible to be.

Was her grandmother right? Did the best marriages start like this? Hadley chewed the inside of her cheek. How did her grandmother know that? She glanced over to see her laughing and clinking a glass of something green with the women at her table. Maybe she didn't know as much about her grandmother's early life as she'd thought. What she did know was that she was always on Hadley's and Wendy's side, and her irrepressible sense of humor and purpose had pulled them through a lot.

It would help pull Hadley through the next difficult year of her life. She had her family. She didn't need to marry Mike Martin. And realizing over peanut butter toast that she loved him had no bearing on the fact that marriage was not in her carefully laid plans.

Hadley swallowed, determined not to think about peanut butter or anything else that made her stomach flip-flop.

"Who else is at our table?" Wendy asked.

"Griffin, Maddox and Mike," Violet said.

Hadley kept her expression neutral. Of course, Mike was part of the group. He always had been. She would see him wherever she went on the island.

"No Justin tonight?" Violet asked Wendy.

"No," Wendy said. "He knows how much I love coming to this with Hadley and Grandma, so he's cheerful about staying home with the kids."

Hadley wondered how she and Mike would work that out. Would one of them stay home with the baby next year? How would they manage the busy summer season with his bike rental going strong seven days a week and all her shifts at the Holiday Hotel? It would take a miracle to pull it off.

"Grandma Penny is wearing off on me, and I'm feeling lucky," Wendy said. "You go sit down and I'll grab a string of door-prize tickets we can fill out."

When Hadley got to the table, Mike got up and pulled out a chair for her. She sat, but he remained standing. He leaned down and his lips brushed her ear. "I'll get you your favorites," he said, and he started to walk toward the buffet tables.

"Wait," Hadley said.

Mike turned. "Don't worry, I know what you like."

"What if my tastes have changed?"

"Have they?" Mike asked, his voice low and his expression serious. "I'm sorry, I didn't think—"

"I'm kidding," Hadley said, forcing herself to lighten her mood. She was trying to be difficult, even though she knew it was silly. Petty, even. People knew about their Christmas entanglement. They knew about the baby. Heck, maybe the whole island expected them to get married and settle into her inherited house together with a tandem bike and a baby seat.

She was there to have fun. She wanted her friends and family and Mike to enjoy the night, too. "You know I'll want the green mashed potatoes, green beans and those little green shamrock cookies from Camille's family."

Mike's shoulders relaxed.

"But I'll come with you," Hadley said. "And help you carry everything."

IT WASN'T EXACTLY an acceptance of his marriage proposal, but Mike was happy to have Hadley by his side even though he would have made five trips to the table to get anything she wanted. It wasn't every day a man got down on both knees and earned a clear cold rejection, but he was putting it behind him.

They'd both had a shock.

Maybe being surrounded by friends and family in a night dedicated to springtime and good luck would thaw Hadley's feelings about marrying him.

"I bought a string of raffle tickets," Mike said. "And I grabbed an extra pen."

"And?"

"I thought we'd fill them out together," he said.

"You could put your name on half, and I'll write my name on the other half?" Hadley asked.

That was not exactly what Mike had in mind. "Or—"

"Oh," Hadley said, interrupting him. "I—"

They paused by the dessert table and stared at each other. Other guests were bumping past, carrying full plates and trying to grab a dessert to balance. But Mike didn't want to move. He wanted to hear what Hadley had to say.

"I'd like to put my grandmother's name on my half of the tickets. She loves winning, and I don't want her to go home disappointed."

"The door prize is a romantic trip for two," Mike said. He was taking a huge chance pressing this line of conversation. He worried that Hadley would turn around and hurry to the table full of old ladies who appeared to be having a marvelous time, judging from all the laughter. But she stayed by his side. "Do you think your grandmother would like to win that?"

"She could give it to Wendy."

"Or you," he said. Not that he wanted Hadley to go on a romantic trip with anyone else.

Someone bumped into Hadley from behind and she stumbled forward into Mike.

"So sorry," the woman said. Shirley was an imposing but dedicated member of the island leadership, and she had a plate stacked with green sandwiches and pickles.

"That's okay," Hadley said. "We're an accident waiting to happen standing here."

Shirley grinned but didn't say anything. Yes, the accident had already happened, but Christmas Island was a close-knit community and Mike knew no one was going to come right out and say that.

"I recommend the shamrock tea," Shirley said and then she moved off toward a table filled with goods from the island merchants.

Hadley gave Mike a half smile, and the tension around his heart lightened. He'd always thought Hadley was pretty in a good friend sort of way. One time in high school, he'd even kissed her. However, she'd laughed as soon as their brief touch of lips ended, and Mike hardly had time to process anything except for a mildly embarrassed feeling that it hadn't gone well. They'd gone back to being friends, but he'd still noticed as Hadley changed from a pretty teen to an attractive woman.

She was very pretty tonight in her green sweater. When she'd stumbled into him and her cheeks flushed pink at the contact, her beauty had hit him like an unexpected gust of fresh air. He hadn't proposed to her because of her looks, and they weren't wildly in love like Griffin and Rebecca or Camille and Maddox, but they were friends. They cared about each other. And Mike was sure everyone on the island expected him to do the right thing and marry Hadley, just as they expected the annual St. Patrick's Day event to get too loud and go on until the Great Island Hotel staff turned off the green lights.

"Let's get food and sit down before we cause a donnybrook by the dessert table," Hadley said. "I'm pretty sure that would hurt our luck."

"You weren't planning to gamble or take chances anyway, were you?" Mike asked. "I mean, you never have. You show up every year and watch other people waste a few bucks and get their hopes up for nothing."

Hadley shrugged. "I don't usually do anything risky, but…" She held his glance and he saw her swallow. People rushed around them and music and lights made a festive atmosphere in the massive tent, but Mike knew Hadley was thinking about a different holiday. Christmas. When they'd made a choice—was it a choice or was it a risky gamble?—that had changed their lives.

"Maybe playing it safe is overrated," he said, breaking the tension. "Unless you mean making the safe choice by getting out of the way of people who want dessert."

Hadley nodded and they walked back to their table where their friends occupied half the seats. Coats hung on all the chairs, so it was obvious the seats were taken but the occupants were off having fun or getting food and drinks. Mike looked forward to this event every year. He always supplied a new kids' bike for the raffle, green if he could find one, and he loved watching the excitement of people who won prizes. Every dollar went back into the community, so, in a way, no one was truly gambling or throwing away money. They were just redistributing it to people they cared about.

On the way back to the table, they passed Wendy who was headed for the buffet.

"Need any help?" Mike asked her.

"If you're offering, sure."

Mike walked Hadley to the table and set down their food and drinks, and then he returned to the buffet where Wendy was loading a plate for herself and another for her grandmother.

"Nice of you to help," she said.

"I actually wanted a chance to talk to you."

Wendy grinned. "Sure, catch up on old times, maybe see if my favorite color has changed or if I've found any great recipes online you might want to copy?"

Mike smiled. "I want to ask about Hadley."

"Gosh, I'm really surprised," Wendy said.

"I asked her to marry me and she said no."

Wendy nodded as if she already knew.

"So, I'm hoping you could—"

"No," Wendy said.

"You don't think I'd be a good husband?"

Wendy added five cookies to a plate and handed it to Mike to hold. "That's up to Hadley."

"But she's your sister."

"And my best friend, but we don't get in each other's business like this. When Justin was thinking of asking me to marry him, he talked to Hadley first to get her opinion." Wendy smiled. "He told me later that she refused to say anything except to tell him that my ring size is a five and a half."

"So what do I do?"

Wendy shook her head. "That's up to you

to figure out. You know her as well as anyone else."

"Almost," he said. "But I don't think a ring would make much difference. We're not starry-eyed romantics. It's more a friendship and a practical thing."

Wendy gave him a long look. "You're right. A diamond wouldn't make much difference."

"Maybe she'll see reason," Mike said.

"Maybe tonight isn't the time to worry about it. Let's make a delivery to Grandma Penny's table and then we'll pretend we never had this conversation," Wendy said. "But I wouldn't hate having you for a brother-in-law, in a practical and friendly sort of way." She turned toward the table of ten older ladies playing a spirited game of cards, and Mike had the definite impression he hadn't gained any footing with the Pierce family.

When Mike and Wendy returned to their table, Violet looked up. "There are some new games this year," she said. Violet turned to Camille. "Did you give Maddox those good ideas or did he find them on the internet?"

Camille laughed. "The internet is an unending source of inspiration, but I also copied some ideas from a fundraiser I helped with back in Chicago. The candy company I worked for at the time was involved with a few charities."

"Would that be the candy guessing game?" Rebecca asked.

"One of them. Also, the green wheel-of-luck game," Camille said. "The title gives it away, but it's true that all the answers to the riddles involve something green."

"Insider knowledge," Mike commented. "I'll almost feel guilty winning at that game."

"Don't. You have to pay five bucks to even play, and the cash goes to shoring up the break wall by the lighthouse."

"The lighthouse isn't green," Mike said.

Violet held up a hand. "And no one is making that ridiculous suggestion. Agreed?"

Everyone laughed and nodded. Although Christmas Island definitely had a fondness for red and green, there had been mistakes in the past when the island leaders got carried away. Painting the docks in the downtown harbor red and green might have worked out better if they'd considered more carefully the symbolism of those colors. Red channel markers were standard on the right when returning to a marina, green ones should be on the left. The misguided design had been caught quickly enough not to cause a nautical disaster, but it had been a lesson.

"Are you repainting your bike shop like you planned?" Camille asked. "It's finally good enough weather to do outside projects. Fingers crossed on no more snow."

Mike had planned to give his bike rental a fresh coat of green paint, two tones with red accents around the windows, just enough to imply the Christmas theme without being overwhelming. He'd budgeted and set aside the money for the paint and hiring a local teenager to help with labor.

But now? Shouldn't he save every penny for the expenses coming with the baby? He glanced at Hadley who was picking at the green-tinted mashed potatoes on her plate.

"I'm not sure this is the year for it," he said.

Hadley turned her head just enough for him to get a glimpse of his face. Her lips parted as if she were going to say something.

"Why not?" Violet asked.

Mike saw Camille elbow Violet, and he hoped for a moment the question would dissolve into the charged air of the island-wide party. Did it really require an answer?

"I'm wondering that, too," Hadley said.

Suddenly, Mike felt as if everyone at the table was scrutinizing him. Were they really going to make him say this out loud? Wasn't it obvious?

Rebecca held up a finger to get his attention. "Next spring, you'll be too busy juggling a son or daughter and getting ready for the summer. This is definitely your year to do this. If you want me to run the return-on-investment numbers for you, I'd be happy to come over and help with that."

"Return on investment?" Mike asked. His plan was more about getting rid of peeling paint than making more money. At least he'd thought it was.

"You need to think long-term now," Rebecca said. Mike had no doubt the entire table had no trouble following her logic. "Chess, not checkers. That's the way to keep cash rolling in and build on your success."

"My success?" he asked. Sure, he kept his head above water, even though he had to make almost all of his annual profit within a five-month period. And he'd been lucky. His bike rental was the only one on the island. What if some entrepreneur decided to compete with him? His profits would be slashed. He wouldn't be able to sustain the work he loved.

"Your business makes money every year, doesn't it?" Rebecca asked.

Mike took a swig from the green-tinted beverage in front of him. Everyone on the island knew his business, just as he knew all theirs. He didn't usually talk about financials with anyone, but he was a family man now, or would be soon. He couldn't think only of himself.

"Can I get anyone a second helping or dessert?" he asked. Retreat was the safest choice. The heat and noise must be getting to him. Impending fatherhood meant he had to be willing to talk about uncomfortable subjects like…baby stuff and…oh, goodness. Was he really ready for a major change in his lifestyle that had served him well since he graduated from high school?

Okay, he was ready in theory but not practice. But it was a holiday, for pity's sake. Maybe they could just relax and enjoy the party. Mike got up from his seat, but Hadley put a hand on his arm. Her fingers felt cool against his skin. Her face was calm and as her eyes met his, he felt a flash of understanding. She sensed his panic brought on by the minor subject of exterior paint.

"Can you bring us a pitcher of ice water and some bowls of pretzels?" she asked. "And then I want to tackle that game where you have to pop the balloons and reveal a message that has to be decoded."

Mike smiled. "Like balloon fortune cookies. But you have to make a wager first so you have skin in the game."

"I'm willing to stick my neck out if I have the right team," Hadley said.

"You are?" he heard Hadley's sister ask. "I thought I was the gambler in the family."

Hadley flicked a quick smile at her sister and returned her attention to Mike. Was she just saving him from an awkward conversation and being a good friend, or did she want to be with him? Did this mean she was reconsidering his marriage proposal?

They'd teamed up dozens of times in the past. Mike flashed back to the island Christmas party where they'd been partners on a life-sized Santa-themed chessboard. They'd had so much fun, they were still laughing about it later that night when she poured him a warm drink at her place.

"I'm your man," he said.

CHAPTER SIX

THE SUN SHONE, the blue water danced with the spring weather and the ferries were running a daily schedule now that it was April 1. Mike drove his pickup off the ferry, easing over the slight hump. He'd loaded eight new bicycles, still in their boxes, into his truck and held his breath on the passage to Christmas Island. The bikes were tied down, but their large boxes made an easy target for the lake wind.

He knew which bike to assemble first. The green one offered as a prize at the St. Patrick's Day island party two weeks ago had finally come in, and the lucky winner deserved a delivery on such a perfect day.

That winner happened to be Hadley's sister. When Wendy's name was drawn at the end of the party, she'd made everyone promise not to tell her husband she'd won the raffle and, incredibly, the island residents seem to have kept the secret. His birthday was coming up, and this was the perfect surprise.

Mike dialed Hadley's number when he parked behind his shop.

"Any chance you're free this afternoon?" he asked.

"Ye-es?" she said, a question in her voice. "Is there something going on?"

"I just came off the ferry with a shipment of bikes, and I'm planning a special delivery of your brother-in-law's prize."

"It's Justin's birthday," Hadley said.

"That's what your sister said."

"I baked his favorite peanut butter cookies."

"And I have a new bike that'll be ready in about two hours," Mike said. "I need to haul all the boxes inside and assemble his, and then maybe take the rest of the afternoon off."

Silence hung on the phone.

"Did you want me to go with you to my sister's?" Hadley finally asked. "I could take the cookies along."

"And then we could do something together," Mike suggested. "Like take Betty for a drive, roll the windows down, have dinner."

"You've thought this through," Hadley said.

"Which is why you don't want to disappoint me. If Betty could hear this offer over the phone, she wouldn't turn me down."

Hadley laughed, and Mike realized how good it sounded. There had been so much tension between them that they'd almost forgotten how to have fun and be friends, even though they'd been doing that their entire lives. Having a baby together didn't mean their happiness or their friendship had to end. Those should grow. The sunny spring day would be the perfect time to renew his marriage proposal, and this time, he had an extra ace up his sleeve.

"What time should Betty and I be ready to go?"

"Two-ish?"

"We'll see you then."

Mike used a dolly to move the unwieldy boxes from his truck into his workshop. Each year, he added to his collection of rental bikes and relegated some old ones to the parts-and-scrap pile. Heavy bike traffic around the island on warm summer days contributed to collisions and accidents, and he'd become a master of sanding and painting to disguise the wear and tear. Once in a while, a tourist mangled a bike too seriously for repair, and his insurance company got a phone call.

Mike whistled while he unboxed the green bike he'd donated as a raffle prize. He needed a busy but uneventful summer of rain-free days when at least ninety percent of his bikes left the shop with a paying customer. Was Rebecca right about that checkers-and-chess analogy that seemed to imply he needed to up his game for the long run? Did his future lie in bike rentals alone, or did he need to make a bolder move?

Golf carts? Guided tours? Personal watercraft? Mike shook his head, unable to wrap his thoughts around such a risky and major change. Instead, he focused on assembling the bike and double-checking the gears so it would be perfect for Justin.

After a quick shower and change upstairs in his apartment, Mike laid the new bike on a piece of foam in the bed of his truck and drove to Hadley's house. Hadley was in the front yard throwing a stick for her dog and holding one hand over her eyes as a sunshade as she waited for Betty to run back to her.

Hadley wore a loose-fitting sweatshirt over yoga pants. She was over three months pregnant. Was she starting to show it? Would she share that with him? He wanted to be part of every stage of parenthood. If she would just accept his offer of marriage, it would make everything so much easier. They could start sharing a house, a life, a health-insurance policy and a last name before their baby arrived. Didn't they need and deserve that time to learn how to be a couple before night feedings and teething and all the other stressful things he'd heard about began to happen?

Hadley heard his truck and turned to him. He hoped that smile was for him and not just because of the weather and her adorable black Lab. Betty bounded over to him and danced with excitement until he got down on one knee and gave her his full attention. "You love me, don't you, Betty?" he asked. If only the dog could persuade her owner to make Mike an official part of the family...

"She loves everyone," Hadley said as she approached.

"Not everyone."

Hadley crossed her arms and nodded. "You're right. She's not going to throw herself at strangers, and she's cautious about men she doesn't know well."

"Smart dog."

"Lucky for her, there are practically no strangers, men or otherwise, in the off-season. Still, I'm glad she's protective."

"She'll be protective of our child," Mike said, his voice low. He got to his feet. "How are you feeling?"

Hadley looked away for a moment. "I'm fine. I just… Well, you're going to notice it anyway, so…" She turned sideways and pulled her sweatshirt close to her body so he could see the slight swell of her abdomen underneath. It was all he could do not to reach out and lay his hand on her belly. The baby that seemed real to him in an abstract, future sort of way suddenly seemed so real he wanted to hold it in his arms. It would be months before he could do that, but holding Hadley in his arms would be wonderful.

If she wanted him to.

"It's exciting," she said, twisting her hands. "I'm not sure exactly what I'm supposed to be feeling, but every day there's something new."

Mike couldn't help himself. He opened his arms, hoping that her admission of her feelings and excitement might be enough for her to want to connect with him, even with just a friendly hug. He held his breath, and he only had to wait a moment before Hadley stepped into his arms, her head pressed against his chest, her wind-ruffled hair brushing his chin. He closed his arms around her and held her close, and he felt the dog sit on his foot and lean heavily against the side of his leg. To his great relief, Hadley wrapped her arms around his waist and flattened her hands against his back. As if she wanted to feel as much of him as possible in one hug, or so he hoped.

Mike and Hadley held each other in the afternoon sunshine until Betty let out a long loud groan and Mike felt Hadley chuckle against his chest.

"Lucky she likes you," she murmured. "But I think she's ready for that r-i-d-e in the t-r-u-c-k she can probably guess is coming."

"Are you going to spell things out in front of our little boy or girl?" Mike said, drawing back and smiling down at Hadley.

"I think it only works for the first four or five years, and then they'll be on to us," she said.

It felt wonderful, holding Hadley, his long-time best friend, in an embrace while they talked about the future. Not just the idea of a baby, not a result of a holiday indulgence, but a future child they would share. He was tempted to ask her right then and there to marry him, again, but he didn't want to take a chance on spoiling the moment. It was too perfect.

HADLEY SAT IN the passenger seat of Mike's pickup with a dog on her lap and a shiny new bicycle in the truck bed behind her. Her brother-in-law was going to love it. Justin's current bike was something he'd had since he was a teen, and at least two of the ten speeds didn't work, something Hadley had seen for herself when she borrowed it one day the previous summer.

"How many speeds does the new bike have?" she asked.

"Twenty-four. It's awesome. If Justin wants, I'll move the hitch for the baby wagon over to the new bike while I'm there."

Hadley laughed. "That sounds like a necessity until Aaron and Macey learn to ride competently. I think this will be the summer Janey takes off the training wheels, but the island roads are a little scary for a newbie with the hills and the potential for careening off into the lake."

"Don't I know it," Mike said. "I lost three bikes last summer to serious damage. The insurance company basically totaled them out like they would a car. At least no people were seriously hurt, but I have taken a closer look at the waivers I make people sign, just as a precaution."

Hadley laughed. "Smart."

"Your family was quite lucky at the St. Patrick's Day event. Wendy won this bike for Justin, and your grandmother won the grand prize of the romantic Bahamas trip for two."

"She did," Hadley said. "She says she's saving it just in case Robert Redford ever comes to the island and happens to be available."

"Good luck to her," Mike said. "You didn't win anything that night, though."

"But I didn't risk anything, either," Hadley said. Aside from the risk of acknowledging her feelings for Mike every time she was near him, she was playing life as safely as she could at the moment. Her own mother had played everything she had when she gave her heart to a man who wasn't staying.

Hadley didn't want to risk that kind of

pain, even though she knew Mike wouldn't run away if the going got tough. He'd stick it out, which would be almost worse if the love was one-sided.

Betty snapped at a bug flying past, swallowed it and then sneezed all over the inside of the truck.

"Oh, ick, oh, goodness, Betty. Yuck," Hadley said, swiping dog snot off her cheek. To her relief, Mike reached under the seat and pulled out a roll of paper towels.

"Thank you," Hadley said. She dried her face and hands and then wiped a string of slobber from Betty's mouth.

"You can roll up the window if you think it's safer," Mike said. "Now that Betty had her first taste of bugs for the year, she might be hard to stop."

"Good idea," Hadley said. She rolled the window almost all the way up, just enough for her dog to breathe fresh air, but not enough to grab a passing fly. "Days like this are a serious reminder that summer is almost here."

"You say that like it's a bad thing," Mike said.

"I don't mean that. It's just that the quiet winter days are nice."

Mike reached over and gave her hand a

quick squeeze. "Next winter, our days may not be so quiet."

"True," Hadley agreed. Instead of long walks in the snow with her dog, she'd be pushing a stroller. In the snow? Hadley considered it as they drove past a pile of dirty snow leftover on the side of the road that hadn't yet melted in the spring sunshine. Maybe a baby backpack. Or front-pack? How old did a baby have to be for one of those? She sighed. She had a lot to learn, but her sister would be her lifeline.

"If it makes you feel better," Mike said, apparently misconstruing her sigh, "we'll probably get at least one more snowstorm and weeks of cold drizzle before summer. There will be quiet times left before the May first starting gun."

"Will you be ready?" Hadley asked.

"We'll have to be," Mike said. His eyes dropped to her small belly covered by her heavy sweatshirt.

"I meant for the summer season," Hadley said.

"Oh. That, too, I guess. I'm still trying to decide if it's worth it to repaint my store. On one hand, I don't think anyone comes to my place because it's pretty. I think they come because I'm the only game in town."

"And you have nice bikes and fair prices," Hadley said.

"But I've been thinking about what Rebecca said at the St. Patrick's Day party. Maybe I need to think about the future. If someone else wanted to compete with me, what would I do? Would I have a selling point aside from the fact that I've been there longer?"

"You have free helmets."

Mike laughed. "They could offer free helmets, too. I think Rebecca is saying I need to make sure I'm putting money back into my business if I want to keep taking it out. I added two more bikes to my order of new ones this year, and I'm thinking of diversifying into mopeds or golf carts or something like that."

He looked over at Hadley, his eyebrows raised as if he were asking a question. He wanted her opinion? Although they'd shared rides, dates, secrets, heartaches and almost everything else over the years, he'd never asked her opinion about Mike's Island Bike Rental. Her first thought was to deflect the question and refuse to get involved. Mike's business was his own, and she didn't have the right to tell him what to do or give suggestions. What did she know about running a bike rental?

"You hate the idea," Mike said. "Is it stupid? I was afraid of that. I—"

"It's not stupid," Hadley said. "In fact, I think it sounds like a great idea. Not everyone wants to or is able to pedal the hills on this island. They might like something with a motor. But I don't want to get in your business."

"You're in it," Mike said.

"No, I have my job at the Holiday Hotel, and you have your work across the street. Just because we share a child doesn't mean we have to start asking each other's permission about our work."

"Not permission," Mike said. "Opinion. I value what you have to say, you know that. How many times have I asked you your opinion? Round up to the nearest thousand," he added.

"Yes, but that's always on little things. Like whether you should bring a coat if we're going somewhere together. You know I always pay attention to the weather forecast."

"I do," Mike said, flashing her a quick grin.

"And you ask my opinion about birthday gifts for our friends and where we could get dinner on a summer night where it won't be too crowded. That sort of thing," Hadley said. Mike wasn't alone in this. Lots of people asked her thoughts because of her reputation for practicality and thinking things through from several angles. She also had a good memory and recalled how many pumpkins were needed to decorate the downtown for Halloween or how much candy Mike needed to buy for the island trick or treat.

She always had things under control. Until she didn't.

"I want your opinion because we're connected as more than just friends now," Mike said.

"As parents," Hadley said, wanting to define the role in one neat word. Why was Mike insisting there was something more than that simple fact? They would share parenting duties as evenly and sanely as possible. Of course, her house would be home base for their child because there was a sunny room sitting there waiting and Mike lived in a one-bedroom apartment over a bike rental. They hadn't discussed housing yet, but there was really nothing to discuss.

"Not just as parents," Mike said. He pulled off the road just a quarter mile away from Wendy and Justin's house. Mike parked his truck between two pine trees and cut the engine. The blue water of Lake Michigan danced in front of them, and Betty pawed at the truck's door.

"Why are we stopping?" Hadley asked. Her brother-in-law's birthday cookies were on the seat next to her, his new bike in the back and they were almost there.

"We should talk," Mike said.

"You could come by the hotel tonight. I'm on duty, but it will be quiet. I think the special is pork chops and mashed potatoes. And pie. I think peanut butter pie, as a matter of fact, and I know you love—"

"About us," Mike said. "Not just about my business or summer or peanut butter pie or even our baby. Us."

Hadley looped a hand through Betty's leash and opened the truck door. Mike jumped out and hurried around the truck to hold out his hand. "I'll take her so she doesn't tug you into the water and get your shoes wet. My roll of paper towels wouldn't help much with that."

Hadley considered protesting that her dog was well trained and she could certainly handle the leash herself. She was pregnant, but she wasn't helpless. Just as she opened her mouth to tell Mike she didn't need his help, two ducks swept low, their feet held out straight below them and made loud landings in the shallow water by the shore. Betty lunged, and Mike grabbed her leash just in time.

Hadley let out a long breath. "Ducks are hard to resist," she said in defense of her dog who was always the best girl. Except when ducks presented themselves tantalizingly in front of her.

Mike gave Betty some leeway and followed her down to the water, keeping his feet carefully out of the lake. The ducks took flight, and Hadley joined Mike, standing at his side.

"There isn't any *us* to talk about," she said. "We're friends. You know I care about you just as much as I always have. And I trust you and know you'll be a great dad. We'll work it all out. Somehow."

Mike nodded and continued looking out

over the calm lake. His expression was so serious that Hadley was afraid he was going to claim that he was in love with her. And then they would really be in trouble. She wanted to get back in the truck and avoid talking. Hadn't they already talked enough?

"It's daunting," she continued practically. "Trying to imagine us both navigating a busy summer season next year and juggling parenthood. Other people do it, and we can, too. My sister's life looks like an utter circus to me, but she manages three kids with a husband who works a lot of hours, especially in the summer."

Mike sat on a log and Betty sat next to him with her nose on his knee. Hadley remained standing, feeling as if she were giving a lecture on how she planned to use her superior powers of organization to manage their way out of the situation they'd gotten themselves into. But she had to. It was the only way.

"There's another way," Mike said.

She held her breath, waiting. What could he mean? Did he not want to share the work of parenting, or did he think they should quit their jobs, hire a nanny, bring Grandma Penny out of retirement? In the dark of night as Hadley had stared at her bedside clock's glowing numbers, she'd run all those scenarios through her head. There had to be a way, or a combination of ways.

"You could marry me," Mike said.

Hadley let out the breath and relaxed her shoulders. Not that again.

"How does that actually help?" she asked. "Is parenthood easier because we have the same last name and matching rings?"

"It would be more than that," Mike said.

Hadley didn't want to hear Mike say he loved her. He didn't. He'd said himself that that wasn't why he wanted to get married. But if he told her he loved her, her wall of resistance would crack and she'd be left defenseless. Those were words she could not hear.

"A lot more," Mike continued. "For one thing, we're friends. Plenty of good marriages started out that way, probably the best ones."

Hadley didn't want to tell him that her Grandma Penny had suggested that plenty of good marriages had begun with an accidental pregnancy. That hardly seemed necessary to explain, especially since she was going to turn him down again.

"And we trust each other, know each other

so well I can probably guess what you had for lunch today," Mike added.

"And I can guess you probably didn't have lunch because you were so excited about your new order of bikes that you worked straight through and didn't eat. You'll have a headache tonight because you don't remember to stop and drink water when you're busy."

Mike grinned. "See?"

Hadley shrugged. "That doesn't prove anything." Or did it? Her grandmother's words echoed in her head. Mike's words were starting to burrow their way into her practical brain. She was in dangerous territory. She'd always imagined she'd marry some day to some nice, sensible, not too dramatic man. Was she really going to live in that lovely three-bedroom house alone until she became devoted to church bingo and knew seventy-five years of island history personally because she'd lived it?

If she were going to marry someone, he'd be someone like…well, like Mike. He was a good guy. Funny, handsome, hardworking, a good friend, loyal, a dog person. There had even been a few times when the light was just right when he looked at her in a way that made her suspect he might...care for her.

"I know I sprung a proposal on you fast the night you told me about the baby. I'm sorry about that. I was shocked and my first thought was how to fix things and make it right."

"I was shocked, too," Hadley said softly. They'd both been through a lot in the past few months, and the next few weren't going to be any easier.

"So I wasn't thinking that night, but I've had some time to think since then, and I think I have a compelling reason why you should marry me. The best reason," he added, looking pleased with himself as if he were about to get what he wanted. He stood up and Betty got up, too, clearly expecting something interesting to happen.

Hadley waited. If he told her he loved her, what would she say? Would she let down her guard and—

"The pact," Mike said. "Our thirtieth birthdays are coming up fast, and we made that compact that we'd get married if no one else had the brains to snap us up by the time we turned thirty."

"The marriage pact we made ten years

ago?" Hadley asked. She felt as if she were a pillow that someone had shaken all the stuffing out of. Empty. But she also felt surprised. Relieved?

"I think it was eleven going on twelve years ago," Mike said. "But it's still good. I'd like to invoke the pact."

"No," Hadley said.

"You're a practical person. You keep your promises. You make decisions based on facts and logic," Mike said. "What could be more logical than this?"

Hadley stared at him. This proposal was even worse than the last one, and he wasn't even down on one knee this time. He wanted to marry her because they were turning thirty and it was practical, logical and the fulfillment of a stupid joke from when they were too young to know that thirty wasn't where life ended. That there would be joy and happiness and chances to fall in love at any age.

"No," Hadley repeated, unable to even explain to Mike how hollow his proposal was. She turned and headed for his truck, hoping that he wouldn't see the tears pooling in her eyes. It was hormones, she persuaded herself as she held open the door and let Betty jump in first. Those tears weren't because she'd received two marriage proposals in a month's time, and neither had come from a place of all-consuming, albeit dangerous, love—the kind of love that brought tears to a person's eyes against her will.

CHAPTER SEVEN

HADLEY HELD OPEN the back door while Maddox and Griffin rolled case after case of supplies into the hotel. It was still early in April, but most island businesses began stocking up for the summer as soon as transportation via boat became safe and easy. Owning a business where everything needs to arrive by ferry requires careful planning, which was something Hadley could appreciate. She'd been looking forward to this week just as she had every year because it was checklist, organization and spreadsheet heaven.

Her kind of thing, and just what she needed in a world that had become a whirlwind of saltine crackers and marriage proposals.

Two proposals. Both an easy no.

"Do you want these cases lined up along the south wall like we did last year?" Maddox asked.

"Yes," Hadley said. "I'll check them off

on the packing slip and invoice, and then I'll move the boxes to storage."

Maddox exchanged a look with Griffin, and Hadley knew what was coming.

"I'm not an invalid just because I'm pregnant," she said. "I can move a box."

Griffin shook his head. "We have a lot of boxes. You haven't seen what's coming off the ferry."

"There's a lot, and they're really heavy," Maddox said, piling on with his brother.

"And—" Griffin began but stopped.

"And what?" Hadley asked.

"We sort of promised we wouldn't let you lift anything."

"Promised who?"

Both brothers avoided looking at her.

"Let me guess. Mike."

"He was at the dock getting an order, too," Griffin said. "He knows you love unpacking shipments and organizing stuff."

"Everyone knows that," Hadley said. Just because Mike thought he wanted to sit in front of the fireplace with her on winter nights for the rest of their lives did not mean he knew her better than anyone else.

He just knew *some* things about her. Like

how much she liked riding with the windows down, finding the first bulbs pushing up in the springtime or having an ice-cold orange soda by the boat docks on summer nights. Her sister didn't garden, her grandmother liked the windows rolled up and Hadley never drank an orange soda with anyone else. It was just their thing.

Griffin interrupted her thoughts. "Mike said he'd come over personally and help you put all these boxes away later today."

Hadley took a deep breath and let it out. Her head felt heavy, and her pulse drummed in her ears. She rubbed her forehead, trying to shove away the dizziness that had bothered her all week.

"Are you okay?" Maddox asked. "Maybe you should sit down. You could use the rolling chair and wheel around to check stuff off. We could prop open the door and you wouldn't have to hold it."

He was being kind and friendly. Both brothers were like that. She appreciated their concern, but she hated the feeling that her life was out of control, her body not entirely her own. Not that she minded that… Sharing her body and knowing there was a life growing right there under her sweatshirt's Christmas Island graphic was unlike anything she'd ever experienced. She put a hand over the image of the island's historic downtown and felt the small bump underneath.

"Don't cry," Griffin said. "I'm sorry."

Hadley hadn't even realized tears were spilling from her eyes.

"It's okay," she said, swiping her tears. "It's just that you're being so nice and I feel so... useless."

"Hardly," Maddox said. "You're making a whole person. We're just hauling boxes of food and drinks off the ferry."

Hadley laughed. "You're right. I really am busy making this person. Maybe I should take the whole summer off."

"That's the spirit," Griffin said. "But you know we'd be lost without you. Let's go with the rolling-chair-inventory plan while I make Maddox carry the heavy stuff inside."

It was a little thing, surrendering on carrying boxes. Hadley relaxed her shoulders and tried to let it go. It was just for this year. Next year, she might have a playpen set up in the corner of the restaurant while she helped unpack and store supplies. Either way, Griffin's words bolstered her. They'd be lost without her.

"Just make sure you give me all the packing slips," she said. "Even the ones they put on the bottom of the box just to test you."

Maddox shoved a brick against the back door to prop it open. "Yes, ma'am," he said, giving her a mock salute as he ducked outside to get more boxes.

Hadley pulled up the spreadsheet with their bulk order, adjusted the margins so it would fit on the fewest sheets of paper and printed it. The order included cases of bottles for the bar that would last, if her records were correct, until the halfway point of summer. To an outsider, it might not make sense to lay out so much money and use up storage space, and if their business were in a nice town on the mainland, they wouldn't.

But when summer days got busy, receiving a huge shipment at the dock and then hauling it and organizing it would make the days a whole lot longer. They'd still have to restock in a big way at least two more times before the island quieted down in the fall, and there would be daily deliveries of fresh ingredients. It was fun, working in a busy island hotel and restaurant where people came and went even though the weekly specials remained the same. Only the locals noticed that every Tuesday had an identical menu, but they politely ignored it as part of the compact of those who live in vacationland.

Hadley took her printout and laid it on the counter next to the stack of packing slips Maddox and Griffin had begun to accumulate. She checked off items, slicing open each box just to see for herself that there really were eighteen jars of pickles or twenty-four bottles of wine. The boxes were stacking up and she found herself with downtime while she waited for Maddox and Griffin to bring more. It was so tempting to move them herself, but even bending over to cut open a box made her head swim.

She heard the back door open but didn't look up from tracking down two mysterious jars of raspberry jam that had been packed separately from the rest, making her believe initially they'd been shorted. It was satisfying to check them off the list.

"I'm glad you're sitting down," Mike said.

Hadley spun around and then regretted it instantly. She put one hand on the edge of the bar near her stool to steady herself, but she put on a friendly nothing's-amiss smile.

"Why, do you have shocking news? Is someone unexpectedly pregnant?"

Mike laughed and then leaned an elbow on the bar right next to Hadley and gave her a long look. "I meant I was glad you're sitting down because I don't want you to overdo it. This isn't the summer for working long hours and extra shifts."

He was being nice and caring, and his eyes were soft and sweet, but Hadley battled irritation, anyway. She was an adult. Yes, the baby was theirs, but her body was hers. She knew when she needed to sit down. She also knew she needed those long hours and extra shifts to save up money. How else would she manage childcare and a full-time job? This was her last summer to pick up shifts, sacrificing nothing but her own leisure time.

"I'm sorry," he said quietly.

"About what?"

He raised one shoulder and then sat down next to her. He folded his hands on the bar and looked straight ahead as if it were easier to talk without looking directly at her, even though they were both reflected in the mirror behind the bar.

"A little bit of everything. I'm sorry I botched a proposal so bad you gave me a hard no. Twice."

Hadley felt as if she should reassure him it wasn't his fault. He seemed to need a kind word. Was the pressure of impending fatherhood getting to him? Or was something else going on?

She wanted to tell him he hadn't made a mess of the proposals, but that would have been a lie. He had. Rushing into marriage as a quick fix or, worse yet, to honor a teenage pact was a huge mistake. Love was the only reason two people should get married. And that was the worst reason in the world if it was one-sided.

She met his gaze in the mirror behind the bar and smiled at him, but she could see her smile was a sad one. This was not going to work.

She reached over and put her hand on his. "We can't sit here at the bar and mope," she said. "It's pathetic."

A hint of a smile replaced his serious expression, and she realized hers matched it.

She looked away from the mirror and swiveled her stool so she could face him. He did the same and she put her hands on his knees.

"I'll admit I was irritated that you conspired with Griffin and Maddox to steal some of the glory of the big shipment day away from me, but I'll let you make it up to me if you want."

Mike put a hand over his heart. "Can I be so lucky that you're going to let me haul heavy boxes and be bossed around for the rest of the day?"

"Yes."

"I could die of happiness," he said, his eyes crinkling at the corners.

"Don't do that," Hadley said. "I'm going to need you to put training wheels on a bike someday for our little boy or girl. Who's better qualified than you?"

He laughed. "Absolutely no one. And now I better do what I promised and start stowing boxes."

Hadley pointed to cases of wine. "Those first because they're expensive and I don't want you getting tired and dropping things."

"I won't let you down."

No matter how tired he was after working

in his shop all day and now helping her, Hadley knew Mike would never let her down. It was one of the things she loved about him.

MIKE SPUN THE wheel of the bike he had secured in a workstand. The bearings needed grease and the shifter was misaligned, but it would be a rentable bike for at least one more season with a little work. He watched the wheel, making certain it didn't wobble and demonstrate being off balance. He felt somewhat more balanced himself after spending the previous afternoon and evening with Hadley and helping her move boxes and inventory supplies. He needed to get his own place ready for summer, but he hadn't wanted to give up the chance to help Hadley.

He didn't want her lifting cases of food and drinks, and he didn't want Griffin and Maddox to have to absorb her work. It wasn't their fault their restaurant manager was on light duty. He and Hadley were a family now and it was his responsibility to watch out for her and their child, even though she wouldn't marry him.

She wouldn't marry him. That thought beat in his head for days. He kept replaying the scene. She'd walked away with her dog and gotten in the truck as if the entire matter were settled. He'd stood with his back to the water, its rhythm reminding him that he was part of the island, reminding him that he needed to breathe. But it had been hard when he'd looked at Hadley and her dog sitting in his truck, waiting for him as if…they belonged to him. But it was more than that. The waves had swooshed back and forth on the pebbles behind him and he'd felt his own blood rushing in his ears as if it were telling him he needed to listen hard.

There was something he was missing.

Mike ran his finger over the bicycle's shifting mechanism to see where it was stuck, and a sharp stab of pain interrupted his thoughts about that moment with Hadley and her dog waiting for him. He clamped his hand over his throbbing finger, but it didn't stop the blood from dripping. *Rats.* He walked to the window where the April light was better and carefully exposed the cut on his finger.

He winced as he examined a wound that definitely needed stitches. He'd need them before he could get back to work. He glanced at the wall calendar. At least it was Wednesday.

He was in luck because the island clinic had a doctor every Wednesday, even throughout the off-season. On other days, the nurse managed nearly every emergency, but it was still a happy accident that he sliced his left thumb wide open early on a Wednesday afternoon.

Mike wrapped a shop towel around his dripping finger, took a swig of water and started on the short walk to the island clinic one street behind Holly Street, the main thoroughfare of Christmas Island. Even on this overcast spring day, birds sang and the air smelled of fresh earth. It was a good day for a walk or a bike ride, if you didn't mind the cold. Not such a great day for an unplanned trip to the clinic, but what day was?

As he approached, Mike forgot his own pain. Wendy's car was parked right by the front door. She would be officially family now, even if Hadley continued to turn down his proposals. Was one of her kids sick or injured?

What if Hadley was sick or something had happened to her? Mike doubled his pace, practically running the last block to the clinic even though the activity made his cut thumb throb mercilessly. He shouldered open the door and found no one in the waiting room or at the front desk.

"Hello?" he called. The door to the exam room in the back was closed, but he heard voices. He strode to the door, but it opened before he could decide to knock or call out another greeting.

The nurse gave him a quick assessing look, but his attention was behind her where Hadley sat on the exam table, her sister in a nearby chair. The doctor was listening to Hadley's heart with a stethoscope. Hadley looked over and saw him in the doorway, and then her gaze dropped to his his bloodied shop rag.

She put her hand to her mouth, and the nurse hustled through and shut the door.

"Is she okay?" he asked.

"Sit," the nurse said. She grabbed his arm and led him to a chair in the front reception area. "Let me see."

"I don't care about me. It's just a cut. Is Hadley okay?"

"I can't talk about other patients."

"She's not just another patient. She's my—"

He hesitated. What was she? His friend, the girl who sat next to him at lunch every day at school even when they were awkward teen-agers, the mother of his future child?

Understanding dawned on the nurse's face.

"The baby is mine," Mike said.

"I see."

"Is she okay?" he repeated.

"Yes, but I should let her tell you that. Her and the doctor."

He got up, but the nurse put a hand on his shoulder and forced him back down. "Let me see your wound first. You won't be any good at changing diapers if you've managed to cut off a finger."

Mike wasn't sure he would be any good at changing diapers even if he had three hands, but he decided not to argue. This wasn't about him. All he cared about was Hadley. Why was she there? The nurse was calm, no one seemed to be in a hurry, no medical helicopter hovered over the island clinic.

The nurse put on a pair of surgical gloves and then peeled away the shop towel, taking dried blood with it and making Mike wince. "You did a number on it. I'd say you're looking at five or six stitches. Let me see you wiggle your thumb and the other fingers, too."

Mike did as he was told, reasoning cooperation would get him to Hadley sooner. Why hadn't they come out of the room? Wendy could at least find him and tell him what was going on.

"Just a moment," the nurse said. She disappeared through a door and came back with a clean bandage. "Hold pressure on it until the doctor is finished with...your...with Hadley."

Before she could turn away, Mike heard the door open and Wendy came out of the exam room. He tried to get up again, but his head swam and heat rushed over him followed by a cold clammy feeling.

"Not so fast," the nurse said. "Have you had anything to eat today?"

He shook his head and took deep breaths.

Wendy took the chair next to him and reached into her giant purse. She pulled out a package of peanut butter crackers and a small bottle of water.

"She's okay," Wendy said, opening the crackers for him and loosening the cap on the water bottle. "Her blood pressure is a little high, which is why she didn't feel well."

"She called you?" Mike said. It hurt, knowing Hadley had called her sister and not him.

Didn't she know he'd be there for her night or day, rain or shine?

"Don't get weird about it," Wendy said. "Eat a cracker so you can get your stitches without passing out." She waited, giving him a distinct *mom* look while he forced himself to eat a cracker and wash it down with the water bottle she'd opened for him as if he were a helpless baby.

He felt helpless. All he wanted to do was make things right with Hadley. For Hadley.

"It's not uncommon," Wendy said. "High blood pressure. And if she takes it easy and keeps an eye on it, she should be fine."

"Should be?"

Wendy put a hand on his shoulder. "Will be. She has all of us to watch out for her."

"You know I will."

"Of course."

"But she called you," he said.

Wendy rolled her eyes. "I'm her sister. I've had three kids. I have some idea what's normal and what's not when you're pregnant. Have you ever been pregnant?"

He heard the nurse suppress a chuckle.

"Fine," he said. "Can I see her?"

"In a minute," the nurse said. She taped the

white bandage around his hand. "This should hold you for a bit until the doctor is available. I don't think Hadley wants to see your bloody hand."

"She's not squeamish," Mike said. He knew Hadley as well as anyone on earth. He'd seen her pull a sliver from under her own fingernail after running her hand down a split-rail fence. She'd brought him a cold pack when they were sophomores and he'd gotten a bloody nose from a basketball in gym class. One time, while the rest of their friends had hesitated, she'd swum with Mike out to an unmoored boat to see if anyone needed to be rescued.

"Not usually," Wendy said. "But she might be a little less stoic right now. She's got a lot going on."

"Oh," Mike said.

"She'll recover. For example, I couldn't even think about peanut butter when I was pregnant, but here I am sitting with you and breathing in your peanut butter breath and I don't even mind that or your gross hand you blundered into cutting."

Mike almost laughed. "We're not even related yet and you're already treating me like I'm your annoying brother."

"We're related," Wendy said. "No getting out of it now."

"I don't want to."

She smiled. "Me, neither."

Mike wanted to ask her what she meant by that. Would she help persuade Hadley to accept his proposal? Certainly, with three kids, Wendy knew how hard having a child was and how much better it would be to have a partner under the same roof.

Not that he'd be far away. And not that he'd shirk his responsibility just because they hadn't exchanged rings and vows. For the first time, he imagined being married to Hadley. Not as an obligation...but actually married. Kissing her after saying I do, going home together. Stealing the blankets at night or letting her steal his pillow. More children?

Mike felt chills roll over him and the nurse moved closer. "Put your head between your legs for a minute. You're as green as spring leaves."

He put his head down, but jerked right back up when he heard the door to the exam room open. The doctor stood in the open doorway.

"Are you okay to come in?" he asked.

Mike got up, ignoring the throbbing in his hand when he moved. "I'm fine."

"We'll see about that in a minute, but first Hadley wants to talk to you."

Mike hurried to the exam room, and the doctor closed the door behind him. Hadley was sitting in a chair next to the exam table, and she looked fine. Beautiful as always, the color back in her cheeks. If he hadn't known better, he would think there was nothing wrong.

The doctor rolled another chair over and pointed to it.

"You two are quite a pair, both ending up in the clinic at the same time."

Mike exchanged a smile with Hadley and he felt as if a bicycle chain connected them, pulling them around and around, but always staying together. Being in the same room with Hadley always felt right. He reached for her hand with his uninjured one.

"It happens a lot," she told the doctor. She curled her fingers into his. "We were born on the same day, and we've been friends all our lives. And now…this."

"I don't usually comment on the personal

lives and decisions of my patients," the doctor said. "But I'd be tempted to say it sounds like it was meant to be."

Mike locked eyes with Hadley, the image of himself married to her fresh in his mind. What if he asked her to marry him because he cared about her and wanted to be with her, not just because it was convenient for the baby or because of a pact they'd made when they were teenagers? Would she say yes, or would she say the words he wasn't sure he was able to hear? That she didn't care about him that way.

Finding out which way she felt would have to wait for another day when they weren't both in the Christmas Island Health Clinic.

"Let's talk about the ways we're going to manage Hadley's blood pressure," the doctor said.

Mike nodded, anxious to hear medical advice and do everything in his power to take care of his lifelong friend, even though he was beginning to realize his reasons were as broad and deep as the blue waters just a block away.

CHAPTER EIGHT

HADLEY HAD KNOWN it was coming, the huge wedding on the third weekend of April. The daughter of a famous athlete had fallen in love with the island as a child, when her family visited for two weeks every summer. It was a credit to Christmas Island that the young woman wanted her wedding in the small church here before the official tourist season got busy. The Great Island Hotel didn't open until May first every year, so the Holiday Hotel and all the smaller bed-and-breakfasts on the island were booked solid for the event.

"We're the epicenter," Rebecca said as she sat on a barstool, chin in her hands. "Every room is booked, there will be pictures on the front porch and the horse-drawn carriages will leave from here to go to the church. The publicity is going to be something you can't even put a dollar figure on."

Hadley laughed. "I would bet that you, out of all the people I know, could figure out a value."

Rebecca smiled. "Okay, yes. But it's more dramatic to say you can't put a price on it. This is going to be an amazing weekend, and I can't wait to see the dresses."

"Getting ideas for your wedding?"

"Mine is going to be a much smaller affair this fall," Rebecca said. "And there will only be a few people from off the island, so the hotels won't be bulging with wedding guests."

Rebecca had been a foster child shuffled from home to home until she put herself through college, where she met Camille Peterson and forged a connection with the island that she'd eventually fall in love with. Marrying Griffin May who had inherited a fortune from Rebecca's employer Flora Winter meant Rebecca could afford the most elaborate wedding the island had ever seen.

But that wouldn't be true to her nature.

"I've found a dress I like," Rebecca said, scrolling through pictures on her phone. She held up the screen toward Hadley.

The dress was an utter outrage against good taste. Huge sleeves almost overshadowed a bodice with easily a million sequins, and the massive puffed skirt looked like a mushroom cloud. Had Rebecca gone overboard as a result of finding true love? The larger-than-life dress was way out of character for her understated, bookish, piano-playing friend. True love seemed like an unacceptable risk if this was one of the consequences.

Hadley swallowed. "It's...not what I thought you'd choose."

Rebecca laughed. "Kidding."

Hadley put a hand over her heart. "You scared me for a minute there."

Rebecca's expression shifted to concern. "I'm sorry, I shouldn't mess with you. I heard about your high blood pressure."

Hadley shook her head. "I can still handle some teasing, but I'm not supposed to be on my feet all day like I usually am at my job. I don't know what to do about it. Summer's coming, and I don't want to be a burden at work."

"That's what I came in here to talk to you about," Rebecca said. "Griffin's afraid to bring it up because he doesn't want to upset you, but I told him you're a smart, strong woman who can handle plain talk and viable solutions."

"Thank you," Hadley said. "I'm guessing you're about to test that theory."

"Yes. Here's the solution. You work at the front desk this summer. Griffin and Maddox usually hire a seasonal person, and that works out okay, they've said. But having someone with a vested interest in the place would be better. And you could sit down."

"But—" Hadley began.

"Your pay rate would be higher to accommodate for the tips you would typically earn working in the restaurant."

"It's okay," Hadley said. "The money, anyway. And it's a very generous offer."

She swallowed. She was being relocated. Relegated to the front desk instead of the job she'd had for years. Things couldn't stay the same. They wouldn't stay the same. Not with another life depending upon her. Maybe it was wise to rip off the bandage and make a change now.

"It's just for the summer so you can put you and your baby's health first," Rebecca said gently.

Hadley nodded. "I know, and I'm grateful for the offer." She ran a towel along the bar's surface and then draped it evenly over a rack.

She straightened the glasses hanging over-heard, shoving one of them farther back so it would be even with the rest.

"It'll be okay," Rebecca said.

Hadley let out a long breath. "It's for the best." She forced a smile. "Being around all the food smells sometimes hits me wrong, anyway. I wouldn't want to ruin anyone's dinner by turning green and running for the restroom."

"That's the spirit," Rebecca said. "The only issue is timing. We've got the giant wedding party arriving tomorrow with extended family, and you're going to have to teach me everything you know about running the bar and restaurant in the next twenty-four hours."

"You?"

"Just for the weekend. I'll be your right-hand woman and do the legwork until we can hire someone to replace you for the summer."

Replace. Hadley forced herself not to dwell on the word. She was getting more than she was giving up. By the time Rebecca and Griffin exchanged vows in November, she would have a baby. Knowing that was worth any sacrifice.

"Lesson one," Hadley said. "Memorize every detail of the menu."

Rebecca smiled. "Done. The academic parts are easy for me. Mixing and pouring drinks is going to be harder, especially when people ask for things I've never heard of."

"Keep your phone handy and search anything you don't know," Hadley said. "That's my secret. What I don't know is the secret of running the front desk. I've filled in a few times, even carried luggage on busy summer days, but I don't know the computer system."

"I can help you with that," Rebecca said. "The restaurant doesn't open for another hour, so do you want to get started? We've got at least one family checking in this afternoon ahead of the rest of the party. They said they'd be on the noon ferry."

Hadley nodded. If she was going to make the switch, she might as well just do it. It was only one family, so it wouldn't exactly be trial by fire like a summer's day would be.

She gave her friend a lopsided grin. "This is going to be the strangest season of my life."

"Stranger than mine when I came to spy on Flora Winter and then ended up engaged to her heir?"

They both laughed. "I think it compares," Hadley said.

For the next hour, Rebecca ran through the check-in process, complete with instructions on how to use the online system she'd installed the previous summer. Although the Holiday Hotel only had twenty-four guest rooms, she'd insisted on bringing it up to date and allowing people to make online reservations instead of requiring them to make a phone call.

Hadley took notes and paid close attention. She wouldn't repay Griffin and Maddox's willingness to accommodate her by doing a shoddy job of running their front desk.

"There's less guess work in this than the restaurant and bar," Hadley said as they took a break and got granola bars and water from behind the desk. "You know exactly how many people are coming, reservations are made way in advance and you don't have to guess whether or not you're going to run out of rooms. In the restaurant, sometimes we make a huge tray of whatever the special is, and every single guest comes in wanting something else. And drinks depend on the weather, desserts depend on the drinks, so it's a roll of the dice sometimes."

Rebecca laughed. "I think the front desk will still surprise you sometimes. You know how many people are showing up, but you don't know how much baggage they're bringing, literally and figuratively."

As if on cue, the sound of a child whining, an adult's voice raised in frustration and a baby crying broke the afternoon silence.

"For example," Hadley said.

"Sign of things to come," Rebecca added.

Hadley didn't know if Rebecca was referring to the approaching family, the summer that stretched out before them or Hadley's future motherhood. She crossed the small lobby and held open the front door as the family of two adults and three children struggled toward them. Rebecca dashed past her and helped get a stroller up the steps.

"Welcome to the Holiday Hotel where it's always Christmas," Hadley said. It was the standard line for the hotel, used in all its promotions, printed on napkins and prominent on the website.

"Is Santa here?" a little boy asked.

The boy's tear-streaked face gave away the

fact that he'd been the source of the whining, and Hadley chose her words carefully, not wanting to set off another round.

"Not today," Hadley said. "But we're always ready just in case."

The dad of the family hauled two massive suitcases and a garment bag while the mom had an infant in her arms, a shoulder bag and one hand on the stroller. A girl who looked just a little older than the tear-streaked boy had a pink backpack and dragged a diaper bag. Rebecca helped the mom with the stroller, and Hadley was about to lighten the load for the dad battling the luggage, but suddenly Mike appeared on the steps and took the largest bag.

"Got it," he said.

"Thanks," the dad said. "Can I offer you one of my kids, too?"

Mike and the dad laughed as they swept into the lobby that suddenly seemed small with all the people and luggage.

Hadley didn't know where Mike had come from. Was he watching from across the street? She didn't need a keeper, someone constantly spying on her to make sure she was taking it easy. Although it was nice that he cared. He'd been so sweet at the clinic a few days earlier, and for a moment the emotion she thought she'd recognized in his eyes was love. She pushed that thought aside, though.

If he loved her, there had been far better opportunities to tell her.

MIKE WAS GLAD to see the Mays had acted fast and already reassigned Hadley to the front desk. He hung back while Hadley checked the guests in, consulting her notes twice and Rebecca once. She'd have to learn a new job, but at least it involved sitting down most of the time.

"It's early in the season, so we don't have bell service yet," Hadley was saying, "but I could—"

"Let me," Mike said, cutting in.

Hadley shot him a look. "I was going to ask Maddox who is right down the street at the candy store and actually works here. He'll be back any second."

"I'm right here," Mike said. He was prepared to do anything to help Hadley, even if it annoyed her. Heck, she wasn't going to marry him, so what did he have to lose by pressing his point?

Hadley raised an eyebrow and then smiled. "Mike will take the heaviest bags. You're on the third floor, but this is a historic building without an elevator."

If Hadley thought he would abandon his effort just because three flights of stairs were involved, she underestimated him. Maybe she underestimated him in a lot of ways, now that they were both taking on a new role and teetering into unfamiliar territory. Would they learn things about each other that the past twenty-five had not revealed? Did parenthood change a person that much?

The mom of three kids leaned in toward Hadley. "Please tell me the bar is open. I've been in the car and on the ferry since five o'clock this morning. I used to be a put-together person, but I'm on the brink of stealing a rowboat."

And there was his answer. The formerly put-together mom had wild hair, flushed cheeks and a stain on the front of her shirt. But she did have three beautiful kids who were probably going to grow up too fast.

"It opens at five," Hadley said.

"I'll help carry," Rebecca said. "My fiancé

and his brother own the Holiday Hotel, along with the ferry you crossed on."

"Family affair," the mom commented.

Rebecca smiled. "The longer you're on this island, the more it seems like you're related to everyone. That's its charm."

Rebecca took the diaper bag and a smaller suitcase and led the way up the stairs. The family followed, and Mike brought up the rear. Christmas garland adorned the banister, and quiet Christmas music played in the lobby. Before they reached the first landing, Mike heard Maddox's voice below.

"I'm back with cookies," Maddox said.

Every day during the tourist season, a glass dome covered a tray of elaborate Christmas cookies on the lobby's check-in counter. Mike had been known to pop across the street and steal one on occasion. At his bike shop, he stocked candy canes throughout the summer and handed them out liberally. The coffee shop had gingerbread mocha all summer long and, of course, the candy store kept a large stock of Christmas-themed cupcakes and candy in addition to its famous fudge.

The island was a year-round Christmas party.

"Can we have cookies?" the little boy asked. "Please?"

His mom paused a moment, and Mike wondered if he was going to learn something important about parenting.

"Please, Mom?" the little girl chimed in.

The mom knelt in front of both kids while balancing the infant on her shoulder. "You've had a long day of travel. If you help us get all our stuff to the room, we'll all wash our hands and come right back to the lobby for cookies."

Both kids shouldered the load they were carrying and marched up the stairs as if they were on a mission, and Mike admired the simplicity of the woman's plan. Would he and Hadley learn to negotiate the highs and lows of being parents? Would they agree on everything? Argue over silly things? Consider hijacking a rowboat just to escape the chaos?

He didn't know. He glanced back down at the desk where Hadley had her head raised, intently watching the progression of the family up the stairs. Her eyes met his and they exchanged a smile. He would have bet a tandem bike she was thinking the same thing he was.

Mike only went as far as the door of the

family's room where he tucked the two suit-cases he carried inside. Then he descended to the lobby where Hadley sat alone behind the desk.

She pointed to iced sugar cookies with glis-tening colorful frosting. "Your favorites," she said. "They even have the edible baubles on them so they have a little crunch."

"You know I love those?"

She nodded. "At the party last Christmas, I picked the silver balls off my cookie and put them on my plate. I saw you steal them and eat them."

He laughed and picked up a Christmas tree–shaped cookie with rows of icing garland and silver balls. Mike bit into it and groaned. "I love Christmas Island."

"I hope those guests feel the same way. They seemed a bit tattered when they arrived."

Mike laughed. "I remember going on a big theme park vacation to Florida when I was a kid. Of course, my brothers were already out on their own, so it was just me and my parents. I realize now that they were too old to enjoy spinning in teacups and riding car-ousels."

Having been a very-late-in-life child, Mike

was born when his parents were in their forties, and his older brothers seemed more like uncles. He'd grown up as practically an only child, and his parents had retired off-island as soon as he graduated from high school. They hadn't been happy initially that he wanted to stay alone on the island and go into debt to start a business, but his success had persuaded them it was a good idea and he still got a thrill from showing off his bike shop's little improvements every time his parents returned for a visit.

"I don't think you're ever too old for teacups and carousels," Hadley said. "Although I might pass on the spinning rides right now."

Mike finished his cookie and strongly considered taking another one from the loaded tray. Maddox had stocked up, and Camille's family bakery just down the street was a never-ending source of treats. Instead of taking another cookie, though, he leaned an elbow on the counter near Hadley.

"So I see you have a new job. How do you like it?"

"It's fine," she said quickly. "Really. It's not hard, and I can probably still find time to do the orders and daily inventory for the restaurant, so I don't leave Griffin and Maddox in the lurch."

"They wouldn't see it that way," Mike said. "But I know they value everything you do."

They were silent a moment, and then Hadley picked up a small white angel-shaped cookie and ate it in one big bite. She handed him a green-and-red-striped napkin and took one for herself. "Next Christmas we'll have a baby."

The simple, honest, raw statement caught him off guard. Of course, he knew the due date, but he was still imagining life beyond that date in small doses. He tried to picture riding a bike with his son or daughter, taking the ferry and laughing as spray doused them on a windy day. Flying a kite, snowmobiling and throwing snowballs.

"We'll have to put out cookies for Santa," he said at last. He wanted to add that such cookies would almost certainly be by the chimney at Hadley's house. What would happen then on Christmas Eve? Would he go back to his small apartment over the bike shop? Would Hadley invite him to stay and experience Christmas morning, their baby's first Christmas?

This was why they should just get married. There would be no awkwardness on birthdays and holidays. It was practical and logical, and it should appeal to Hadley who was one of the most organized and pragmatic people he knew.

As Mike pondered future Christmases, the thought of walking away from Hadley on Christmas Eve to spend the night alone left a hole in his stomach not even a tray full of Christmas cookies could fill.

CHAPTER NINE

HADLEY PULLED OUT a length of yellow yarn and cut it off. "Hold the flowers exactly where you want them," she instructed her niece Janey. At six, Janey was finally old enough to join the bicycle parade in downtown Christmas Island as part of the island-wide celebration of May first.

May Day. Hadley smiled as she thought of the many different historical meanings of the holiday. Christmas Island took a pure approach to the date. It was the official start to summer, and the entire island joined the party.

Janey held a bunch of silk flowers on her bike's handlebars while Hadley secured it with yarn leftover from one of her grandmother's many crochet projects. There was enough yarn to wrap all the bikes on the island and probably the lampposts downtown, too.

"Mom says we have to hurry so we're not late to the blessing of the feet," Janey said.

"Fleet," Hadley corrected. "The pastor will bless the fleet, which means all the boats from the island."

"So they won't sink," Janey said.

"That's what we hope. I also hope you don't ride too fast. We don't want your flowers to fly away," Hadley said.

"That would be pretty if flowers flew out behind me like I'm a fairy princess."

Hadley smiled. She vividly remembered riding her bike in the May Day parade when she was as young as Janey. Every summer, she and Wendy had matching bikes and their mom had lovingly woven silk flowers onto the baskets and wheels. She secured them so well some of the flowers were still clinging to the spokes by the middle of summer.

"You are a fairy princess," Hadley said. "Do you want to add more flowers to the basket?"

Her niece nodded, and Hadley tied as many yellow daffodils and pink roses as possible to the bicycle's pink plastic basket. If her baby was a girl, she might be doing this same thing again in about six years. Boys rode in the parade, too, but they usually had streamers instead of flowers, even though flowers were a more traditional May Day choice.

"Will you watch me in the parade?" Janey asked.

"I sure will. I'll be standing downtown with your mom. And then we'll all go down to the harbor to watch the blessing of the feet."

"Fleet," Janey corrected, giggling.

Two hours later, Hadley waited on the front steps of the Holiday Hotel as the parade of island kids on bikes made its way down Holly Street. Mike led the parade as the grand marshal, a title he'd held since he bought the bike rental shop right out of high school. He wore a huge top hat with red and green flowers glued all around the brim and a red velvet vest trimmed with white fur as a nod to Santa.

Mike rang the bell on his bike and waved to the crowds, and the kids came behind him, some wobbling, some still using training wheels and also quite a few competent riders—mostly older brothers and sisters who'd been assigned to keep their younger siblings on the parade route.

Grandma Penny grabbed Hadley's arm and pulled her down to the level of her folding chair. "He's so good with kids," she said as she pointed at Mike.

"He's good with bikes and being silly," Hadley said.

Mike executed a pop-up wheelie, tossed his hat in the air and caught it, and then stood on the pedals of his bike and did a sweeping bow for the crowd.

"It's his moment in the spotlight," Hadley added.

"I think he'll be a wonderful father," Grandma Penny said.

"Yep," Wendy said, giving Hadley a sarcastic grin. "All it takes is bike skills to be the dad of the year."

"I'm not even thinking about this today," Hadley said. "I'm enjoying the weather, the parade and all the fun stuff."

"Me, too," her grandmother said.

Betty sat obediently by Hadley's side, watching the bikes go by, until Janey cycled past. Betty jumped to her feet and wagged her tail when she recognized the girl and Janey almost crashed into another bike when she took one hand off the handlebars and waved to her family.

"Heart attack number three hundred and seventy-four," Wendy said.

"Who's counting?" her husband, Justin, asked.

"Children are a blessing," Grandma Penny said.

In past years, such banter would have slipped by Hadley like the early May breeze. Children hadn't been on her radar, at least not anywhere nearby, and in previous years she'd simply enjoyed her role as aunt.

"Can't see," her nephew, Aaron, complained, and Hadley reached for him and picked him up, propping him on her hip. The three-year-old put his head on her shoulder, content with his new view of the parade.

"Is he too heavy?" her brother-in-law asked.

Hadley shook her head. "He's just right."

After the parade passed, her group moved with the crowd down the street to the marina where nearly every slip was full. Griffin and Maddox had their ferry docked among dozens of smaller pleasure craft. Kayaks, rowboats and even two intrepid paddle boarders braved the cold waters of the lake. An equipment barge with a dump truck and a backhoe loaded on it floated next to a string of sail-boats, masts shining in the sun.

The pastor from the island church took the microphone and delivered a solemn speech about the perils of the lake followed by a cheerful blessing filled with hope for a good boating and fishing season. Janey took Hadley's hand and very carefully pronounced, "Fleet."

Hadley smiled. "We could ask the pastor to bless our feet, too."

Janey shook her head. "Not today. I'll ask at church tomorrow."

Hadley suppressed a laugh and wondered if she should warn her sister. Before she got the opportunity, Wendy and Justin took their kids closer to the water where some children's games were set up on the wide green lawn sloping up from the marina. Grandma Penny settled onto a park bench near Hadley, and Betty went over to stand guard with the older woman.

Hadley took a moment to stand and enjoy the view of the marina and feel the warmth on her shoulders. She'd been going easy at work for the past week, taking the time to put up her feet and making sure to get plenty of water and rest. The morning sickness had subsided, and she was beginning to think summer would be okay. Small, but significant, changes added up, and it was the new story of her life. The reward would be worth it.

"I put my boat right at the front," Mike said as he pedaled to a stop beside Hadley and took off his ridiculous flowered hat. His cheeks were flushed with the heat and the excitement of the parade, and he looked exactly as he had when they were teenagers. It was only a month until their thirtieth birthdays, a date she'd once considered a turning point but now thought would be just a turn in the road.

"*Flounder*?" Hadley shaded her eyes and looked where Mike pointed. A faded orange fiberglass boat with an outboard motor was tied next to a sleek white powerboat. Mike had hand-painted a picture of a giant fish on the side along with the boat's name. It was the least elegant watercraft in the entire marina, and it had a definite list to starboard.

"She's looking good," Hadley said with a grin.

"Just as beautiful as the day I found her behind a barn in Traverse City," Mike said.

"And she's floating."

"Never any doubt. I charged the battery for the bilge pump before I put her in yesterday, but I think *Flounder*'s got some fishing trips left in her for one last season."

"Last?"

Mike nodded. "I think I'll sell the boat at the end of the year."

"Why?" Hadley asked, although she suspected she knew the answer. Mike had owned that boat for seven or eight years and it had barely been seaworthy all that time, and now he was talking of selling it?

"The truth is…" Mike began and then he stopped and looked out at the marina filled with boats. "The truth is I'm getting rid of it before your grandmother is tempted to borrow it and take her old lady friends out for some fun."

"Very funny," Hadley said. "You don't have to sell your ugly boat just because you'll be a dad."

"It's not ugly," Mike said. "But it's also not a family boat. I can't take my kid out in that."

Hadley hadn't thought about Mike taking their child out in a boat at all. At least not for a long time. And she certainly didn't want to spend the May Day Festival pondering it.

"If you're so concerned about Grandma Penny," she said, "you could go fetch her some coffee and cinnamon rolls from the church tent. She looks pretty comfortable on that park bench, but I know she loves a treat."

"I'll bring some for you, too," he said. "Don't tell anyone, but I like you more than I like your grandmother."

"She'd be destroyed," Hadley said. "She's leaning on me to ma—" She cut herself off abruptly.

"To do what?" Mike asked.

"Nothing," Hadley said. *Rats*. She'd almost just told Mike her own grandmother thought she was a fool for not accepting his marriage proposal. If Grandma Penny knew she'd turned Mike down twice, she'd have to pop a few antacids and crochet an extra few rows before she could settle down to sleep that night.

"Maybe your grandmother is right," Mike said, his eyes and voice serious.

"She's right about a lot of things," Hadley said. "Especially the bake sale in the church tent and how quickly it sells out."

Mike put a gentle hand on Hadley's upper arm. "Why don't you sit down with your grandmother, and I'll bring you both something."

"I can go myself."

"You should save your energy. The greenhouse barge comes in this afternoon, and you wear yourself out every single year planting your flowers too early and then panicking about them getting frosted."

"Maybe this is the year I'm going to know better," Hadley said.

Mike smiled. "We'll go buy your plants, and I'll try to persuade you to leave them in your garage at night for two weeks. As usual."

Hadley smiled as she walked away, and then she did as he suggested and sat with her grandmother and her dog, watching the island festivities with the promise of pastries in her near future.

"Does anyone else think this is a monopoly?" Mike grumbled to Griffin and Maddox as they all waited for the flower barge to dock. Every May Day Saturday, the massive greenhouse on the mainland loaded a barge with annuals, perennials and hanging baskets and sent it to Christmas Island. The scene at the dock was a polite feeding frenzy as locals discreetly stepped in front of their neighbors to get to the prettiest hanging baskets and most lush trays of petunias first.

"I told Maddox not to be too polite this year," Griffin said. "We need the best hanging baskets for the Holiday Hotel, and I don't care whose toes he has to trample."

Mike laughed. He knew there was no way either Griffin or Maddox May was going to elbow a fellow islander over a basket of ivy geraniums, no matter how perfectly the colors might complement their hotel.

"I don't think anyone even notices my planters out front," Mike said. "All they want is a decent bicycle at a fair price. Petunias aren't going to impress anyone."

"Not true," Camille Peterson said as she came up with Rebecca and Hadley. "Petunias are incredibly hardy and fragrant and I think they've impressed more people than you…" She let that word dangle for a moment before adding, "think." Mike laughed. They'd all been friends for so long he didn't care if Camille thought flowers made him more impressive than he was.

Heck, it had never been his mission to impress anyone. He just wanted to be a good neighbor, a successful businessperson and a solid friend. And now a dad.

"I want red geraniums this year," Rebecca said. "The Great Island Hotel has all those porch planters filled with them, and it's a good look. I doubt they'd mind if we copied the look at the Holiday Hotel, and I definitely want to try them at the Winter Palace."

Mike was certain that any flowers would be unnecessary at the Winter Palace, the Victorian mansion named for Flora Winter, who had recently bequeathed it along with millions of dollars to Griffin and Maddox.

"Violets are the only flower worth fighting over." Violet Brookstone joined the group watching the flower barge tie up. "Obviously," she added. "I'm filling the planters in front of my boutique with purple and yellow ones this year, and if anyone thinks they're beating me to the violets, I brought Jordan along for muscle."

Jordan shook his head, a lopsided grin on his face. "Please don't make me fight anyone. I'm hoping for a promotion at the hotel one of these days, and a police record would really wreck my prospects."

"No one's going to jail," Hadley said. "What happens on the island stays on the island."

The flower barge's crew finally finished securing it, and at least one hundred island residents waited while the greenhouse's staff set up a folding table with a cash register and put on green aprons. The crowd surged forward, and Mike stuck to Hadley's side.

"You didn't mention what you wanted," he said. "I'll stick with you and all you have to do is point and I'll grab anything you like."

Hadley slipped her arm through his, and the subtle move sent a rush of happiness through him. Her fingers wrapped around his arm seemed to say that she counted on him, trusted him. "I want pink flowers this year," she said.

Pink? Mike wondered briefly if Hadley was trying to tell him something. Did she have reason to think they were having a girl? She wasn't scheduled for the ultrasound that might reveal the gender of their child for another couple of weeks. He had already enlisted help in his shop that day so he could go with Hadley to the clinic on the mainland.

"Don't get all weird," she said. "I had red and white last year, yellow the year before, and pink the year before that. It's pink's turn. That's all."

Of course, that was all.

"I almost forgot how systematic you are," he said. "Next year, I'll grab yellow flowers and you won't even have to ask me."

"You'll remember?"

Mike grinned. "I'll put a reminder in my phone." He put a hand on the center of her back as they stepped onto the barge with the dozens of other islanders, and he followed her lead as she went directly to the trays of flowers she wanted without even wavering or looking at signs.

"They were in the same place last year," she said. "They must have a system for loading the barge."

Hadley pointed to what she wanted, and Mike picked up two flats and took them to the register area. Hadley followed him with a hanging basket dangling from each arm.

"I would have gotten those for you," he said.

"They're for you. I thought these would be perfect on the lamp posts in front of the bike rental."

He noticed she didn't say *your* bike rental. She didn't say *our*, either, but little by little the signs suggested his and Hadley's lives were getting more entwined. And she cared about his curb appeal?

"Thank you," he said.

"I don't want you to get outshone by the T-shirt shop. Last year, they had petunias rolling out in every direction."

"I appreciate you looking out for my interests," Mike said. "Should I try petunias everywhere?"

"They're water hogs. These baskets will be low maintenance so you can focus on the bikes. I'll pop over and water these on a schedule, so you won't even have to think about them."

It was such a minor thing, her choosing plants for his business and offering to take care of them, but Mike felt as if she'd just offered him her heart and her hand in marriage. He swallowed and took a deep breath in an effort to manage his expectations—expectations that he shouldn't let run away with him.

"How many more flats do you want?" he asked. "You could stay here with the plants while I go back on the barge and get more."

"Just one," Hadley said. "I'm planting pink flowers at my grandmother's duplex, too."

"Does she already know this?"

"She can probably guess. She knows the schedule."

Mike laughed and dodged back into the crowd of people stooping over flats of flowers and browsing among the baskets and planters. The fresh earthy smell from the plants mixed with the lake's aroma. All around him, people were talking, laughing, helping each other carry awkward flats of flowers, most of them dripping water. Despite his friends' chatter, people weren't competing with each other. Christmas Island was a place where your neighbors might know all your business, but they'd also mow your lawn for you if you were unable to. It was a perfect place to grow up, and just as perfect of a place to live as an adult.

"Grandma's first?" he asked when he returned to the checkout line. Hadley had her credit card in hand. Should he offer to buy her flowers, just lump them in with his? He didn't want to push her, especially not when they were having fun. Today felt like old times, when their friendship came easily and there was no one on the island who made them feel as comfortable as they made each other.

An unexpected pregnancy had come between them, but couldn't it just as easily go the other way and make them closer?

"The timing is good," Hadley said. "If we stop by there now, she'll be watching a NASCAR race on television so she won't try to come outside and insist on helping."

Mike laughed. "I didn't know she liked racing."

"It's only been the last few years since she stumbled on the Daytona 500 on television. I think living on an island helps her appreciate the simplicity of going round and round a confined space on the track. Plus, she likes the drama of the drivers and their personal lives, and I wouldn't put it past her to make a friendly wager with MaryAnna on occasion."

"Who would have guessed it?" Mike said.

"Well," Hadley said with a laugh, "if I start watching stock car racing every weekend when I get to be in my eighties, I want you to stop me."

Her eyes met his and he could identify the exact moment she realized the implication of what she'd just said. That they'd be together in fifty years. The laughter in her eyes didn't exactly fade, but it shifted enough for him to know her words had impacted her, too.

"Next," the person behind the cash register said, interrupting the moment and stealing his chance to tell her he hoped she'd be there to remind him where he'd left his shoes when they were grandparents.

CHAPTER TEN

HADLEY'S EXPERTISE ROWING a canoe and her desirability as a partner in the annual May Day Weekend's Sunset Canoe Race was legendary. She'd been on the winning team five years in a row before losing to Maddox and Jordan the previous year. This year's contest should have been her sweet taste of revenge and redemption.

But she didn't put her name in the drawing for boat partners. Not this year. The fun part about the canoe race was that contestants never knew who they were going to get as a partner until the drawing right before the starting bell. Grandpas got paired with teenagers, divorced couples got accidentally matched, siblings or cousins ended up in the same boat, and once, quite memorably, a pairing led to a marriage proposal right on the dock.

Hadley loved the thrill of not knowing who her partner would be, but her doctor had advised her to take it easy. She'd already attended a bike race, bought and planted flowers, and eaten at the festival tent. She'd sit this one out for her own health and that of her baby's.

But it was still fun to watch. They were all at the marina as Rebecca drew a name from the box set up on a table. She was the first to draw, and the president of the chamber of commerce, Shirley, enthusiastically announced the first pairing. Rebecca and Bertie, who was on the brink of retirement after thirty-five years running the island post office, would share a canoe for the evening race.

Some people in the crowd chuckled, but Hadley thought her friend's chances were good. Rowing a canoe didn't necessarily depend on physical vigor. It was much more about rhythm and paying attention to your partner, and a man who'd survived a lifetime of service reliably receiving and delivering island mail had to know a lot about working with people and keeping afloat.

Hadley sat on the grass with her dog. Betty pawed at a bug, but her ears were alert, monitoring someone coming up behind them. Hadley didn't even have to turn around to know who it was.

"I brought you a chair," Mike said.

"Thank you, but I don't mind sitting on the ground."

"It's damp. It'll be cold." He offered her a hand and gently tugged her up and then unfolded the cushioned camp chair he'd brought.

"I hope you won't end up damp and cold before the night's over," Hadley said.

Mike flashed her a grin. "That depends on who I end up rowing with. Maybe I should sit this year out, too."

"Can't," Hadley said. "They'll have an uneven number and you committed."

"I did," he said, nodding. "If I win the prize, I hope you'll have a late date with me."

"I could," Hadley said. First prize was always a dinner for two for each of the winning partners. "But we'd technically be three for dinner."

Mike's mouth opened and he stared at her in the evening light. She'd been aware that he was a good-looking man. Attractive. Nice dark hair and eyes, a manly jawline, often with a bit of beard stubble. Broad shoulders and a long lean body. The thought of him rowing a boat with anybody else gave her a shiver of dissatisfaction.

In the late day glow with the island's earthy smell all around them, Hadley suddenly felt a whoosh of wanting to hold Mike in her arms, not just as a quick friendly hug. More as a sign that he was...hers.

"This is new," he said.

Had he guessed her thoughts? Did he know that she wanted to grab his hand and take him away from the marina and the silly but fun canoe race and have him all to herself?

"Joking about our situation," he clarified.

Hadley smiled, half with relief that they were talking about the baby and not her feelings, despite how they were tangled together, anyway. "I'm not kidding, though. There really would be three of us at the table."

"Do we have a name for the third person?"

She shook her head. "No ideas yet. How about you?"

"I'm waiting," he said.

"Until the ultrasound." Hadley nodded. "Me, too."

"Contestants please come and draw for partners," Shirley's booming voice pierced through the murmurings of the crowd around them.

"If it's a girl, how about Shirley?" Mike asked.

Hadley laughed and shook her head. "That name is quite gloriously taken on this island."

Mike smiled. "You're right. But now I should go and face my fate," Mike said.

Hadley was sorry to let him walk away. The farther into her pregnancy she got, the more comfortable she felt talking about it. With her sister, she'd been candid. But with Mike, there were so many layers that they'd done a lot of dancing around the details and spoken in generalities.

"I'll be watching," Hadley said softly, wishing she could be in that canoe with Mike. They were good partners, always in tune with each other, seldom even having to talk about their route or their strategy.

Things would be okay as long as she continued to think of him as a partner. A solid friend who happened to share in the life of her child. She watched Mike line up with the islanders choosing names at the table near the life jackets, and she simultaneously hoped he'd get an amazing partner and win that dinner for two and also that he'd end up with someone hilarious so they could share a good laugh about it later.

The next person to draw a name was a teenage girl, Sharon, whom Hadley knew because she was a part-time dishwasher and server in the restaurant at the Holiday Hotel. Because Hadley was a good listener, Sharon had confided in her about the senior boy who didn't know she existed and how her mom thought she was too young to date and never understood anything. Hadley had been sympathetic but offered no advice. She wasn't going to get between a mother and daughter.

Sharon drew a slip of paper, and her expression when she pulled her own mother's name from the box was a masterclass in drama. Hadley sucked in a breath. Luckily, Sharon's mother was behind her daughter and didn't see her daughter's reaction. The mom raised both fists in the air and said, "Yes!"

Clearly, the mom thought this was the best pairing in island history and Sharon thought it was the worst. Hadley sympathized with the girl's teenage plight, but she'd also give almost anything for one more day with her own mother, even if they had to row a canoe that entire day. Her mother wouldn't be there to see her grandchild or give Hadley advice or spoil the baby with too many hugs.

She sighed and Betty moved closer and put her nose in Hadley's lap.

"It's all good. Right, Betty?"

Instead of an answering groan of sympathy, Betty's head snapped up as Hadley's brother-in-law flopped down on the grass next to her.

"Wendy sent me," he said. "She says I have to represent the family since your grandma's no longer allowed to row after tipping a canoe two years ago, and you're sitting this one out."

"What about Wendy? She likes paddling."

"The kids are tired and cranky, and she's letting them eat in front of the television while they watch an endless movie about princesses or castles or something."

Those three little angels must be exceptionally tired and grouchy, Hadley thought, because her sister never gave in and let them eat in front of the television. Was that what parenthood did? Did it wear you down, or did you just adapt? She pictured herself on the rug in front of her television, sharing a bowl of popcorn with a child on her lap. She had a nice stock of kid-friendly DVDs for when her nieces and nephews visited. It would be fun to have someone to watch an animated film with where a happy ending was guaranteed.

"An evening in front of the television sounds kind of nice," Hadley said. "Or are you getting the better deal tonight?"

"That depends on whose name I draw."

"Whose name are you hoping for?"

"You would be my first choice, obviously," he said. "But I'm prepared for disappointment. I just don't want to disgrace myself too much because people have expectations."

"Because you're related to me?" Hadley asked with a smile.

"Because I'm a park ranger. And I'm related to you."

Hadley nodded toward the table. "Go draw a winner."

As Justin approached, Mike also walked up to the table to draw a name. If her brother-in-law was lucky, he'd get Mike as a partner because, although Mike was better on a bike, he had excellent coordination in a canoe, too. Hadley knew this from rowing with him in this very race two times and also from fun excursions on pretty days in the early or late season when they could both take a break from their tourism-intensive jobs.

Her brother-in-law would do well with Mike or nearly any member of their friend group. Camille Peterson and her sisters, their friend Violet and most islanders were decent on the water. Justin, however, did not appear to be lucky. He chose the name of a complete stranger, someone visiting the island for the weekend. Of course, it was an open contest, and anyone could sign up, but it seldom happened that a person from off the island joined in. Hadley recognized the name from the hotel registration. The woman was in her midfifties with short gray hair and well-defined arms.

She looked like she could handle a canoe and just about anything else. An author, she'd brought along copies of her recent self-help book to leave at the hotel desk for any guests looking to *Conquer your Goals in Thirty Days*. Hadley had tucked one of the books in her purse and planned to put her feet up and read chapter one as soon as the busy May Day weekend was over. Being pregnant seemed to be a crash course in thinking about goals, short- and long-term.

Justin, to his credit, kept a friendly expression when he drew the name, and he amicably shook hands with the author. They stood aside while Mike drew the name of his partner in the canoe race. "Shirley Harte," he read aloud.

"Yes!" As the president of the local chamber, Shirley was a fixture at every community event. Bingo, trivia night at the local bar, the pumpkin decorating contest, the July Fourth fireworks.

She loved Christmas Island with the strength of a bear hug. And she was notoriously competitive.

"Gonna kill ya," she said to the other teams lined up. Hadley had heard those words from Shirley before, and so had most of the other island residents. Shirley wasn't violent, but she certainly loved a challenge.

Mike glanced over at Hadley with an expression of longing and unfulfilled wishes. Like a child begging for a balloon at a theme park or a dog salivating over a pot roast. Mike wanted Hadley for a partner in that canoe, she'd bet her desk organizer on it, but he was getting in a tiny watercraft with Shirley and her big personality.

MIKE STOOD NEXT to his canoe as streaks of pink and orange light began to mix with the blue sky. The canoe race was short, just one lap out to the lighthouse and back. A strong rower could make the trip in twenty minutes. Stragglers who got too far off course would be flagged by the harbor patrol or towed in.

He had no idea what was going to happen, although if enthusiasm could win a race, he had the ideal partner.

"Who'd you draw?" Mike asked Justin. "Island visitor?"

"Author staying at the Holiday Hotel," Justin said. The gray-haired woman was over in the life jacket area getting fitted and buckled in. "She wrote some self-help book about getting everything you want in thirty days."

Mike chuckled. "I hope she knows how to paddle a canoe."

"No idea," Justin said. "Next year, I'm volunteering to stay home with three tired, grouchy kids instead of ending up in a boat with a stranger."

"Or worse yet, Shirley," Mike whispered.

"I'd be happy to trade," Justin said. "Shirley is a beast when it comes to competitions, and she's been known to trade to up her chance of winning. Trading's allowed if it's mutual."

Mike eyed the woman walking back toward them sporting a bright orange life jacket. She had the tenacity and follow-through to write a book. That had to say something about a person. Did she really know the secret to getting what a person wants in only thirty days?

Thirty days from now he and Hadley would both turn thirty. He wanted to celebrate that milestone by doing the smart, practical thing they'd both agreed on a decade ago, even if they'd made the pact half-jokingly. Why wouldn't Hadley marry him? Hadn't he shown her he wanted to be a strong parent in their child's life? Didn't she know he cared about her? Did anyone, except perhaps her sister, know Hadley better than he did?

What was he missing?

"Hello," he said, sticking out a hand to the island visitor as soon as she approached. "I'm

Mike Martin, owner of Island Bike Rental, and I've just persuaded my friend here to trade partners with me."

"I'm Miranda Mitchell. Why do you want to race with me?" the woman asked.

Mike flashed her what he believed was a winning smile. He didn't want her to think she was getting in a canoe with a lunatic, but then again, she had come to an island and signed up for a race without knowing anyone.

"Do you think you could teach me the secret of getting what I want in thirty days?" he asked.

"While we're paddling this canoe?"

"It's a start," he said.

"I should tell you to buy a copy of my book, but I could give you some pointers if you use your hometown advantage and make sure we don't come in last."

"I'll do my best," Mike said.

"And that's the first step toward getting what you want," Miranda said.

They got in their canoes and took up their paddles. Right before they launched, Hadley came over with her dog.

"Good luck," she said. "Betty and I will be rooting for you."

"Not for your brother-in-law?" Mike asked.

Hadley laughed. "He has Shirley in his canoe. He doesn't need a cheerleader."

"Gonna annihilate ya," Shirley said cheerfully from the neighboring canoe.

Hadley walked away with Betty by her side.

Mike's partner turned around from her seat in the front of the canoe. "I believe I can guess what it is you want."

"I've already asked her to marry me twice."

"Why?"

Before Mike could answer, the canoe race started with a whistle. Splashing, laughing and one loud cry from the crowd as an imbalanced canoe tipped into the harbor distracted Mike from telling his rowing partner about his coming fatherhood.

"Right, left, right, left," Mike said, chanting evenly and delighted when Miranda paddled as if she'd done it a million times. They were heading in a straight, neat line for the lighthouse, pulling ahead of the rest of the pack.

"You didn't answer my question," Miranda said without missing a stroke.

"She's pregnant," he said.

"So?"

"So that's why I asked her to marry me."

"I see."

"And you don't think that's a good enough reason?" he asked.

"Does she?"

"Apparently not," Mike said.

"Why else?" Miranda asked.

"There's a pact."

He thought he heard her breathe out the words, "Oh, boy."

"We have the same birthday. June first. We agreed back when we were teenagers that we'd get married when we reached the ancient age of thirty if we hadn't found anyone else. That's only thirty days away now."

Miranda flicked him a glance over her shoulder. "And you think the method outlined in my book will help you convince that beautiful woman with the dog to marry you in time for birthday cake?"

"Ouch," Mike said. He was tempted to splash his rowing partner in response to the cold water she'd just thrown on his matrimonial plans.

"There's nothing I can do to help you until you figure out the real why," she said. "That's on you."

"I have two good reasons."

"Neither of which are good enough," Miranda said.

Mike dug deep with his paddle, hoping to get this canoe trip over with fast. It wasn't enough that they were winning handily. He wanted out of the boat with the woman who clearly couldn't see the perfect logic of his plan. Maybe he should try again with Hadley. He didn't want to go home alone on Christmas Eve, didn't want to plant his and her flowers and live separate but connected lives.

They executed the turn at the lighthouse as if they'd rowed together across the Atlantic.

"How'd you learn to paddle a canoe like that?" Mike asked.

"How did you learn?" she returned.

This woman really was a tough customer.

"Experience and practice," he answered.

"Same here. Although I did condense all my initial practice into thirty days because I'd always wanted to canoe and didn't want to look like an amateur."

"Why?" Mike asked.

"No one wants to look like a beginner," Miranda said.

"I mean why did you always want to canoe?"

Miranda's laugh rang out over the calm water of the Christmas Island harbor. "Now you're playing my game," she said. "I like it here. I may just see if I can stay for the whole month while I work on my next book. That way I can be around on your birthday to see if you ever figure it out."

Mike's shoulders only ached a little, but he was anxious to cross the finish line. Would Hadley be waiting? Would she be impressed by his win, even though he could only take half the credit? They'd have a late dinner together somewhere with an outdoor table where Betty could catch a stray firefly while they dined over candlelight.

Lamps turned on in downtown Christmas Island as the dusk deepened. The red and green channel lights welcomed them back into the harbor, even though it was still technically bright enough without them. Holiday lights twinkled in the trees on the marina's lawn, their red and white bulbs freshly strung for another tourist season that was just beginning.

The hope of a perfect summer hung in front of Mike like a lantern beckoning him in to shore. Better yet, he could make out a woman and a black dog standing by the dock, waiting for him. He flashed back to that moment after his second proposal when Hadley and Betty had waited for him in the truck while the waves whispered to him, and he felt as if he could finally hear the words that had been there all along.

He and Miranda cruised into the slip first, someone blew a whistle, and he heard his name and his partner's being announced over the loudspeaker as the audience applauded. He got out of the canoe first, making sure to keep it steady so he didn't tip his rowing partner into the harbor. Mike offered Miranda a hand and helped her out of the boat.

"You're the best canoe partner I've ever had," he said. "It only took you thirty days to get that good?"

She smiled. "It took me thirty days to get what I thought I wanted, but then I kept on going because it made me happy."

Hadley came up and gave him a friendly hug and her dog licked his knee and jumped around on the dock, clearly aware of the excitement in the air. He glanced over at Miranda in time to see her mouth the word *why*.

As the sun dipped low over the island and he had one arm around Hadley, Mike had a moment of clarity so strong he could have seen the stars and planets with a naked eye.

He loved Hadley. That was his *why*.

If only she felt the same way.

CHAPTER ELEVEN

ON A WEEKDAY morning after the busy May Day weekend, Hadley decided to do something out of character. She knew very well that it was seven o'clock, but she didn't get out of bed. She pushed her long dark hair off her face and closed her eyes, shutting out the bright sunlight coming through the lace curtains. Her bedroom walls were yellow, a color her grandmother had painted them and Hadley had never changed.

It was pretty and cheerful. The room next door, though, was not cheerful. The wallpaper in there was, quite possibly, as old as the house itself. Growing up, it had been her mother's bedroom, and Hadley and Wendy had shared the larger room down the hall. Their mother hadn't wanted to fuss about the wallpaper, claiming she was never in there, anyway, so it wasn't worth the trouble.

Now that Hadley intended to use it as a nursery, that wallpaper had to go.

Later.

Instead of popping out of bed, she gave in to the luxury of running her hand over her baby bump and imagining holding a sweet-smelling baby in her arms as they watched the snow fall next winter.

Betty nosed into the room and whined, wagging her tail. Hadley closed her eyes, hoping the dog would take the hint. She heard the soft thump as the dog sat down and then her tail swishing on the hardwood floor.

"You're still there, aren't you?" Hadley asked. "I wish I could put your energy to good use stripping wallpaper."

She shoved off the blankets and stood, taking a moment to get her bearings before heading down the steps in her nightgown to let her dog into the backyard. As she passed the front door, she heard a quiet knock. She paused, leaned back to peek through the narrow window alongside the door. Mike's truck was parked outside.

Hadley sighed. "How about using the front yard this morning?" she asked Betty.

Betty trotted to the front door and waited while Hadley opened it.

"Good morning," Mike said cheerfully. He held up a white bag and a drink carrier. "I brought breakfast sandwiches from the Christmas Carol and decaf tea."

"You're drinking decaf tea?" she asked.

"One decaf tea, and one strong black coffee I could drink outside if the smell is too tempting. Sorry, didn't think about that."

Hadley laughed. "It's fine. Come in." She left the door open for Betty and went into the kitchen with Mike. "You know it's my day off, right?"

"Yes," he said. "That's why I'm here. I'll do anything you want, up to and including scooping Betty's poop out of the yard."

"Good," Hadley said. "That's first on the list."

"I'm serious," Mike said. "I want you to be able to take it easy, and if I know you, you have a detailed to-do list for your day off because you know how busy we're all going to be starting roughly next week."

Hadley sat and opened the bag. She pulled out two warm sandwiches wrapped in white paper. "Are these the same?" she asked. Betty came inside and followed the smell of food to the kitchen. She sat next to Mike and put a chin on his knee.

Mike nodded. "The usual."

Hadley opened the wrapper and took a bite, taking her time and chewing slowly, a trick she'd learned early in her pregnancy in case a wave of nausea came from out of nowhere.

"Is everything okay?" Mike asked. "I don't think I've surprised you in your nightgown before. You're usually work clothes and ponytail by this time of day."

Hadley shrugged. "I was going to treat myself to sleeping in, but my brain was awake and so was my dog. I was about to give up and do the work-clothes-and-ponytail thing."

"And your list?"

Hadley took another bite and chewed slowly, considering the offer of help and how to best use it. "How do you feel about wallpaper?"

"I hate flowers and texture. Other kinds are okay. Some of the stuff up at the Great Island Hotel is a bit much, but—"

Hadley interrupted him with her laughter. "I mean stripping wallpaper."

Mike took a long swig of his coffee. "I said

I'd do anything, and that's only slightly worse than poop-scooping."

"Maybe it will fall right off the walls," Hadley said.

Mike laid the back of his hand on her forehead. "No fever, so you must be in your right mind. Do you remember helping me pull off that pink wallpaper that was in my bathroom?"

"It wasn't the ugliest thing about your apartment," Hadley said.

"You don't have to be nice to me just because I brought you breakfast and I'm offering free labor for the day," Mike said, his grin wide. "And I have a secret I never confessed to before."

Hadley leaned back in her chair and tugged her nightgown down over her knees. "I think it's too early in the morning to reveal terrible secrets."

"This one's relevant. I told you at the time that I'd finish stripping the wallpaper after you helped me do the first two walls. But I lied," Mike said. "I painted over it on the other two walls."

Hadley laughed. "I knew that."

"How?"

"I've used your bathroom. The wall with the wallpaper seams showing through the paint is right next to the toilet. You can't help seeing it when you're unrolling bath tissue. I think the crack at the seams might be getting worse as time goes by."

Mike swished his lips to the side and stared up at the ceiling. "All this time, I thought I was getting away with something, and you knew all along. I guess that's a reminder I can't hide anything from you."

"Same here," Hadley said.

Mike locked eyes with her across the table and there was a long pause. Distantly, Hadley heard the morning ferry's whistle.

"Good to know we won't bother hiding anything," Mike said, his voice low and gruff. "You go ahead and take your time with your tea, and I'll run to my place and get those scrapers and the scoring tool we used when we did half of my bathroom."

"Do you hate doing this?" Hadley asked, prepared to let him out of it and find some other way to beautify that room.

"I would hate having you do this by yourself, and we both know there's no easy way out if my bathroom's coming apart at the seams has taught me anything."

Mike got up and Betty followed him as he left the kitchen. He paused in the doorway and looked back at Hadley. "Is it okay with you if she rides along?"

Hadley nodded. "She'd love that."

Mike put an affectionate hand on the dog's head. "This is why I've never gotten a dog. I can just borrow yours whenever I want one."

"I never thought about it like that," Hadley said.

Mike smiled at Betty. "You have the best dog. Nothing I could get would come close."

As she watched Mike open the side door of his pickup for Betty, it occurred to Hadley that they'd had a soul-baring conversation about wallpaper and dogs, but it was really about something bigger. The unspoken things they were hiding in their hearts. How were they going to manage being parents without altering the friendship that had always bound them?

It didn't seem possible.

She watched Mike and Betty drive off and swallowed back her tears. There was too much work to be done, and days off were scarce.

Hadley trudged upstairs and put on an old stretched-out pair of yoga pants and a T-shirt and pulled her hair into a low ponytail. Even if Mike did the hard parts, she wasn't going to sit by and let him pick away at years' worth of wallpaper by himself.

THEY'D ONLY BEEN at work for two hours, but Mike had bits of glue and paper stuck underneath what little was left of his fingernails. Wetting down the walls with a sponge helped, but he still had to pick his way inch by inch around the high parts while Hadley did the low parts.

"I think I've changed my mind," she said. "This paper is beautiful. No wonder no one has removed it before."

"Very funny. I think I'm finally getting a strategy down," Mike said. "Look." He held up a fragment of wallpaper that was at least six inches square. "Finally getting it off in big chunks."

They worked in silence for a few minutes, and then Mike took the sponge and wet down a fresh section of wall. "I was thinking," he said. "We have less than a month until our thirtieth birthdays."

He was actually thinking about how he could use thirty days to win Hadley over to the idea of marrying him, but he was holding that ace up his damp, sticky sleeve.

"So we should do something wild to celebrate our last month in our carefree twenties?" Hadley asked. "Like the Roaring Twenties? We could dress up. You could be a gangster and I could be a flapper and we could learn to do the Charleston."

"I think you need a break," Mike said.

"I'm perfectly fine. What did you have in mind when you brought up the impending doom of our thirties? And don't—" she held up a hand "—bring up that silly pact again."

"Believe me, I won't," he said.

Did Hadley look relieved? Puzzled? Interesting. If she thought he was going to take an awkward stab at another marriage proposal, she was going to be disappointed.

He sighed. Wasn't he there proving himself as husband material by bringing breakfast, taking the dog for a ride in the car, cleaning up after the dog and now tackling an agonizing home-improvement project? What else would it take?

Maybe he should ask one of his married

friends. He'd already tried talking to Wendy at the St. Patrick's Day event, but she'd made it clear he was going to have to figure this one out on his own.

"You look as if you're considering the gangster-and-flapper idea," Hadley said. "Or the Charleston. You're not a bad dancer. You might be able to pull it off."

"I believe I would," Mike said. "But I was thinking we should do little things. Simple pleasures. We could approach the geriatric age of thirty as if every day is a celebration."

Hadley laughed and pointed around the room. "We've already started."

"This doesn't count."

Hadley put down the narrow paint scraper she was using to peel strips of wallpaper from the corner by the window. She sat on a stool and stretched her lower back, twisting to get her hands behind her. Mike walked over and turned her stool so her back faced him. "Let me," he said. He kneaded her shoulders and worked his way down her back, gently massaging until he felt her relax.

"I could live with this kind of celebration for our last month of being twenty-something," Hadley said. "And we could really live it up by you rubbing my feet."

"Anytime," Mike said. "I'm all yours."

He felt her tense at that statement and then relax again. Maybe she was softening toward him? If he kept up a thirty-day charm offensive and showed her how much he cared for her, how long would it take for her to decide marriage to him wouldn't be so bad?

The thought warmed him, but his happiness was sharply interrupted by barking and then yipping from outside. Mike reached over Hadley's head and pulled aside the curtain. Betty was rolling around the yard, rubbing her face on the grass.

"What's the matter with her?" Hadley asked, rising, her voice sounding strained.

Mike started to say he didn't know and was preparing to run downstairs and help the dog when the smell hit him.

"Skunk," he said. "Smell it?"

"In the middle of the day?"

"I overheard talk at the hardware store that there was a bumper crop of baby skunks this year. She must have surprised a mother skunk."

"Oh, my God," Hadley said, her mouth

open in shock. "Poor Betty. What do we do?" She was halfway to the door of the bedroom, but Mike was right on her heels.

"Let me go out there. I'll rinse out the bucket and fill it with fresh water if you'll grab some towels."

Mike went into the upstairs bathroom and dumped out the wallpaper water and then refilled the bucket in the bathtub. Hadley pulled old towels from the bottom of a cabinet and held them out to him. As awful as the situation was, he was glad Hadley was letting him help. If he hadn't been there, she would have handled it, but she didn't need any extra stress in her life right now.

"This is terrible," Hadley said, her voice quivering. "My poor girl."

"Poor us," Mike added. "It takes a year to get skunk smell out of the thick fur on a lab."

"Has this happened to you before?"

He nodded, one hand on the banister at the top of the stairs. "When I was a kid. It seemed awful at the time, but it turned out okay. It'll be okay, Hadley."

"Thank you," she said. "I—"

"I'm here for you," Mike said. "And your smelly dog."

Hadley's pained expression softened.

"Whatever you do, don't let her in the house, no matter how much she cries. She'll go right for the couch and rugs to try to rub that smell off. Let me try to get her cleaned up and then she can spend the night in the garage."

Mike dashed down the steps, bent on rescuing the sweet dog as quickly as he could so its sweet owner wouldn't worry too much. The moment he went through the door, bucket and towels in hand, Betty rushed him and rubbed her face on his pants. She knocked the bucket over and he dropped the towels.

So much for looking like a hero. He soaked a towel in the water that remained in the bucket and carefully wiped Betty's face and eyes, just in case she'd gotten a blast of skunk scent in the face. As he did so, he heard the door open behind him.

"No," he said, turning toward the sound as Betty rushed the door, but Hadley, still inside was fast enough to pull it shut again, proving she had listened to Mike's warning. Hadley's face in the window, hand over her mouth, showed her surprise but also a hint of amusement at his plight.

He approached the door. "Is your outdoor

spigot turned on for the year?" he yelled to be heard through the glass. Mike knew that, like everyone else on Christmas Island, Hadley shut off and drained the lines going to her outdoor hoses so they wouldn't freeze in the winter. Hadley nodded.

Mike took the bucket, with Betty at his heels, around the side of the house where Hadley kept the hose for watering her outdoor plants. Skipping the bucket, he began hosing off the dog and wiping her down with the towels.

"This is only step one, girl," he said to the dog. "We'll try to get as much off as we can, and then we'll look up the internet recipe involving mouthwash and soup or something like that, and we'll do what we can for you."

Betty stood still and gave him long sad looks while he scrubbed the thick fur around her neck.

"You got it all over me, so we're in this together," he said. "Maybe I'll spend the night in the garage with you. It's better than picking off wallpaper one square inch at a time. And maybe it's a good thing this happened now and not next year when there'll be a baby at your house."

He spoke low and reassuringly to the dog,

keeping up a string of conversation to keep her calm while he scrubbed and hosed her black fur.

"You'll have to help with the baby, you know," he said. "I'll be counting on you to keep everyone safe, which means I hope you learned from this adventure. It's your job to wake people up if a smoke detector chirps, and if a stranger comes to the door, you know what to do, right?"

Either he was losing his sense of smell, or the skunk odor was fading. Mike gave Betty a break from scrubbing and sat on the ground next to her. He was soaked to the bone, anyway, and the sun felt good.

"I heard everything you said to my dog."

Mike turned toward the door, hoping Hadley hadn't come outside and risked getting soaked and skunked. She had the window in the door open and her face was veiled by the window screen.

"Did you hear the part where I told her she'd have to take over the wallpaper job?"

Hadley laughed. "No. But I heard the rest. Thank you for being so sweet, Mike."

"I'm just helping out a friend," he said.

"I'm more than a friend."

Mike leaned back on both elbows and smiled at her. "Maybe I was talking about Betty."

Hadley laughed, and the sound made him so happy it almost erased the skunk smell burning his eyes.

CHAPTER TWELVE

WENDY SANK INTO a chair in the Holiday Hotel lobby. "The kids are at Grandma's for an hour, but I don't want to leave them there any longer," she said.

"They love visiting Grandma," Hadley said. She saved the work she'd been doing in the reservation system and came around the desk. She took the glass dome off the tray of Christmas cookies. "Want one?"

"I want three," Wendy said. "But I'll just take one. A big one."

Hadley laughed and chose a large gingerbread lady wearing a green-and-red-checkered dress. "It's almost too pretty to eat."

"Almost," Wendy said. She bit the head off the cookie and smiled. "That's wonderful."

Hadley waited for her sister to get to the reason for the mid-morning visit. Wendy usually reserved hour-long visits with Grandma for times when it was an absolute necessity.

"Is it true that you made Mike spend the night in your garage a few days ago with your skunk-sprayed dog?" Wendy asked.

"Sort of," Hadley said. "Poor Betty surprised a nest, and Mike was at my house peeling wallpaper in Mom's old room. He elected to stay with her in the garage."

"You're getting the nursery prepared," Wendy said.

Hadley wasn't ready to talk about the nursery and all the details it would involve. She still couldn't picture a baby living in that room, but she hoped when she found out the gender, the baby might come into focus in her mind.

"Beginning with the wallpaper," Hadley said. It was a start. "How did you hear about the skunk incident?"

"Mike called Justin to ask if he knew any secret park ranger methods of getting the smell out."

"Did he?"

Wendy shrugged one shoulder and finished off the gingerbread lady. "They get their information from the internet just like everyone else."

"I didn't make Mike stay in the garage. He

was being nice. Poor Betty was upset, but we didn't want to let her in the house quite yet, so we set up a camp cot for him and I moved her bed out there. It was a warm night and I brought them both breakfast in the morning."

Wendy laughed. "It's good baby practice for Mike."

"In case our baby gets sprayed by a skunk?"

"No. For all those sleepless nights where you would honestly lie down in traffic just to be horizontal and close your eyes," Wendy said.

Hadley didn't have to ask her sister if she was exaggerating. Having taken night duty with her nieces and nephews a few times to help out, she knew that up-all-night feeling, and the odd sensation of wandering the house at three in the morning thinking she was the only person in the world who was awake. That was going to be her life in a few months.

"You look so serious," Wendy said, leaning forward in her chair and putting her hand on Hadley's knee.

"Having a baby is serious."

Wendy smiled. "But it's also magical and wonderful and joyous and sometimes even hilarious. For example, just this morning, Janey explained to Macey where babies come from."

Hadley put a hand over her mouth. "Do I want to know?"

"I hid around the corner and listened, and it was pretty educational. She told Macey that she used to think babies came from eating wedding cake, but now she's figured out that's not it. Now she thinks babies come when someone wishes very hard, but you have to be old, so she told Macey they shouldn't bother yet."

Hadley laughed until a tear ran down her cheek and she got the hiccups.

Wendy fetched her a glass of water and patted her on the back. Hadley sputtered and held up a hand. "I'm all right," she said, still smiling at being pronounced old by her six-year-old niece in her sage advice to her four-year-old sister. Hadley loved those kids as if they were her own. How much more could she possibly love her own baby? It didn't seem possible to fit all that love into one heart.

"Everything okay?" Hadley recognized Griffin's voice and waved a hand toward him. He and Mike stood in the hotel lobby next to the chair where Hadley sat. Mike wore his usual bike shop uniform of faded jeans and a Mike's Island Bike Rental T-shirt stained with bicycle grease.

"I'm good," Hadley said. "Wendy just told me something funny that made me laugh until I got the hiccups, but I'm fine."

"You sure?" Mike asked. "You're pretty pink."

Wendy poked him in the chest. "You mean pretty."

"That, too," Mike said. "Beautiful, actually."

Hadley swallowed and looked up at him. "You think I'm beautiful?"

"I know you are," he said.

Had he ever said anything like that to her before? Maybe a casual comment if they were dressed up for some island function. He might have told her she looked nice or even pretty. She could probably dig up those memories, even though she hadn't taken them seriously. Mike was her friend. They hadn't strayed into romantic territory in over a decade, not since that high school kiss that ended in laughter and led to a silly thirtieth birthday pact. Unless one counted the encounter after the island Christmas party, of course.

"I think you're being influenced by my new perfume," Hadley said. "Skunk Scent Number Five." She held up the back of her hand and offered him a sniff.

Everyone laughed, and Hadley was glad to have broken the brief tension caused by Mike telling her she was beautiful in front of her boss and her sister. If they had been alone, how might she have handled that statement? But they weren't.

"Fabulous," Mike said. He took her hand and drew in a long dramatic breath. "A touch of earthiness mixed with danger. Very appealing."

Hadley pulled her hand back, but she couldn't hide her grin. "What are you doing here in the middle of the morning when you should be across the street handing out bike helmets?"

"I have new brochures and coupons I was hoping to put in your registration packets as usual," Mike said. He held up a stack of colorful papers with a rubber band securing them. "Do I need to see the manager?"

"The owner is standing right next to you," Hadley said. Mike could easily have given the flyers to Griffin outside. Had he come in just to see her?

"No way," Griffin said. "I put you in charge of the hotel for the summer so I can spend all my time working on my second ferry dock."

Hadley cocked her head at Griffin. "You put me in charge of the front desk."

"Same thing," he said. "Moving you out of the restaurant has opened my eyes to your organizational skills, and I'd be wise to make you general manager of the whole place."

Hadley sucked in a breath. It was only the third official season for Griffin and his brother owning the Holiday Hotel, and they'd spent a considerable amount of that time renovating it. This would be their first full occupancy, full speed summer.

"Are you serious about that?" Hadley asked. On one hand, the work would be more significant than the restaurant and bar manager and server job she'd held for years, beginning when she was a teenager. She'd enjoyed the work and just…never left. Maybe it was time to get a more grown-up job now that she was turning thirty and having a baby?

"Yes," Griffin said. "But we'll talk about it when you're ready. Sorry to spring that on you."

Hadley smiled. "I'm getting used to surprises."

"I know what you mean," Griffin said. His surprise had been an inheritance of three-million dollars and an island mansion, but Hadley wouldn't trade hers for all that wealth. Griffin grabbed his jacket from a hook inside the door and left, and Mike walked over to the counter and put his stack of flyers by the cookie tray. He lingered over the pile of books the visiting author had left on the counter.

"You can take one of those," she said. "The author left them out as complimentary copies. She says this place inspires her and she's staying a month."

Mike picked up the slim volume and tucked it under his arm. "I should get back to work," he said.

Hadley nodded and smiled at him. She didn't want to run him off, but she was curious about her sister's visit that had a one-hour limit. After Mike left, she motioned for her sister to sit down.

"I'm glad you stopped in to say hello today," she said, prompting her sister to get to her real reason.

"I had something I wanted to suggest to

you, and you can take it or leave it, but I'm laying it out there," Wendy said. As the older sister, Wendy had offered advice and counsel before, but they were only two years apart in age and Hadley usually felt as if they were on an equal footing. Although Wendy knew more about kids and Hadley knew more about running a restaurant, and now a hotel.

"Do you hate my hair?" Hadley asked. "I've let it get really long, and I swear it's growing ridiculously fast right now. Is it the wrong look for a…mature woman?"

Wendy laughed and reached out to touch a long lock of Hadley's dark hair. "Your hair is gorgeous, and you can let it get as long as you want. I actually wanted to help you out with your clothes."

Hadley looked down at her clothes, suddenly self-conscious. Her waist had expanded, and her usual pants were a no-go. She'd tossed some of the tops and blouses that were fine for working in the bar where she always wore an apron into a storage bin. They didn't look right for her front desk job, and the ones that were a little nicer didn't button. Today, she wore black stretch pants, flats and a Holiday Hotel polo shirt she'd found under the desk that appeared to be a sample from a graphics company wanting the hotel's business. It was cut for a man and two sizes too big even with her expanding belly.

"I'm taking suggestions," Hadley said.

"I worked at the bank all through my first pregnancy, so I have some nice maternity clothes. They're in a plastic tub in the back of my closet, but if you want to come over and go through them, you might find something you like."

Hadley sighed. Maternity clothes. She loved the idea of having a baby of her own but she hadn't allowed herself to picture waddling around in maternity clothes.

"Nothing you own is going to fit by the end of the summer," Wendy said. "Trust me on that."

"Nothing fits very well now," Hadley admitted. She swallowed. "When can I come over?"

"Anytime, but you're coming, anyway, on Sunday for Grandma's eightieth birthday dinner. I can get Justin to entertain Grandma and the kids while you and I go upstairs and go maternity shopping in my closet."

Hadley felt tears sting her eyes at the thought.

"This is one of those times I miss Mom," she said. "She'd be all about going maternity-clothes shopping and would probably offer to sew a whole wardrobe for me."

"I can't sew, but I have some cute clothes you're welcome to. I'm never going down that road again, especially now that Justin and I are outnumbered."

Hadley laughed and her sister stood up to go and pulled her up for a long hug. "We're having Grandma's favorite noodle casserole and the girls are helping with the cake. Will you bring a salad and rolls?"

"Absolutely."

"And...you could bring Mike along, too," Wendy said. "He's technically part of the family now."

Hadley's heart fluttered in her chest. A promotion offer, maternity clothes and now Mike was invited to a family birthday. It was a lot for one Wednesday morning.

"I'll ask," Hadley said. "And thank you."

"I'm your sister," Wendy said, keeping one arm around Hadley. "And our kids are going to be cousins, and everything's going to be okay."

Hadley nodded. She should tell her sister

Mike had proposed a second time, but she might burst into tears and cry all over her oversized polo shirt, especially if Wendy said what she thought her sister would say. *Marry the guy. You could do worse. You're going to need a committed partner, and why not make it your best friend whom you secretly...* Well, Wendy knew her well, but she didn't know that. And Hadley was keeping that secret close to her heart where it was safe and wouldn't cause too much trouble. Letting herself love Mike could only lead to heartache for them both.

The last guests to check-in for the day had their keys and island maps, and the front desk was clean, organized, and ready for the next morning when there would be four checkouts. She had an envelope for each group that held their ferry tickets along with a coupon for a discounted return visit.

The front desk hadn't been sloppily run, Hadley thought, but the summer employees hired to work it had simply completed assigned tasks instead of owning the job. She owned it now, at least for the next five months until she went on leave. Luckily, her leave would coincide with the quiet season on the island during which the Holiday Hotel was technically open but with a limited capacity. It rarely had guests outside of weekends in the off-season. Maybe she could bring her baby to work and help out? She owed Griffin and Maddox May her loyalty, considering they'd changed her work assignment to something she could manage better at the moment.

And maybe permanently. She swept a cloth over the gleaming wood of the check-in desk and locked the drawer. It was nice meeting guests and helping them organize their trip. Was it better than serving them drinks and recommending specials? She glanced in the doorway of the restaurant as she prepared to leave work at five o'clock. The piano would be silent until later in the evening, and the late afternoon light streamed through the front windows of the restaurant.

She missed it, the place where she'd worked for ten years, but it was right around the corner from the front desk that she'd already organized to her satisfaction. She could do this, roll with the changes.

As she left the front door of the Holiday Hotel, prepared to walk home on the warm weekday evening, Mike looked both ways and dodged bicycles as he jogged across the street.

"I tried to come over earlier, but it was busy. I was afraid I wouldn't catch you before you left work," he said, a little breathlessly.

His cheeks were flushed, and his hair was mussed as if he'd run his fingers through it. It was still a bit long from the winter.

"You haven't gotten your summer buzz cut yet," she said before she even thought.

Mike smiled. "I was hoping you'd use Betty's clippers and do it for me again."

Hadley laughed, remembering that time three years ago when he'd come over as she finished shaving Betty on a hot spring day, and he'd suggested she just buzz off his hair, too. "That was a disaster. Shaving my dog for the summer was not the job experience I needed for cutting your hair. You wore a hat for a month."

"I like hats," Mike said. "And it wasn't your fault. I think Betty is more cooperative than me. I kept making you laugh."

"Either way, I think I'll stick to hotel management."

Tourists brushed past them on the sidewalk

and Mike took Hadley's hand and guided her onto the stone path leading to the steps of the Holiday Hotel. "Let's have dinner together," he said. "You're done with work, and I'm almost done. My summer helper can check in the bikes that are still out there."

"I have to go let Betty out," Hadley said. She noticed the quick look of disappointment on Mike's face as if he thought she was going to turn him down. Had she ever turned him down for dinner or anything else? She couldn't remember.

"Is there some special occasion?" she asked.

"Yes," Mike said. "We only have twenty-five days until we turn thirty, and I'm already behind on celebrating each one of them with something special."

"The skunk incident distracted us," Hadley said.

"We can restart the countdown with tonight's dinner," Mike said.

"And…then what?"

"You'll have to wait and see. But first, tonight's plan." Mike rubbed a hand affectionately down her arm. "Name the place and we'll meet there in an hour."

"Mistletoe Melt," she said, giving in to dinner but not necessarily the plan of a daily countdown to their milestone birthday. "Those giant sandwiches sound so good I'm not sure I can wait an hour."

"I'll hurry," Mike said. He gave her arm one last pat and then jogged back to his bike rental.

Less than an hour later, Hadley sat across from Mike on the outdoor patio of the Mistletoe Melt, wearing one of her favorite ocean blue tops that still fit. Their table overlooked the water, and the evening breeze ruffled their menus as they considered their choices.

"They have some new combinations this year," Mike said. "But you can't argue with a burger that also has eggs and home fries on it."

"As hungry as I am, I have to use some self-control. Not everything settles as well as it used to these days. I'm going with a grilled chicken on whole wheat with a salad on the side."

"You're going to steal half of my fries if you don't order your own," Mike commented, not even looking up from his menu, but Hadley could see his grin, anyway.

"Of course," she said. "But I have the moral high ground of not having given in and ordered them."

Mike looked up and his smile widened. "What's mine is yours."

Her heart melted at his simple declaration, which she knew, from experience, to be true. He'd always been there for her, and now they were linked together forever. Hadn't they always been, though?

"How is your blood pressure?" he asked, pulling Hadley's thoughts back to the practical here and now.

"It's fine. I stop by the clinic every few days and have the nurse check it. The very low dose of blood pressure medication combined with a change of jobs is doing the trick."

"Do you need anything from me? A ride to the doctor or extra help?" Mike asked.

Hadley smiled at him. "I'm doing okay. Really."

Mike let out a long breath. "I'm glad. But you only have to ask. Anything, anytime. You know that."

Hadley nodded. "I do."

A server wearing a red and green apron and a green baseball cap with a sprig of plastic mistletoe on the brim appeared next to the table with a notepad in hand. "What can I get you?" he asked.

Mike took his eyes from Hadley and smiled at the server. "We'll have everything," he said.

Although he was joking, Hadley almost believed that she and Mike already had everything.

"I'll put that order in right away," the server said.

Hadley laughed and held up a hand. "I'm pacing myself with the grilled chicken and a side salad."

Mike placed his order for something wildly greasier, and the server left.

"Pacing ourselves," he said, his words more a question than a statement.

"I'll indulge at my sister's house on Sunday night. It's my grandmother's eightieth birthday party and we're having a big family dinner." This was the moment she had to cross over the friend line and take a chance. "And you're invited."

Mike's expression changed to something serious. "I've never been to one of your grandmother's birthday parties."

"Well, you're basically family now," Hadley said.

"Basically?"

"Your child will be Grandma Penny's great-grandchild."

Mike gave her a long searching look. "Is that the only reason I'm invited?"

Hadley shook her head and swallowed. She considered telling him he was invited because he was more to her than just a friend, more to her than the father of her child. But his expression was so intense she was afraid he'd drop to one knee and go for the third proposal to cement his spot in the family, and she knew it wouldn't come with a declaration of love, just as the other ones hadn't. It was a beautiful night, and she didn't want to ruin it.

"That's not the only reason," Hadley said forcing a smile. "My sister asked me to invite you."

Mike regarded her for a moment as if he were trying to decide whether or not to play along. Finally, he rolled his shoulders and sat back in his chair. "Wendy was always the nice sister. And she never steals my food."

"But," Hadley said, raising her glass of

water to him, "you don't share a birthday with her."

"In only twenty-five days," Mike said.

His smile was a bit mysterious, and Hadley wondered if there was more to his plan than simply a birthday countdown. Did he think he'd wear her down by being a good friend and then she'd agree to honor that goofy marriage pact on their thirtieth birthday? He was setting himself up for disappointment, but Hadley did have to admit to herself that the next twenty-five days could be a lot of fun.

CHAPTER THIRTEEN

MIKE WENT TO the only florist's shop on Christmas Island the morning after his dinner at the Mistletoe Melt with Hadley. The shop occupied a sunny place next to Violet Brookstone's boutique, with a coffee and pastry shop on its other side. The Peterson family's Island Candy and Fudge shop was right across the street, and this section of downtown Christmas Island smelled like heaven.

"Hello, Jennifer," he said to the shop's owner, a middle-aged woman with salt-and-pepper hair and bright blue eyes. She had been friends with Mike's mother, and he knew they still kept in touch. Mike had called his parents just a few days after he'd discovered he was going to be a father because he was excited to tell them and because he knew they'd find out somehow and it had better be from him.

"I just had a text from your mother yesterday," Jennifer said. "She sent me a picture of her grandkids' visit to their retirement home in Florida, and I sent her one of last weekend's May Day celebration."

"She misses those fun island things," Mike said. "But she has golf year-round and no longer owns a snow shovel, so it's a good trade."

"I bet she'll start visiting again when she has a grandbaby on this island," Jennifer said.

Mike smiled. "I hope so." His parents already had plans to visit during the Christmas season because they were excited about being part of his baby's first Christmas. It still seemed surreal that he would be a father by then and would have his own family. He pictured a family photograph with him and Hadley and their baby sitting in front of a Christmas tree.

"What can I get for you today?" Jennifer asked. "Are you looking for some flowers to brighten up your shop or maybe a gift for someone?"

"Flowers," Mike said. "What do you have twenty-four of that would make a nice bouquet?"

Jennifer contemplated her taller glass-fronted cooler filled with flowers. "I get fresh shipments on Mondays and Fridays this time of year. If you can wait until tomorrow, I'll have an even better variety."

"Today is day twenty-four," Mike said.

Jennifer gave him a curious look, her held tilted but her eyes kind. As the only island florist, she provided flowers for every occasion, and even though she knew everyone on the island, she was also discreet enough not to press people on their reasons.

"I have twenty-four carnations, but they're not all the same color," Jennifer said.

"That could work."

"I have a dozen fresh white daisies that you could mix with a dozen pink or yellow carnations, and it would be a beautiful bouquet. They're not fussy flowers like roses or orchids, but they're pretty and cheerful. And not expensive, especially this time of year."

Hadley was pretty and cheerful, and he couldn't imagine anyone describing her as fussy. Punctual, organized, detailed, yes. But not fussy. She would like the practical choice of inexpensive but happy flowers.

"That's perfect," he said.

"Would you like to carry them with you or have them delivered to…someone?"

Mike considered the question. It would be nice to have an excuse to pop into the hotel lobby and say good morning to Hadley, but having the flowers delivered would seem special. And everyone on the island knew he and Hadley were…associated.

"Let's go with delivery. Can I write a note to go with them?" Mike asked.

"Of course," Jennifer said. She pointed to the rack of small cards with matching envelopes. "Take your pick. There are cards for birthdays, anniversaries, weddings, babies, and just saying I love you."

She waited, obviously curious about which card he'd pick. He let his fingers linger over the one with hearts and an *I love you* message, then over a happy-birthday card. He knew Jennifer was watching, and it was kind of fun to make her and everyone else on the island wonder what was going on with him and Hadley. More than one person had hinted to him that they should get married, but he'd said nothing, respecting Hadley's privacy and her refusal. Twice.

Mike finally selected a card with the words *Thinking of You,* which was a true, if inadequate, statement. He picked up a pen from the counter and wrote *24 days until the big day*. He wrote Hadley's name on the little envelope, then stuffed the card inside and sealed it.

"What color ribbon would you like on the bouquet?" Jennifer asked.

"Green. Christmas green. It's her favorite color."

Jennifer beamed at him, obviously delighted that he knew Hadley's favorite color.

He paid for the flowers and hurried back to his bike shop in time for the first wave of tourists coming off the eight-thirty ferry. These early-season weekday visitors were usually coming with tour groups, eager to get outside after a long winter.

The first people through his door were a vibrant retired couple. As Mike found two bikes that would be a good fit, they told him all about their cross-country road trip that had begun in their Ohio hometown. They'd traveled up through Michigan, were staying on the island for two days and then continuing via a northern route west to California. They planned to be on the road all summer, heading home via the southwestern historic Route 66 and then finally back to their Ohio home.

"We had our kids young and saved up so we could enjoy retirement," the wife said as she swung a leg over her bike.

"Helmets," Mike said, handing her a red one and her husband a blue one. "Gotta stay safe on the journey."

He watched as the couple leaned their bikes toward each other to exchange a quick kiss before pedaling off for a day of exploring the island. He and Hadley had biked every inch of the island, but their kissing had been limited to only two occasions. Maybe that was the missing ingredient. If he asked for a kiss, would she be reminded that she found him irresistible? As the affectionate couple pedaled away, Mike glanced across the street at the Holiday Hotel where he saw the florist's assistant climbing the front steps with flowers in hand.

Maybe she would be moved by the pretty flowers and she'd want to kiss him. He'd wait five minutes and then stop in for a quick visit.

Before the five minutes were up, his phone pinged with a message.

You shouldn't waste your money on flowers.

Mike sighed. Practical Hadley would, of course, think that spending money on something transitory, no matter how pretty, was frivolous.

It's never a waste of money to show you I care about you.

There. If that weren't the perfect response, he'd eat a bicycle tire. He hovered in the front window, still considering a trip across the street. His message plus the flowers had to be a winning combination.

I think you just want someone to suffer with as you cross the threshold into your 30s.

The message was accompanied by a smiley-face emoji, but it didn't leave Mike laughing. So, fine. Hadley wasn't going to get gushy over cut flowers. She appreciated the kind they bought from the flower ferry and planted in her yard, but Mike realized that was probably because they would last for months and be a wise investment in addition to being pretty. As well as he knew Hadley, he should have seen that one coming.

Am I still invited to your grandmother's birthday party?

Dinner is at 5 at Wendy's. I'll meet you there.

We could go together

I may stay later than you because Wendy and I have some things to sort through

Mike sent her a thumbs-up emoji, surrendering to whatever plan Hadley already had for the birthday dinner and accepting with grace the fact that he'd been invited.

Baby steps. He almost laughed aloud when he thought about that expression and how true it rang in their case.

HADLEY ARRIVED EARLY to her sister's house with the hope of centering herself before Mike appeared. Lately, he'd affected her balance. She'd been thinking of him when she put away the dishes from the rack by the sink. Was that why she'd put the cups in the bowl cabinet? She needed to keep her feelings for Mike in check, or what kind of a mess would she be when she had a baby on one hip while putting away dishes?

"Can I help with anything?" she asked her sister when she entered Wendy's kitchen.

"Not with cooking, but I have a sit-down job for you." Wendy pointed to a Cinderella jewelry box on the breakfast table in her kitchen. "You're good at untangling things, and you'd be saving us a lot of crying if you could separate Janey's necklaces."

Hadley pulled out a chair and opened the lid on the box. A cheerful tune played, but the disaster inside was anything but happy.

"How did this happen?" Necklaces were twisted and knotted together with bracelets, all the chains a hopeless coil.

"Aaron shook it. A lot. He liked the sound it made, and I didn't realize he was doing it until I heard the fighting upstairs."

"Janey wasn't pleased?" Hadley asked.

Wendy laughed. "Epic meltdown and she swore her brother would never be allowed in her room again as long as she lives."

"Poor Aaron," Hadley said.

"If you value his life, you'll untangle everything so Janey can wear her favorite unicorn necklace for the birthday party."

"Good thing I got here early," Hadley said. Using a systematic approach, she took everything out of the jewelry box and tried to separate the strands on the table. The unicorn necklace had a fine silver chain that was looped and knotted around a pink bead necklace, a charm bracelet and a long gold chain with a small *J* in a heart. She let out a deep breath. This was a problem she could solve with logic and patience, so she began following the chain of the unicorn necklace and freeing it as she went.

"Grandma's on the back deck watching the kids blow bubbles," Wendy said. "She convinced them that every bubble is a birthday wish, so they're going at it with gusto."

"They're such sweethearts," Hadley said.

"And Grandma's smart. It'll keep them busy until dinnertime, and all I have to do is rinse their hands in a big bucket of warm water I already put on the deck."

Wendy dug through a kitchen drawer and put some towels on the counter. "Grandma also mentioned she has that Bahamas trip for two she won at St. Patrick's Day, and she wanted to know if I had ideas about who might appreciate it."

"I'll babysit if you and Justin want to take it," Hadley said.

"And I'd babysit if you wanted to get away next winter to someplace warm."

"I think Grandma should take one of her friends and live it up," Hadley said. She was not ready to think about a romantic trip anywhere. Her life was as booked and complicated as she could imagine. Hadley freed three inches of chain and re-evaluated her pile, moving the pink beaded bracelet out of the immediate work zone.

Wendy laughed. "I asked her not to bring it up at dinner."

"Thanks."

"Do you want me to go with you to your ultrasound next week?" Wendy asked. She opened the oven door and peered in, her back to Hadley.

"Yes," Hadley said. "But Mike wants to go, and, well, I guess…"

Wendy turned toward her and straightened up, big oven mitts on her hands. "He should go," she said gently. "He's the dad and you two should do this together."

Hadley smoothed out a crease in the chain,

being careful not to break the delicate links. "It'll be strange."

Wendy laughed. "Get used to that. You've got a lot of surprises coming your way."

"I know," Hadley said. She unwound a blue sailboat charm from the gold chain of the *J* necklace and unexpectedly loosened a whole six inches of gold chain. "Excellent," she said.

Wendy had turned her back to put breadcrumbs on top of the casserole. "Since when do you think surprises are excellent?" she asked. "You're a planner."

"I was talking to the necklace," Hadley said. "I don't think I'll ever love surprises, even when I accidentally surprise myself. I put dishes in the wrong places in my cabinet this morning."

Wendy cut her a quick glance over her shoulder. "And?"

"And I'm going to move them back when I get home." Hadley didn't tell her sister that she'd considered leaving the cups and bowls mismatched and mingling on shelves they'd never shared. It had been a passing impulse and she knew she wouldn't be happy in the long run making reckless changes, no matter how small they were.

Betty got up and went to the back door where she whined and bounced on her front paws.

"Did she just figure out that the kids are outside?' Wendy asked. "I'm surprised she didn't want to go straight there."

"Not when all the good food smells are coming from this room."

"I've got her," Wendy said. She let Betty out the back door while Hadley continued her project. She was so close to freeing the unicorn necklace. Just a few well-played moves and the knots should loosen. Head bent over her project, she saw a red T-shirt slide into the chair across from her in her peripheral vision.

Hadley looked up and smiled at Mike and then she realized his shirt was wet. "What happened?"

"Bubble war," he said. "I went straight to the backyard when I got here five minutes ago, and I became the target. I had no idea how wet bubbles are when you stand in front of one of those battery-operated blower things and let three kids assault you."

"Sorry about that," Wendy said.

"Don't pity me too much. I sort of started the war," Mike said.

Wendy laughed. "You've got to be a sticky mess. Do you want to borrow one of Justin's T-shirts?"

Mike laughed. "Nope, this was my own fault, and it goes with the territory. I'm practicing for being a dad."

"You'll be great," Hadley said, the words coming automatically from her mouth but they were also coming from her heart. She knew he would be a good dad. He'd play board games, hide Easter eggs, dry tears and search for missing socks. They exchanged a long glance across the table, and for a moment Hadley forgot she was on a mission to untangle necklaces.

Instead, she was trying to untangle her feelings.

"Looks like you've got quite a project," Mike said, his eyes dropping to the jewelry tangle in front of Hadley. "Do you need any help? I'm better with bicycle chains, but I could give it a shot."

"I've got this under control," Hadley said. The jewelry *was* under control, even if her emotions weren't. She turned her thoughts to the unicorn necklace's silver chain and meticulously worked the length of it through one final knot until it was free.

"Twenty-two days left until our thirtieth birthday," Mike said so quietly Hadley doubted her sister heard it as she rummaged through the refrigerator. He'd sent her chocolate candies, dropped off assorted colored pens and markers, and had emailed her a list of fun things to do on the mainland—all corresponding with the countdown numbers—with a promise to take her anytime she wanted. Did Mike think a countdown was the way to persuade her? Sure, she had a reputation for liking order, lists and yes, countdowns. But this was different. This involved her heart and the rest of her life.

Janey burst through the kitchen door declaring she was starving, but then she saw the necklace Hadley held up and ran over. She gave Hadley a big soapy hug and held still while Hadley fastened the necklace for her.

"You're the best aunt," Janey said.

"Dinner's ready," Wendy declared. "Mike, will you round everyone up and get them to the dining room table?"

The simple act of her sister deploying Mike reminded Hadley that he was part of the family now, and she needed to manage her feelings because the dinner was about her grandmother's milestone birthday—not her.

During dinner, Justin entertained them with a story about one of his new coworkers who'd recently relocated from Arizona and continued to be blown away everyday by the sheer volume of fresh water everywhere in Northern Michigan. Mike told a funny story about a tandem bike incident, and Grandma Penny revealed that MaryAnna had gotten her a fish tank for her birthday and she needed help acquiring both fish and names for the fish.

"I got you something very different," Hadley said. She gave her grandmother a card after they finished their cake. "It's the yarn project of the month club. Every month this year, they send you a pattern for something like a hat or scarf and the yarn to go with it."

"A surprise every month," her grandmother said, clapping her hands together. "I love getting mail, and I love trying new things."

"I know," Hadley said, laughing. She also liked getting mail, but she had never shared

her grandmother's inclination for the unexpected.

"We got you slippers and a new bathrobe,"
Janey said, handing over a brightly wrapped
box.

"You're supposed to let her open the gift
instead of telling her what's in it," Wendy
chided.

"I'll still be surprised by the color," Grandma
Penny said.

"It's purple," Macey supplied.

Everyone laughed, and the birthday girl
opened her gift to reveal a beautiful lavender bathrobe with matching slippers and she
delighted her grandchildren by putting on
the robe over her clothes and switching out
her sneakers for slippers. The party wound
down, and the evening light shifted, and
Wendy came over to Hadley and said, "I'll
have Justin drive Grandma home so we can
get started with our project."

Mike stood up. "I'm headed downtown. I'd
be happy to take Grandma home."

"Are you sure you don't mind?" Wendy
asked.

He smiled. "Not at all. I don't even care
if she wears the purple bathrobe. If anyone

sees us, I'll tell them I have a sassy new girl-friend."

"You should be so lucky," Grandma Penny said.

After they left, Justin volunteered to do bathtub duty, and Wendy and Hadley retreated to the back of Wendy's closet.

"I'm sure glad you can use these clothes," Wendy said. "I'm done with them, but I held on to them, hoping to find just the right person to give them to."

"Bet you never thought it would be me," Hadley said.

"Never say never," Wendy said. She pulled a bunch of hangers off the closet rod and took them to the bed where she arranged them so Hadley could see them. Not that she was a stranger to the clothes. She remembered her sister wearing the outfits and had even bought some of them for her as gifts.

"I always thought you looked very pretty in this one," Hadley said, holding up a dark blue top with elbow-length sleeves and a ruffle along the bottom.

"I may have looked pretty for the first seven or eight months, but after that, I was a watermelon on legs, just trying not to burst at an inappropriate time."

Hadley laughed. "I'm never getting that image out of my mind."

"How about these capri pants?" Wendy said. She held up a navy and a khaki pair. "They'd be good for work, and they have a magical elastic waist that never let me down."

Hadley didn't want to overthink the watermelon analogy or the need for a magical elastic waist, but she surrendered anyway and hauled almost every one of her sister's maternity outfits to her car. On the way home, she glanced in the rearview mirror at the clothes piled in the back seat—even a colorful T-shirt that said Baby on Board. That one topped the list of things she thought she'd never be caught dead in.

She met Betty's eyes as the dog sat obediently in her place in the cargo zone at the back.

"Never say never, Betty."

The dog put her nose on the back of the seat and gave her a sympathetic stare as they drove along the quiet island road back to their pretty house. Hadley pulled into the garage and opened the back hatch to let Betty out, but she left the piles of maternity clothes on the back seat for the night. A deep exhaustion weighed down her shoulders as she carried in the leftover casserole and piece of birthday cake her sister had insisted she take home. She stowed them in the fridge and dragged herself upstairs, but as she passed the room that had been stripped of wallpaper and was waiting for the next stage of renovation, the weight lifted.

Her baby was going to make everything worthwhile. Even, perhaps, wearing that Baby on Board top.

CHAPTER FOURTEEN

A FLAGPOLE ANGLED out from beside the entrance to the Christmas Island post office a few doors down from Mike's bike shop, and the breeze caught the flag as he walked past. The stars and stripes brushed his head and knocked off his Mike's Island Bike Rental hat. As he stooped to grab it before it ended up in the gutter, he saw the sign on the door of the post office.

Help Wanted. Postmaster. Apply Within.

Bertie was a fixture on Christmas Island. He'd been the postmaster all of Mike's life, but all the locals knew he was retiring after thirty-five years of service. Mike had overheard Bertie talking about his government pension and his plans to do more fishing and visit his grandkids now that he'd have time on his hands.

What pension would Mike have after thirty-five years? Worn-out bicycles? A building that would need at least one more, if not two, roofs by then? Windows that would be older. A fading sign in the front window advertising the daily or weekly special. He stopped right there on the sidewalk in front of the post office and stared at his reflection in the door.

He wasn't living for himself anymore. He needed a more secure position that came with health benefits, a steady year-round paycheck and a retirement that would add up to more than a supply of helmets and spare bike parts. As he stared, the door swung open and Bertie waved him in.

"I've got packages for you," the older man said. "Big boxes but they don't weigh much."

"Wire bike baskets," Mike said. "I keep ordering them. Those are always the first thing to get damaged in a collision, and I've got some bent ones to replace."

"Never a dull moment when you own your own business," Bertie said.

"Are there…" Mike hesitated. Should he ask? Was this an impulse or was it fate? Had that flag hanging outside the post office snapped him in the head for a reason? "Are there a lot of dull moments here in the post office?" he asked.

Bertie lifted up a section of countertop and walked through it, and then he disappeared into the back room for a moment before returning with a big box.

"Not dull," he said, "but some days are quieter than others, especially in the winter." He leaned an elbow on the counter and looked around the small post office with a wistful expression. Posters advertising commemorative and holiday stamps hung on the walls. A scale and cash register took up space on the end of the counter. Post office boxes with bronze faces and key slots occupied an entire wall of the place that had looked exactly the same for as long as Mike could remember.

"I'm going to miss it," Bertie said. "The smell of stamps and packing tape, seeing all those letters and packages and wondering where they came from and what's in them. I'm not a hero and I've never saved anyone's life, but I'm proud of making sure people get their mail every day, even during November storms and madhouse tourist season."

Mike smiled. "You've earned that retirement."

"I think so, but it's going to be tough finding a postmaster who wants to spend his life on an island," Bertie said. "Two candidates have already fallen through after they visited and saw how small the post office is and realized they'd need to meet the ferry and the plane every day in all kinds of weather."

Mike already lived on the island, and he was no stranger to the ferry and the island airport. How hard would it be? Sure, it would mean spending his days in this small post office instead of his shop. He wouldn't have bicycle grease under his nails, and he'd have to change his wardrobe. Wouldn't own his own business anymore. Could he adjust?

"What are the qualifications for the job?" Mike asked.

Bertie tilted his head and gave Mike a long grandfatherly look. "Do you know someone?"

Should he admit what he was thinking? Bertie was a kind soul, but he was also a talker. The news that Mike Martin was sticking his neck out and applying for a job for the first time in his life would travel. What would people say?

What would Hadley say? Maybe this decision would persuade her that he could be husband material, willing to change his life and make a sacrifice for his family. He was almost thirty. Was it about time he settled into a job that was steadier than renting bikes to tourists?

"Maybe," Mike said.

Bertie reached beneath the counter and pulled out a piece of paper. "Here's an application if you want to pass it along to anyone. It's a good, steady job for the right person."

Mike nodded his thanks and wedged the application between the two boxes so it wouldn't blow away when he went back outside. He'd been on his way to the ferry docks because Griffin had texted him that a tourist abandoned a rental bike on the ferry the night before. The bike could wait a few minutes while he stowed the packages. When he returned to his bike shop, there was an envelope taped to the back door that led only to his office.

A large *18 Days* was written on the outside of the Holiday Hotel envelope, and it took Mike a moment to realize it had to be from Hadley. He pulled the envelope off the door and held it between his teeth while he opened the door and went in with his boxes. He slid the post-office application from its spot between the boxes and tucked it under his desk calendar.

Inside the envelope was a printout of the daily special in the dining room of the Holiday Hotel. On a yellow sticky note, Hadley's neat handwriting said, *Meet me for dinner at 6:30. Rebecca is playing tonight, and I don't want the tourists to have all the fun.*

Mike smiled. Interesting. Hadley had decided to play the countdown game. He shouldn't be surprised that she would want to have some control.

He pulled out his phone and texted three words. I'll be there.

WENDY'S CLOSET HAD provided treasures in the form of stretch pants that didn't look like stretch pants and tops in various sizes. Hadley knew she was in for a lot of change and seeing the broad spectrum of clothing sizes reinforced the truth.

As soon as she closed the front desk for the day with the last check-in accommodated and the books balanced, Hadley ducked into the employee restroom off the lobby and switched her blouse to the pretty dark blue one with the ruffle. She had plenty of room to expand in the top, but it also looked nice and neat over her gray stretch pants. Her face was getting a bit fuller and her hair longer.

And she was starving. She folded her work polo shirt into her shoulder bag and met Mike the moment she left the restroom. He wasn't wearing his usual T-shirt advertising his business. He appeared freshly shaved and showered and wore a short-sleeved green Henley. He must have dashed up to his apartment over the bike rental and made an effort. Was it because she'd invited him and given him time to plan his approach?

"There's my beautiful dinner date," he said, holding out an arm for her as if he were there to escort her into a ballroom.

"Are you here for me or because I sent you the specials?" she asked, taking his arm.

"You know me well enough to know the answer is both."

Hadley laughed. "I'm hungry enough to eat both our meals, so you might not want to sit too close to me."

Mike glanced down at her as they walked into the familiar dining room. "I always want to be close to you."

She stumbled as she crossed the threshold

and Mike slid his arm around her to steady her. "I'm fine," she said. "I just didn't pick my feet up."

"Long day?"

She nodded. "But not a bad one, especially since I've had a good dinner to look forward to." She led them to a table by the front windows where they could watch the evening tourists strolling past. She sat first and then Mike chose the chair next to her instead of across from her.

"I'm glad you decided to play my countdown game," he said.

She smiled. "We're in this together."

"And what are we going to do when it's our big day?"

Hadley considered the question. If he was asking if she would reconsider their marriage pact, he was beating around the bush. Or maybe just giving her space and time. Or he could have changed his mind and he thanked the stars at night that she'd turned him down. Twice.

"Share an ice-cream cake like we do almost every year," Hadley said, sticking to a safe answer. "Mint chocolate chip is my current favorite, and if it has chocolate fudge icing, I might not even mind turning thirty."

"Why don't we get that for dessert? The bakery usually has an ice-cream cake in stock, and they'll still be open."

"Too indulgent," Hadley said.

Mike laughed and shook his head. "No such thing."

Rebecca came through the dining room doors and gave Hadley a little wave before heading to the baby grand just off an open area of the restaurant where couples occasionally danced. Hadley had seen plenty of dancing, especially on summer nights when couples were celebrating an anniversary or during the epic Christmas in July week.

Hadley had only danced on special occasions herself, and only when she was off duty. Rebecca lifted the lid on the piano and sat on the bench. Moments later, the opening bars of a smooth love song floated throughout the restaurant, just loud enough for people to appreciate her excellent playing but soft enough not to interfere with conversation. Griffin credited Rebecca's music with bringing in business on weeknights that had previously been quiet, and Hadley agreed.

Rebecca was a treasure and she and Griffin's love story had caused a collective sigh all over the island, second only to the one caused by Camille Peterson and Griffin's brother, Maddox. Their reunion after being apart for seven years had been the sweet ending befitting the owner of a candy store.

"You look serious but happy," Mike said. "And if it's the promise of ice-cream cake putting that expression on your face, I'll happily buy you one every day."

"It's not ice-cream cake, but I was thinking about something sweet."

"What?"

She considered making up a response, but she and Mike had always been honest with each other in their long friendship. *Until recently*, Hadley thought, but there was no way she could tell Mike that she was in love with him and that was the reason she couldn't marry him. What was he supposed to do with that information? Mike was good at fixing things, and he was a hard worker and a devoted friend, but even those qualities wouldn't help him make himself fall in love with her if he wasn't.

And she had to face the reality that he wasn't.

Things had changed for her, but not for him, and it wasn't fair to impose her feelings on him.

"I was thinking about Rebecca and Griffin and what an incredible summer they had last year. I'm sure neither one of them saw that coming."

"Does anyone ever see it coming?" Mike asked lightly. He nodded politely at the young woman waiting tables who came by with glasses of ice water. She stayed and recited the specials before promising to return for their orders in a few minutes.

Tourists wandered in and the restaurant began filling up with chatter in addition to the piano music. At the table next to theirs, a young couple who appeared to be just out of high school shared an appetizer plate. Hadley noticed them laughing and talking and the shy glances they exchanged. How long had they been dating? From appearances, she'd guess they were newly dating. If the young lovers noticed the nearly thirty couple at the neighboring table, what did they think? Did Mike and Hadley look like an old married couple to them, expecting child number one or two or even three?

Hadley stole a glance at Mike and caught him looking at her, and she laughed. Maybe they weren't so different from the new love-birds at the next table.

"What?" he asked.

"I'll tell you later."

"When we're dancing?"

"I…" Hadley hadn't expected Mike to ask her to dance. This wasn't a party or a special occasion or even a formal date. Of course, she was the one who'd asked him to dinner under the guise of the daily countdown.

"We've danced before," Mike said when Hadley hesitated. "And I'm not any worse than the last time."

Hadley smiled and took a sip of her water. "You're a good dancer. I may be a little clumsy or off balance, though."

"That's what I'm here for," Mike said.

Their server returned, and they both ordered the chicken marsala and spring vegetables special. While they ate, Hadley watched tourists going by, some holding hands, some pushing strollers or wheelchairs, everyone going somewhere to enjoy the beautiful island evening. Hadley felt as if she were observing the diners inside the restaurant, too, because she was so accustomed to being on duty, working the bar, delivering food to tables. She knew the entire routine and the menu, but she felt outside of it somehow. Just as expected, at 7:30, Rebecca took a ten-minute break from playing the piano. When she returned to the bench, the light level in the bar had shifted to mellow low lighting.

"Now that we've eaten and they turned down the lights, we could try a dance," Mike said. "And you can tell me what you were laughing about earlier."

"It was really nothing."

"Then it won't take long, and we can talk about the nursery after that."

Mike said it as if they were deciding on their dessert choices. No big deal. *Just the nursery for our baby, future parents that we are. Sure, why not have dinner and dancing as if there were not two rejected marriage proposals hovering over our table?*

"Okay," Hadley said.

Mike stood and offered her a hand. She put her napkin on her empty plate and followed Mike over to the small dance floor where two older couples were already dancing to the lively piano piece Rebecca was playing.

"Uh-oh. They look like they've taken lessons and they know what they're doing," Mike said. "I'm just going to hold onto you and follow you around the dance floor until you get tired of me."

Hadley put both hands behind Mike's neck and he slid his arms around her. He was warm and his arms felt safe and familiar.

"The young couple next to us," Hadley said, leaning in close so her lips almost touched his ear. "I was smiling because they looked as if this was one of their first dates. They kept exchanging these shy glances. It was cute."

"We were doing the same thing," Mike said. "Which makes sense because we just started dating."

Hadley laughed. "We've had dinner together three hundred times."

"But not as…"

He didn't finish the sentence, and the words hung in the narrow space between them as they moved slowly together to the music. Neither of them put a label on their relationship, but Hadley was sure Mike's thoughts were turning the question over and over, just as hers were.

At the end of the song, Hadley said, "I'm ready to sit down and finish my drink."

Mike nodded and released her, but he took her hand as they walked to the table. Was it just the polite thing to do because they were dance partners?

"We should have dessert, too," he said as they took their seats.

Hadley shook her head. "It sounded great a little while ago, but I'm ready to call it a night."

Mike shrugged one shoulder and shot her a lopsided grin. "We can get a treat on the mainland the day after tomorrow when we go for the ultrasound appointment."

She'd been looking forward to the appointment with a mix of excitement and nervousness. The experience itself was outside her comfort zone but thrilling. Going through it with Mike at her side was something she was sure she wasn't ready for but couldn't wait to try it, anyway. Her life had become a complex maze of excitement and trepidation.

"The pie shop downtown," Hadley said. It was a logical choice. Right on the way back to the ferry from the medical center where they would both see their baby for the first time and discover if they were having a girl or a boy.

"And we could stop by the big home store and get things for the nursery. I want to get going on that project, and when we know the baby's gender, I think it'll be easier to pick stuff out and plan it," Mike said.

Hadley wanted to protest that of the two of them, she was the planner and organizer. And it was her house, her spare bedroom that would be the baby's room for the next…how many years? Ten? Twenty? A lifetime? She herself had grown up in that house and she was still there. She imagined their child as an adult, making choices, moving on, making mistakes. As she pictured the next decades, Hadley knew one thing for certain—rolling with the changes was the only way she was going to be happy.

"I've started a list," she said.

Mike smiled. "I'm sure."

"But it's fairly general since I've never done this before, and there will be plenty of things we need to figure out."

"Together," Mike said.

Hadley nodded. "Can I pick out the curtains and bedding?"

Mike reached across the table and curled his fingers around hers. "I wouldn't want it any other way."

CHAPTER FIFTEEN

MIKE PICKED UP Hadley early enough that they were the first vehicle to roll onto the eight o'clock ferry. In fact, they were the only vehicle leaving the island that early. When they returned later in the day, they'd be sharing the deck with tourists and their vehicles, but they almost had the boat to themselves on this sunny morning.

He waved to Maddox, who waved back and then climbed the steps to the ferry's pilothouse. Mike had made this trip too many times to count, but today's mission was a first for him—and for Hadley.

"The lake's nice and calm today," Hadley commented as Mike set the parking brake and took off his seat belt.

"Are we calm?" He'd almost skipped his morning coffee because he didn't need that caffeine on top of the energy pulsing through his body.

"Excited and a little bit nervous, but basically calm. I think," Hadley said. "This is my second time having an ultrasound, so I have some idea of what to expect."

Mike knew she'd gone with her sister a month earlier when her blood pressure was high, but it had been too soon to determine the baby's gender.

"I'm glad you asked me to go along today," Mike said.

Hadley gave him a smile. "You have every right, and I…want you here."

"Good," Mike said. He swallowed. Having paternal rights was one thing, but Hadley choosing his company was even better.

"Do you want to get out and pick a bench or sit in the truck on the way across?" Hadley asked.

"I'm comfortable here if you are."

In answer, Hadley unrolled her window a few inches, took her travel mug filled with decaf tea from the cup holder in the center of the truck and leaned back.

"The last time we made this trip with my truck together was December, when we went to pick up that rocking chair for your grandmother's Christmas gift," Mike said.

Hadley nodded. "That was a stormy day, and it was a good thing we both have good sea legs. I wasn't sure the ferry would even be running that day."

"I called Griffin early that day to ask," Mike said.

"Did you do that for me?" Hadley asked.

Mike nodded. "I knew it was important to you." The truth was he'd do about anything for the residents of Christmas Island. They were a close-knit bunch of people out of necessity and the shared camaraderie of enduring long lonely winters and busy, chaotic summers. Hadley had just been a friend back in early December. A good friend. One whom he'd once kissed and been rebuffed by and then settled into an easy companionship with. He hadn't even thought much about their *married by thirty* pact in years.

Until that Christmas party when their casual companionship changed, replaced by something new.

So new that Mike could scarcely name it, but it felt like need and hope and longing and the promise of spring and the first snow all wrapped into one package that was too big to fit in his heart.

What the heck was he going to do about it?

"Grandma says she loves that rocking chair," Hadley commented, interrupting his thoughts. "But she doesn't use it much because the arms interfere with her crocheting somehow. I may ask if I can borrow it for a while."

"We can buy our own," Mike said. The use of the word *our* felt a little risky and very personal—but also right. They could share a rocking chair and a baby and…everything.

"We'll fill up your truck fast if we go big like that," Hadley said. "Maybe we should take this one step at a time and see what the ultrasound says. We could be having twins."

Mike sucked in a breath and Hadley laughed.

"Do you have any reason to think that?" he asked.

Hadley shook her head and sipped her tea. "Not at all, but I'm getting used to surprises and things that are out of my control."

"I guess it's like sitting in a vehicle on a ferry. I'm in the driver's seat, but there's no point in even putting my hands on the wheel," Mike said.

Hadley raised both shoulders. "Enjoy the ride?"

"Just one question," Mike said. "Does this count as the celebration of fifteen days until our birthday?"

"Certainly," Hadley said with a smile. She raised her tea as if she were offering a toast. "What better way to say farewell to our twenties?"

They sat back and watched the mainland come into focus as the ferry approached the dock. Driving off the ferry toward the medical center with Hadley at his side felt like the opening act of a movie. In only an hour, they'd know more about the contents of that movie, and Mike took deep steadying breaths as he backed into a parking space. He wanted to fold Hadley into his arms and ask her, one more time, to marry him before they went inside, but he didn't.

Inside, they were shown into a waiting room where two other pregnant couples sat.

"When are you due?" one of the other women asked Hadley before she'd even had a chance to settle into her seat.

"Oh," Hadley said, her voice sounding a little surprised as if she weren't accustomed to hearing that question. All their island friends knew and, Mike guessed, hotel visitors didn't ask the lady behind the counter questions like that. "October," Hadley said. "Early October."

"I'm due in August," the other pregnant woman said. "I'm having a boy, which is why I didn't have months' worth of morning sickness like I did when I had my girl."

"Same," the other lady said. "But I'm due in September. And having a boy this time definitely made me feel less hormonal than the first one. Of course, I guess that could be because it's my second time around. Is this your first?" she asked Hadley.

Hadley nodded, and Mike was awed both by how easily these women shared details and by how weird it felt. Weird but okay. He was about to get a glimpse inside Hadley's belly, so he better get used to the strange feeling of personal subjects.

Both other couples got called back one at a time until Hadley and Mike were left alone in the sunny room.

"This is it," Hadley said. "Our last time imagining a boy or a girl. We're going to know in just a few minutes."

"I'm still hoping for triplets," Mike said. "But only if you are, too."

Hadley laughed. She reached for his hand and gripped it as if she wanted to draw strength and courage from him. Impulsively, he leaned close and kissed her cheek as he breathed in her scent.

"Okay, lovebirds, it's your turn," a woman in the doorway said.

Hadley and Mike looked up, and Hadley kept her grip on his hand.

"Let's get a look at your beautiful baby," the woman said as she turned and beckoned them down a hallway. "I'm Connie, and I'm your ultrasound technician. The full report will go to your obstetrician, but you'll know a lot before you leave here today, and I'll be sending you home with pictures and video, too. Is this your first child?"

"Yes," Hadley said.

"Well, then, you're going to be absolutely enthralled by what you see today."

TEN MINUTES LATER, Hadley was sure Connie was right. She was already amazed, enthralled, and totally in love with the tiny image on the screen. She chanced a look at

Mike's face, and she was pretty sure he was going to pass out if he didn't take a breath. His eyes were glued to the screen, too.

"She's recording this for us so you might want to blink and breathe," Hadley said.

Mike turned a startled expression to her and blinked three times. "You're right. I'm just…in love."

Hadley knew exactly what he meant. She was in love with everything at the moment. Her baby, the idea of being a mother, the father of the baby…all of it. Her love was so powerful that she almost believed she could marry him and keep their relationship going on the strength of her love alone. And that thought was so scary she pushed it away.

"Are you ready to find out the baby's gender? Because I think I can give you a clear picture from this angle," Connie said.

"Ready," Hadley said. She glanced at Mike. "Are you?"

"Absolutely," he said.

Connie concentrated on the computer screen as she moved the ultrasound tool over Hadley's skin. "I can tell you what I'm *not* seeing, and it's pretty clear you're having a girl."

"A girl," Hadley breathed. "A little girl."

She would never have admitted she was hoping for a girl, and she would truly have been just as happy with a boy. But a girl was—

"Oh, my god, I'm having a little girl," Mike said.

"Breathe," Connie told him. "Other men have survived it."

"I'm excited about it," Mike said. "I know she'll be as beautiful as her mother."

In answer, Hadley reached for his hand and held it for the rest of the scan.

An hour later, Hadley and Mike stood in front of a wall of paint colors at the home store.

"That room gets the morning sun, so it'll be nice and bright no matter what color we pick," Mike said. "But we're going with pink, right?"

The fact that Mike knew that room faced east was no surprise to her. He knew all the nooks and crannies of her house, just as she knew which doors in his apartment over the bike shop tended to stick when the summer humidity hit. Those things were givens, assumptions instead of surprises. Unlike the emotion that swelled her throat when she'd seen her baby on the computer monitor and the matching wonder in Mike's eyes. Her own emotion she could handle, but seeing it reflected on Mike's face had magnified the power of her love for both her baby girl and her daughter's father.

Her daughter. She would have a daughter. Hadley's eyes burned with tears and the paint colors all blurred together. Pink and yellow and green and blue swirled, and she put a steadying hand on her baby bump.

Strong arms encircled her, and Mike's hand on the back of her head held her gently against the firm wall of his chest.

"Whatever it is, it's okay," he said. "It's all going to be okay."

She nodded against his shirt just enough for him to know she'd heard him.

"And we don't have to paint the room pink if you don't want to," he said. "I just assumed—"

She shook her head and pulled back enough so she could see his face.

"It's not the paint. It's just…everything." She swallowed. "In a good way."

Mike brushed back her hair and his fingers lingered on her cheek. He smiled. "I think I know exactly what you mean."

Hadley took a deep breath and felt strength

fill her body. At that moment, the baby kicked, and she impulsively grabbed Mike's hand and guided it to her belly so he could feel it, too. His large fingers splayed across her middle and they locked eyes when the baby kicked against his hand. It was the first time Hadley had invited him to touch her baby bump, and his mouth opened in surprise. Tears flooded his eyes and she laughed.

"We can't both cry in the paint aisle."

Mike swallowed. "Yes, we can. We're a team."

She knew what he meant. He meant he'd be there for every step and each happy and sad moment. But she didn't want a teammate. She was so in love with him as they stood connected, his hand on her belly touching the new life within. If she took the ultimate risk and told him she loved him, what would he say?

Knowing Mike, he'd be a good friend and say the words right back, followed by another marriage proposal. He was a problem solver, and if he knew she loved him, he'd see no obstacle to marriage.

Except the most important one. He didn't love her like that in return. She couldn't let herself surrender and risk both their hearts and future. It was better to stick with her plan. Plans had almost never failed her.

CHAPTER SIXTEEN

THE MORNING AFTER her ultrasound, Hadley paused on the sidewalk in front of the Island Boutique. Hadley stepped close to the window to look at the summer dresses in the mother/daughter display. There were two sets of mannequins in the large window in adult and child sizes. One set mother-daughter pair wore flowered dresses, a yellow background with pink and green flowers, each of them with a wide sash at the waist and a hem that dipped below the knee. Hadley sucked in a breath. In a few years, she and her daughter could be wearing those dresses. She swallowed back a wave of emotion as she pictured herself standing, holding hands, perhaps with a picnic basket over one arm. They'd have matching sun hats, too, just as the models wore.

She turned her attention to the other set of mannequins, which wore blue-and-white-striped capri pants with white eyelet loose-fitting tops. Instead of hats, the models wore red headbands that matched their red espadrilles.

Hadley imagined herself and her daughter going to the Fourth of July fireworks in exactly those outfits, even planning what snacks they would take to enjoy as they sat on their blanket in the downtown park, waiting for the show. She always packed mosquito repellent, a dew-resistant layer to put under their blanket, a flashlight, and a jacket. She'd done it for so long she hardly needed the list she kept. That list would grow, anyway, and include an extra toy, perhaps a pillow, for her little girl. And ear muffs, just in case the fireworks were too loud.

As Hadley stood, picturing future summers with a sense of wonder and longing, Violet Brookstone opened the front door of her boutique.

"I could put those mother-daughter outfits on hold for you, but you'll have to wait a few years if you want to wear them together," Violet said.

Hadley smiled. "It would give me something to look forward to after getting out of these maternity clothes."

Violet leaned on the open door and crossed

her arms. Just a few years younger than Hadley, Violet had established herself as the island fashionista and sewing expert. She'd made curtains, recovered porch pillows and sewn wedding gowns. The Santa and Mrs. Claus costumes on an island known for Christmas had to be the real deal, and Violet had special-ordered high-quality red velvet and white faux fur to make them both traditional and one of a kind. She even embroidered them with gold metallic thread. Anyone visiting Christmas Island during the holidays needed to take a second look just to confirm they were only costumed characters.

Hadley envied her friend for her sewing talent and for knowing exactly what career path to take. Even as a child, Violet had made dresses for her dolls and her friends' dolls and had started making her own clothes in the sixth grade. She had a definite calling.

Did Hadley have a calling? All she'd ever wanted was an idyllic island life with her family and friends. Working for a hotel and welcoming guests to the island was a good career path, but Hadley hadn't really thought much about her future until her future became tied to the tiny baby she was bringing into the world of Christmas Island. And tied to Mike.

"You have plenty to look forward to," Violet said. "I'm a little bit jealous, to tell you the truth."

Hadley laughed. "Yes, my current state of wondering where my feet have gone and preparing to be a single mom is an enviable one."

"You'll be a mom," Violet said. "You'll have someone who is completely yours."

"You have—" Hadley stopped herself before saying Violet had Jordan Frome, her best friend with whom she was so inseparable the island considered them to be a single unit.

"My brother?" Violet asked. "Ryan is off distinguishing himself as the engineer of the year somewhere. He doesn't need me sewing on his buttons or making sure he remembers to eat lunch."

Hadley was glad she hadn't finished her sentence. Didn't Violet know that Jordan needed buttons and lunch, too, or was that not part of their relationship? Hadley hadn't sewn on any buttons for Mike, but she'd helped him with projects at his house and taken him lunch. They'd shared nearly everything two humans could share, and their relationship was evolving with their baby's every heartbeat.

For a moment, Hadley missed the easy friendship they'd had with the intensity of a summer storm. They would never have that again. She wished she could go back in time six months and spend a carefree day with Mike, one in which they didn't have the weight of their decisions hanging over them.

"I'm thinking of doing a father-son display in June in time for Father's Day," Violet said. "But those aren't nearly as fun for me. I can make men's clothing, but I'd rather make dresses and blouses any day of the week."

"Fathers have daughters, too," Hadley said. "Maybe you could make a little girl's dress and a matching neck tie for her dad."

Violet nodded and smiled. "That's a good idea. So, next year or the year after, you can get matching outfits with your daughter. And Mike, too! All three of you could match. You could even do a Christmas card photo shoot with matching outfits. I love those. They're so unapologetically dorky and wonderful."

Hadley blew out a breath. "I don't think I can plan that far ahead, especially since I'm still trying to keep up with the train I seem to be on. I got on at Christmas, and I think it's going faster with every day that passes."

Violet tilted her head and studied Hadley. "When did you know?"

"That I was pregnant? That's easy. Just in time for Valentine's Day."

"No," Violet said. "I mean, when did you know that your friendship with Mike—something that had lasted for years—was ready to…become something else?"

Hadley concentrated hard on the flower pattern on the yellow dress. She'd spent so much time focusing on the results of that night that she hadn't allowed herself much room to process what led up to it.

"Is it something else?" she asked, trying to inject a casual tone in her voice. "We're still friends."

"But you—"

"I know what we did," Hadley said. "But it doesn't change what we are."

"Did you…want it to?" Violet asked. "Change what you are to each other?"

Hadley wanted to brush off the question in every way possible. She wasn't ready to answer it for herself, and she certainly didn't want to influence anyone else. Was Violet asking for a reason? At that moment, Jordan rode past on his red bicycle and dinged the bell.

"I'm on my way to the grandest hotel on Christmas Island," he called.

"Can't believe they let you in," Violet yelled after him, and he gave her a backward wave as he continued riding down the street.

"I should get going, too," Hadley said. "Even though the Holiday Hotel is only the second grandest hotel on Christmas Island, my job awaits."

Violet's smile turned serious. "You don't have to settle, you know."

Hadley froze. Was she settling by working at a smaller hotel? Would she be settling if she chose to accept Mike's proposals? Heck, had she denied herself the chance at something truly spectacular by choosing to stay on Christmas Island instead of leaving as half her classmates had?

Having a baby made her rethink everything about her life and she hated questioning her heart, her mind and every decision she made.

"I mean you don't have to settle for any of these dresses," Violet said. "I made these myself, and when you and your daughter are ready for yours, I'll make you something special, exactly what you want."

Hadley rolled her shoulders and let some tension go with it. Placing an order and getting exactly what she wanted restored her sense of balance. She could choose the color and pattern and slide the mother-daughter outfits right into her neatly organized closets.

If only everything were that easy. If there were a matching outfit for Mike... She didn't have control of his closet.

"As soon as I figure out exactly what I want, I'll come knocking," she said.

"But you do know," Violet said. "In your heart."

Hadley shook her head. "Everyone seems to think it's so simple. Marry Mike Martin. He already asked, he's my friend, he's my daughter's father. Why not?" She struggled to keep her voice low and calm. Only a few people walked along Holly Street so early in the morning, but she wanted to remain collected. Wasn't that what she always did? Keep organized and moving forward with a plan and action steps?

"That is what everyone thinks," Violet said. "But only you know what's in your heart."

"I'm working on that," Hadley admitted.

"It's hard," Violet said. "Which is why I steer clear of matters of the heart and stick to fashion. I'm a specialist in how things look on the outside."

Violet gave Hadley a little wave, turned her closed sign to open and retreated into her boutique.

THE DAY OF the island-wide bike race was finally here, and all Mike could think about was the picture on the computer screen a few days earlier at the ultrasound center. It was a perfect Sunday morning, and hundreds of bikes lined up at the start line in front of his bike rental.

"Head in the game," he muttered to himself. There was so much noise and excitement all around on Holly Street that no one could hear him. But he heard himself. Loud and clear. This was the fifth year of his charity event that helped build the Christmas Island Foundation. The money could go to any community need as determined by a board. In the past, his bike event had donated cash to restoring the clock tower on the lawn near the marina, a new roof on the island clinic, repairing downtown sidewalks and adding new bike racks in front of island restaurants and hotels. This year, the cause was close to his heart. New playground equipment at the island school would replace the worn-out structure that had been there since he was a kid and developed rust, splinters and a definite creaking sound when too many kids tried to swing at the same time.

Kids. The lucky ones who grew up on the island didn't have immediate access to a lot of things the mainland had to offer, but they weren't actually missing a thing. Maybe they couldn't go to a fast-food restaurant because there weren't any chain restaurants on the island. Maybe they didn't go roller-skating or to a movie theater. But they had an entire island to roam and a close-knit community watching over them.

His daughter would enjoy all the amenities of growing up on Christmas Island, just as he and Hadley and the rest of their friends had. And it would only be a few years until his baby girl would start kindergarten and play on the structure today's charity bike event would help fund.

"Do you have any more zip ties?" Griffin

asked. "I'm running low, and we have a lot more bikes that need to have their race placard attached."

"In my shop. There's a box on the bench next to the blue toolbox."

"Got it," Griffin said. He loped off, and Mike was grateful for good friends who would take time out from their own businesses on a beautiful late May morning to help out a good cause.

"Put me to work."

Mike turned at the sound of Hadley's voice. "I thought you'd be at the hotel."

Hadley smiled. "I wouldn't want to miss this, so I'm going in a little later this morning."

"Then you should be resting."

She laughed. "I'm not an invalid. I can do something to help. Last year, I rode the bike with the basket full of water bottles and handed them out along the course. I wish I could do that this year."

The previous year had been blistering hot, and a few overly enthusiastic bikers had surrendered their spot in the race to sit under shade trees until someone went and found them when they didn't check back in.

"Not so hot this year," Mike said. "And I do have a job for you. Can you sit at the registration table and help out until the race starts and then keep an eye on the finish line and help record what place everyone comes in at? I don't want any disputes, and you're excellent at details."

"You're giving me sit-down jobs," Hadley said.

"You and my daughter."

"Maybe she wants to ride."

"Next year," Mike said. "We'll get one of those baby wagons to pull behind our bikes, and you can hand out all the water bottles you want."

He wanted to savor that image for a moment, him and Hadley and their little girl enjoying a peaceful ride around the island, but the sound of a crash from the starting area grabbed his attention. He glanced over and saw a tangle of four bicycles.

"Mike to the rescue," Hadley said.

"Part of the job," he said.

"Part of who you are," she returned.

He didn't think about what she meant by that, but it sounded like a compliment. He strode quickly to the bikes in a heap at the starting line. Three were kids' bikes and one belonged to an adult who'd chosen a poor parking spot to await the race's start. He offered a hand to one little boy and picked up the boy's bike with the other. He righted the other two small bikes and disentangled the pedals from the wheel spokes of the adult's bike.

"Thanks," the woman said, and Mike realized it was the author, Miranda Mitchell, who was staying at the Holiday Hotel. "How is your project going with trying to get that pretty lady to marry you?" she asked.

Mike grinned and lowered his voice. "I still have ten days left, and if I'm not successful, I may have to leave your book a bad review."

"Have you read it?"

"The first three chapters."

"And then?" she asked.

"Then I got busy running a bike rental, a charity bike race and preparing to be a dad in the fall."

"Is that all?" Miranda smiled. "I've heard a lot about you."

"From Hadley?"

"She may have mentioned you, but I've heard your name come up when I've inserted myself into conversations with locals. They call you Good Guy Mike. The guy who always does the right thing and would give anyone the shirt off his back."

"I'm not a saint."

She laughed. "I certainly hope not. That wouldn't be any fun at all. But I do wonder why, if you're Mr. Helpful, everyone likes you and you're not bad to look at—"

"Thank you."

"You're welcome. But if you're all those things, what's the missing piece to the puzzle of putting an engagement ring on the finger of your beloved."

"She's not—"

"Your beloved?" Miranda asked.

"She doesn't think so."

"Why not?"

Mike let out a long breath. He had a thousand other things to be doing at that moment. The race would start in five minutes. He had to make a short speech, blow the whistle and check on all the volunteers making it happen. Explaining his suddenly complicated relationship with Hadley to a near stranger would require the luxury of time.

"She doesn't want to marry me, that's for

sure. And Hadley is the most direct and honest person I know. Practical. No-nonsense. Believe me, if she loved me, she'd come right out and say it."

"You think so?"

Miranda's smile was too knowing for him to appreciate that early in the morning. Did he really have to explain himself to someone he didn't know? No one else on the island asked him such probing questions.

"Well, I don't have an engagement ring, anyway," he muttered.

"Get one."

Mike cocked his head. "You make it sound so easy."

She laughed. "It's both the easiest and the hardest thing in the world to go after what you want. And right now, I want to win my age category in this bike race, so I hope I don't have a wobbly wheel after my mishap here at the starting line. I'll have to smoke those kids out of the gate so they can't catch up to me and crash me again."

Mike grinned. The tenacious lady probably would burn rubber and leave her fellow racers behind. He admired Miranda's courage and the way she believed in herself. Maybe he needed some of that courage, too.

As he considered her words, Shirley from the chamber of commerce rode up on a tandem bicycle with her husband on the back. "Gonna kill ya," she said cheerfully to the other riders at the start line.

Mike wanted to laugh, but his mind was on an engagement ring. Maybe just asking Hadley and giving her logical reasons wasn't enough. There had to be a missing element to his proposals, and if he didn't figure it out, he was in grave danger of going down on one knee and telling her he was in love with her.

If she rejected him after hearing those words, there was no way for them to go forward together, as parents, on an island where he could never escape the fact that he loved her, but she just thought he was a grown-up boy scout in return.

CHAPTER SEVENTEEN

HADLEY LEANED AGAINST the door frame of the baby's room and grinned as she watched Mike and Justin assemble a new dresser. Her brother-in-law had offered his assistance before he and Wendy went out for dinner and left their three kids with Hadley.

"If the instructions were in English it would help," Mike said.

Justin reached over and grabbed the large, folded paper from Mike's hands. He turned it over and pointed. "English is on the back."

"Maybe that's the front," Hadley said, and she laughed.

"Not helping," Mike said. "I was planning to let Macey and Janey paint my fingernails this evening, but maybe I'll tell them you want your toes done."

Hadley's smile shifted to a grin. "Maybe I do. It's getting harder for me to see my toes and to bend over."

"From what I hear, that's only going to get worse," Justin commented. He applied a handle to a dresser drawer and tightened the screws. "And I wouldn't let Aaron near anything involving paint. He has more enthusiasm than discretion."

"He's three," Hadley said.

"I know it goes with the territory, and I guess he needs to do something to get attention since he can't get a word in edgewise with his sisters doing all the talking for him," Justin said.

"I'll try to have a nice long talk with him tonight," Mike offered. "While the girls do Hadley's nails."

Hadley sat in the room's only chair and looked around. It was late afternoon and clouds had blocked the sun most of the day, but the room was still pretty and cheerful. She and Mike had settled on a coral color that was in the pink family but more subtle. Hadley had picked out curtains and bedding with seashells and cute sea creatures for a beach-themed nursery. After all, her baby was going to grow up on an island, so the clam-shaped pillow and sandcastle rug were a perfect introduction to the watery world that would make up her life.

"Are you ready, Justin?" Wendy's voice came up the stairs and Justin glanced at his watch.

"You better get going," Mike said. "And thanks for your help."

Justin laughed. "You would probably have been better off with Hadley's help, but I'll get points with my wife if I tell her I was the pivotal member of the assembly team."

"Think she'll believe you?" Mike asked.

Justin gave him a friendly shoulder punch on his way out. Hadley followed him downstairs and tried to shoo her sister out the door for her date on her eighth wedding anniversary.

"We're fine," she assured Wendy. "Your kids are angels, and Mike's picking up a pizza after you leave. I may even keep your kids for the entire weekend."

Wendy shook her head. "If you weren't pregnant, I might hold you to that, but they're a handful. You have to work your way up to three kids slowly, one at a time."

As soon as she said the words, Wendy

glanced up at Hadley and put a hand on her arm. "Sorry. I don't mean to say… I mean—"

"It's okay," Hadley said. She put a hand on her belly. "This girl may be my only child, or I may fall in love with a millionaire visiting the island and have five more children."

Wendy gave her sister a half smile. "Thanks for giving us a date night." She hugged Hadley. "And we'll be happy to return the favor anytime. My kids are so excited to have a cousin they'll probably be begging me to bring my niece home for a sleepover."

"You'll be the best aunt in the world," Hadley said.

Justin leaned in and kissed the top of Wendy's head. "Ready?"

"You bet," Wendy said. "We'll be back in a few hours."

Hadley went into the living room where Macey and Janey were making a puzzle on the coffee table. "Where's Aaron?"

"Uncle Mike took him upstairs," Janey said. "He said he wanted a helper."

"Excellent." Hadley sat on the couch behind her nieces. They both had long dark blond hair brushed neatly into ponytails that bounced and swung with their movements.

Would her daughter have her dark hair? She imagined a third little girl with a ponytail claiming a spot at the coffee table and grabbing puzzle pieces. Hadley pulled the chain on the floor lamp next to the couch so her nieces wouldn't have to strain their eyes.

"What do you want on your pizza?" she asked.

"Uncle Mike already asked us and wrote a note in his phone so he wouldn't goof up," Janey said.

Of course, he had. Mike tried to please everyone and do everything right. Even if that meant marrying her whether he loved her or not. What if, instead of her, he was the one who fell in love with someone visiting the island and wanted five more children? It wasn't right for her to lock him into a marriage any more than it was right for her to choose security over love.

She'd never have to worry about Mike being there for her. But it would kill her to share a towel rack and a closet and a toaster and…a life…knowing her husband had married her because he was a stand-up guy. Not a guy who was in love.

As she pictured herself grocery shopping

with him or going through the motions of a perfunctory good-night kiss, Mike came down the stairs, one hand on the railing and one wrapped around Aaron perched on his hip. "We're going on the pizza run," he said. "I called in the order and got your favorite toppings on one of the pizzas. Eight slices just for you to celebrate eight days until our birthday."

He didn't have to ask Hadley what her favorite toppings were. It was one of the many things he knew about her. If only he knew the most important thing weighing on her heart.

"THIS IS MY least favorite thing about owning my own business," Mike said. He killed the engine and tossed out the anchor.

Griffin May sat on the gunwale of Mike's small boat and laughed. "The lake gives and takes away," he said. "The first day I met Rebecca, she'd tried running for the ferry and she made it, but her suitcase didn't. I'll never forget seeing her sprawled soaking wet on the deck of my boat demanding I go back and dredge up her luggage."

It was almost sunset, but Mike and Griffin had finally found time to take Mike's boat around to the northern side of the island where a tourist had tried riding his rental bike out into the lake. Presumably on a dare from friends, he'd somehow pedaled down an abandoned concrete boat launch until the water was up to his ears before abandoning the adventure—and the bike. The bike renter had returned to Mike's shop the evening before, confessed and forfeited his deposit. Luckily, the Northern Michigan water was so crystal clear Mike could see the red bike ten feet down. Because it was the third week in May, the air was warm, but the lake water was still ice-cold.

"I'll hold the rope, but you're the one getting in the freezing water," Griffin said.

"Lucky me," Mike said. "I'm not sure this bike's going to be worth saving after spending twenty-four hours underwater, but I can't just leave it there. It wouldn't be right."

Griffin shrugged. "The fish might have some fun with it, and it might eventually wash up on shore, but you're right. Can't just leave it."

"I'll never know how he managed to get this far out with it," Mike said. "The guy must have been riding like a maniac." He leaned over the side of the boat and stared down into the water. "Maybe I should rent kayaks instead of bikes. Or how about those pedal boats tourists seem to like? My shop is close enough to the water that I could probably pull it off."

"You're the only bike rental on the island," Griffin said. "You can't let people down."

"Someone else would come along and rent bikes," Mike said. "It's not like it's rocket science. They sign a waiver, we find them a bike that fits them, give them a bottle of water and a helmet, and then wait for them to come back at the end of the day."

"It was your dream to own your own business ever since we were kids, and you've built it up from basically nothing. You started with six bikes, and now look at where you are. Don't sell yourself short and talk down your accomplishment. You've never done that before," Griffin said.

"I've never had a daughter on the way before."

The boat bobbed gently, and it should have been soothing to Mike to be out on the water with his longtime friend. Griffin leaned on the sidewall of the boat and crossed his arms.

"Are you worried about having a kid and running your business?"

Mike nodded. The light was fading, and he really should get going. Jump in the water, hook a chain to the bike and get it pulled up. But he needed to talk to someone. "A bit terrified, actually," he said. "It's not the long days and being busy, you know I don't mind that. But I wonder if it's enough. If Hadley and I both have jobs that keep us busy in the summer and are dependent on income from tourist season, how will that work? We need childcare, a steady income, two parents who aren't run ragged from May through September."

"You'll figure it out," Griffin said. "Everyone does."

Mike shook his head. "I don't know how."

Griffin laughed. "I don't think anyone knows how to be a parent until they do it."

"My dad was pretty old by the time I came along," Mike said. "And I wouldn't say he did typical dad stuff. He mostly told old stories about his time in the navy, and I tried to listen, but I always felt like an afterthought. It was like my older brothers had gotten all the good parenting and there wasn't much left for me. I want to do better than that."

"You will. You're young and I don't think the navy will even take you, especially if you're stalling instead of being brave enough to get in the cold water."

"Very funny," Mike said. "Are you and Rebecca going to have kids?"

"I hope so. Can't let my brother have all the fun."

"I'm glad Maddox and Camille finally got things worked out," Mike said. Although Maddox and Camille were two years younger than he and Griffin, it was a small island. Everyone knew about Maddox breaking Camille's heart, having his son, Ethan, with someone else and then finally reuniting with Camille. Almost everyone in Mike's generation and friend group was finding love and getting married. It wasn't too late for him, but there was only one person he wanted to be with.

"Me, too," Griffin said. "We're so busy with the ferry expansion and the hotel, I don't need Maddox to be distracted by anything right now, and Camille is good for him and Ethan. She understands the demands of a family business better than anyone, and I can't complain about the cookies and fudge."

Mike thought about Hadley. She didn't run her own business, but she'd always been supportive of his. She'd even pitched in and worked for him a few times when his summer employees called off or it was a particularly busy day and she happened to be available. One time, he'd had a nasty bout of the summer flu, and she'd run his bike rental for two days while he laid in bed in his apartment over the shop.

"Hadley will understand, too," Griffin said.

"I know."

"But that's not what you're worried about."

"I'm worried about everything. Being a good dad, providing financially, being a good teammate to Hadley."

Griffin laughed. "Teammate?"

"What else do I call it? She won't marry me. I've asked her twice."

Griffin's mouth opened and his eyebrows shot up. "Rebecca told me about the one proposal."

"There were two proposals, and the second one went worse than the first. I'm afraid to try that again."

"Unless…" Griffin began.

"What?"

"Unless something has changed."

Mike sucked in a deep breath and looked out at the expanse of blue water. "That's exactly it. Everything has changed."

"For you or for her?"

Mike swallowed. "I don't know about her."

"Have you asked how she's feeling?"

"No. The thing is, at first, I was just intent on doing the right thing. I didn't want Hadley to think I wouldn't pull my weight as a parent, and I didn't want her to have to worry about anything. It seemed so simple. If we got married, I'd be there to mow the lawn and clean the gutters and go pick up dinner and rock the baby to sleep."

"She could hire someone to do those things," Griffin commented.

Even though Griffin's tone was friendly, his words stung. "I would do them better," Mike said.

"Agreed."

"And then I thought about our pact, the one we made back in high school that if we weren't married by our thirtieth birthdays, we'd marry each other because it was better than getting old and lonely."

"Very romantic," Griffin said.

"But practical. You know Hadley. She's the most logical, orderly person on the island. I was sure she'd see reason when I asked, but she basically laughed in my face. And now we only have seven days left until our birthdays."

Griffin smiled. "The light's fading, so you better get to the part about what's changed."

"I always loved her, you know. As a friend and a person."

"Everyone loves Hadley."

"But not everyone's in love with her," Mike said. "It feels like someone is squeezing my heart in their fist whenever I think of her or see her."

"I know that feeling," Griffin said. "That was me last summer."

"Does it get better?"

"Yes, but you have to actually do something about it. When did this start?"

"It's been gradual, kind of like waves coming in, but there have been a few rogue waves. The night of the canoe race, I got hit by one, and then last week when we went for the ultrasound, and I saw our daughter for the first time."

Griffin nodded. "That had to be big."

"Life changing. Incredible. And that's what I'm worried about. You know? What if I'm in love with the idea of being a dad, or the baby herself, or…is it Hadley? How do I know for sure if I'm in love?"

Griffin laughed. "I know that water is cold, but I don't think you're just stalling. If you're sitting here telling me about your feelings…something we have honest to pete never talked about even though I've known you since birth, I think the idea you're in love has some merit."

Mike kicked off his shoes and picked up the chain. "I should probably take the plunge and hook this bike before it gets dark. On the way back to the harbor, maybe you can give me your wisdom and tell me what the heck I'm going to do about my situation."

"No way. I'm not giving you any advice except to be honest with yourself and Hadley. If you think you can be her teammate and conceal the fact you're in love with her, then you're going to explode before your daughter graduates from kindergarten."

"But she won't marry me," Mike said. "And the thought of her marrying someone else someday… I can't do it."

"Maybe things have changed for her, too," Griffin suggested.

Mike's heart lightened and the squeezing feeling lessened. Could Griffin be right? Was it possible Hadley had changed her mind, too, and would now see him as more than a partner?

He jumped overboard into the shockingly cold water and hooked his chain around the bike frame. He climbed back onto the boat, and he and Griffin pulled the bike to the surface and over the side. Mike examined the bike that had spent a day underwater. Aside from surface rust, it didn't seem damaged. He'd have to check more thoroughly when he got back to his shop.

Mike toweled off, pulled in his anchor and took the wheel for the return trip to the Christmas Island marina. The sun had disappeared into the lake, and it was getting darker. Griffin stood beside him and flipped on the running lights.

"Thanks," Mike said.

"I know your brain is elsewhere, but I don't want to get run down by another boat, and we both have a lot to live for. Unless you're serious about spending your life behind the counter of the post office."

"Hey," Mike said. "How did you know about that?"

"Bertie is a talker. He told me all about it. Seemed a little disappointed, though, that I wasn't interesting in applying since I was his first choice and all."

"You're making that up," Mike said.

Griffin shrugged. "Actually, Rebecca was his first choice, but I'm lucky enough to have her working for me. I wasn't sure I believed Bertie about your application, but I'm guessing it's true."

"It wouldn't be the worst job," Mike said. "It's year-round, steady and I wouldn't be out here fishing bikes out of the lake."

"This is the fun part," Griffin argued. "Does Hadley know you applied?"

"No."

"You sure?"

"Well, I didn't tell her, but since you know, she might have heard, too. Do you think she'll be happy about it?"

"Has she asked you to change your occupation?" Griffin asked.

"No."

"But you think it will persuade her that you're husband material."

"It won't hurt."

Griffin shook his head. "I don't think you know what she would consider good husband material, and I can't help you out because it's not something we discuss at work. But I would recommend you say something to her about the postmaster thing before she hears it from someone else. Hadley likes to feel like she's in control of herself and her entire orbit."

"I guess you're right."

Griffin clapped him on the back. "And, who knows? You might be so lucky that it's always been her dream to be married to a postal worker and she'll be the one proposing to you this time."

CHAPTER EIGHTEEN

SOMEONE FROM HER tiny graduating class was returning to Christmas Island to get married and have a reception in the ballroom at the Great Island Hotel, and there was no way Hadley was going to miss it. The food and decorations would be elegant and tasteful, and it would be a great chance to catch up with old friends. She also knew the evening would be a test. Friends she hadn't seen in months or years would come home for the event, and she'd have to respond to their curiosity. Hadley steeled herself for the inevitable questions as she parked outside the hotel and smoothed her maternity dress before going inside.

The wedding of Andrew Reed, who'd graduated with Mike and Griffin, fell only six days before Hadley and Mike's thirtieth birthday, and earlier in the day, Hadley had received a note telling her to look in the employee break-room freezer at the Holiday Hotel. In a plastic carton, she found a mint chocolate chip ice-cream pie with fudge topping cut into six slices.

Hadley wished she hadn't eaten one and a half pieces of the ice-cream pie, but she congratulated herself on the control it had taken not to finish the second piece. To keep her stomach settled, she planned to eat sparingly and selectively from the wedding buffet and then have a very small piece of wedding cake later in the evening.

Preplanning her interactions with Mike was trickier because there wouldn't be just their usual circle of friends. There would be wild cards, people who may not even know about the baby. She squared her shoulders and entered the ballroom, prepared to seek out a table and walk straight to it.

No luck. She hadn't taken five steps before she ran into Meisha, a student from Hadley and Mike's class who had only returned to Christmas Island a few times since graduation. Hadley could tell from the slight roll in Meisha's walk and the reckless grin on her face that she might be a beverage or two beyond polite conversation.

"Hadley, I can't believe you're still right here on the island where I left you."

Hadley swallowed. She was quite happy being right there on the island, Meisha's leaving notwithstanding. Although they'd had a friendly relationship in school, partially out of necessity because they lived on a small island, Hadley hadn't been sorry when Meisha and her propensity for gossip had moved away. Gossip on an island could only go around a finite number of times before it got back to its subject.

"And you're...here," Hadley said. "I'm sure everyone is excited to catch up with you. It's been a few years, so why don't you start by telling me everything you've been doing." Hadley sincerely hoped Meisha would launch into a description of her life and all she'd have to do was smile and listen without having to say anything.

"I already heard about you and Mike Martin," Meisha said. "But I didn't believe it."

"This baby bump says it's true," Hadley said as she put a hand on her belly. She knew she could have said something more subtle, but what was the point? The truth was the truth, and it was no one's business but hers and Mike's—even if a long-lost acquaintance swaying with a colorful drink in her hand seemed to find Hadley's relationship with Mike such a surprise.

"Well, good for you," Meisha said. "I guess. I just never saw that coming in high school, but what did any of us know back then?"

"True," Hadley said. Maybe Meisha had matured and this wasn't going to be awkward.

"So, are you guys going to get married?" Meisha asked.

Hadley groaned inwardly. Why did people seem to choose that avenue as their first reaction? The twenty-first century was well underway, and she was more than capable of managing her own life and her daughter's without a ring on her finger.

Maybe she should have claimed swollen ankles or indigestion and skipped the wedding reception.

"There you are," Rebecca Browne said as she came up and linked arms with Hadley. "We need you over at our table because no one wants to go to the buffet until our whole party is here." Rebecca smiled at Meisha. "It would be rude."

Hadley began walking away, arm in arm

with Rebecca. She leaned in and whispered, "Did you all really wait for me? There was a late check-in at the hotel."

"I know," Rebecca said. "Griffin told me, and he also suggested I rescue you from Mei-sha the Meddler."

Hadley laughed. "I haven't heard her called that in years."

"I told Griffin it wasn't very nice. People who gossip just need to feel better about themselves, and that's why they talk about other people," Rebecca said.

"I'm glad you rescued me, anyway," Hadley said. "I didn't want to answer the age-old question about marriage again. People on the island have stopped asking me that, with the notable exception of Grandma Penny who would marry Mike herself if he'd ask her. When I run into people I haven't seen in a while, though, I have to go through the whole story again."

Rebecca smiled and pulled Hadley down next to her at a table decorated with a hurricane lamp and fresh flowers. "It's so unfair. Mike can run into people and they don't ask him questions because he's not the one who's obviously pregnant."

"Obviously?" Hadley asked.

Rebecca nodded. "You're a full five months along now. Your dress is very pretty, by the way."

Hadley glanced down at the green cotton knee-length dress with airy eyelet sleeves. "It's one of Wendy's and she says she's never using her maternity clothes again, but I'm still being careful not to spill anything on it."

Camille Peterson came over with her sister Cara and joined Hadley and Rebecca at their table. "We're not spilling on ourselves tonight?" Camille asked. "How will we know we had fun?"

"Pictures," Rebecca said. She held up her phone.

Hadley shook her head. "None of me, thanks."

"Come on," Camille said. "You look beautiful, and you'll want pictures of yourself when you were pregnant to show your daughter someday. You should make a scrapbook of your entire pregnancy so you'll remember it."

Hadley tilted her head and considered her friend Camille. "That sounds more like something Chloe would say." Camille's sister was the sentimental one.

Camille laughed. "She's worn off on me over the years."

Cara leaned forward. "I was at the horse barn earlier today, and I had to run to the post office to get a package of medicine from the vet on the mainland, and Bertie told me about Mike."

The way Rebecca and Camille both swung their heads and gave Cara an identical look put Hadley on emergency notice. "What about Mike?" Hadley asked. "Don't tell me he's been seeing a vet on the mainland about some unknown medical condition."

"No," Cara said. She glanced at her sister and Rebecca, and then closed her mouth.

"Okay, what?" Hadley asked. "What's the talk at the post office about Mike? I know he's not on a wanted poster there. He's never left Christmas Island, so the FBI can't possibly even know his name."

"It's just something Bertie has been telling a few people," Rebecca said. "About his retirement. You know they're looking for a steady, dependable person to take over as postmaster, and there aren't a lot of candidates who want to live on an island."

Realization dawned on Hadley. Mike's talk

about being there for her and being a good partner and provider. Had he really considered taking on an extra job? It was foolish. He wouldn't have five spare minutes for six months out of the year. When was he supposed to take his turn pushing the stroller or blowing raspberries on their baby's belly?

"Mike is the new postmaster?" she asked.

Camille waved both hands in front of her. "No, they haven't appointed anyone. But the word is that Mike applied."

"Without telling me," Hadley said.

"Did you tell him before you changed jobs at the hotel?" Rebecca asked.

Hadley sat back in her chair. "No, but he found out right away. There aren't any secrets on this island and he's right across the street."

"The post office is down the street," Cara said.

Suddenly, the room seemed too hot and close. Even her friends didn't provide the comfort they usually gave. Did everything have to change just because one thing—albeit one major thing—was changing? Hadley stood. "I'm going to step outside for a minute and get some air."

Rebecca opened her mouth to say something, but at that moment Hadley spotted Mike coming across the dance floor. He saw her, too, and he smiled and waved and started moving in her direction. Perfect. She was going to give him a piece of her mind, and she didn't care who heard it. Everyone seemed to know their business, anyway. She'd only gone a few steps when Mike's faster strides brought him to her, just a few feet away from the table where her friends still sat.

"When were you going to tell me about the post-office thing?" she demanded.

Mike's smiled faded. "You heard."

"Why didn't you tell me?"

Mike took a step back. "I think it was only about a month or so ago that you told me you didn't need my permission to change jobs. That we didn't need to consult each other on those things."

Hadley swallowed. She had said those words. But that wasn't the whole point.

"How would you run your bike business?" she asked, hoping that a practical argument would diminish some of the hurt she felt from finding out from a third party.

"Maybe I wouldn't," Mike said. "I could sell it and embark on a new career."

"But you love owning your own business," Hadley protested.

"I love the idea of having something that belongs to me and that I can be proud of," Mike said. "And now I have...our baby."

She was almost certain he'd been about to say that she belonged to him. That she was his. And that thought was too much to process at the moment. If he thought they belonged to each other, she shouldn't have gotten such momentous news from her friends.

"I heard about it from three *other people*," she said, emphasizing the last two words. She heard her own voice rising and confused feelings competed in her chest. She wasn't just angry that Mike hadn't told her, she was hurt. "Other people," she repeated. "Even though I'm your—"

"My what?" Mike asked.

"Your..." Oh, goodness. How did she answer that question? Friend? Baby momma? Parenting partner? Person who loved him unrequitedly?

And that was the root of it. She loved him, and he didn't even love her enough to tell her what he was thinking of doing. Not just changing his bath towels or even trading in his old pickup, but a major change. A job, for pity's sake. He could have told her that. He owed her that.

"Hadley?" he prompted. "What am I to you?" His voice was so soft she was sure she was the only person in the room who could hear it. She felt as if she and Mike were the only people in the room, anyway. All the noise and flowers and music were like a blurred background around the edge of a photograph and she and Mike were in the middle of the picture.

"How am I supposed to answer that?" she said, her own words barely a whisper.

Mike stepped closer. "With what's in your heart."

Hadley was almost certain he could read her feelings in her eyes. He knew her so well. If she tried to say anything at that moment, she was afraid she would tell him she was so in love with him it hurt. And it *would* hurt, because no matter how sweet and good he was to her, he didn't love her. Not the way she loved him.

She couldn't think of anything to say, so she did the only thing she could.

Hadley raised onto her tiptoes and kissed Mike right on the lips. She'd meant it as a quick friendly peck, a kiss that was practically an excuse to get out of an awkward conversation. But even as her lips touched his, she knew she'd made a horrible mistake. It wasn't just a friendly peck. From the first second of the kiss, every rush of emotion and feeling—the same kinds that had put them on the road to parenthood after the island Christmas party—she knew she couldn't stop at just a brush of lips.

His arms encircled her, and she kept on kissing him as he responded as if it were something he'd been waiting for all his life. It was a mistake, a huge error if she didn't want her heart to be any more involved and vulnerable.

Mike would be misled. He'd probably interpret her kissing him as an acceptance of his marriage proposals or at least encouragement to try again. Worse, the kiss might be just physical for him, without the deep churning in the chest that proves it's true love. The kind of love that is both physically painful and yet something Hadley didn't want to live without.

Someone in the room applauded and someone else whistled. The reality of what she and Mike were doing at someone else's wedding reception shocked Hadley into breaking the kiss and drawing back so she could see Mike's face.

His eyes were half closed and his lips were parted. He looked as if he'd walked into a brick wall and was dizzy from the impact.

"I'm sorry," Hadley said. "I don't know what… I just…" She shook her head and gave up on words. There was nothing words could do in this situation, so she turned and walked straight out of the ballroom, right to her car, got in and drove to her sister's house.

She'd planned her dress, shoes and a tiny piece of cake, but she hadn't planned to kiss the father of her child and sow confusion with one long perfect moment she would regret.

MIKE TRIED STAYING at the wedding reception, at least until the buffet dinner and cake. But it was no use. His friends teased him about the kiss. Curious glances from Hadley's friends—who were mostly also his friends— burned a hole through him. He wasn't the one who initiated the kiss, but he hadn't resisted it, and then he was left wondering what on earth he was going to do about it.

And why. Why had she kissed him? He'd

backed her into a corner, that was for certain. Words and logic failed her. And so she'd raised up on her toes and given him a lot to think about without saying a word.

Mike left the party just thirty minutes behind Hadley and went straight to her house. There was no car in the driveway and no answer at the door aside from Betty barking and whining when she heard his voice. He'd bet anything Hadley was at her sister's house, but she'd be back before it got too late. For one thing, she wasn't a night owl. And she wouldn't leave Betty alone too long.

He knew where the key was hidden, but he couldn't just invite himself into her home. It was too personal. So instead he let Betty out and they sat together on the front porch where they could watch the sunset and a strip of lake as the crickets began their evening song and the thirsty mosquitoes came out.

Mike slapped at a bug on his arm. "Do you think it'd be okay to go inside?" he asked the dog. "Or we could get in my truck, but we'd have to leave the windows up or the mosquitoes would get us."

Betty snapped at a bug in midair and ate it.

"I guess I could go home, but I wanted to

make sure Hadley was okay." He scratched Betty's ears. "She kissed me and probably regrets it, and I don't want her to go to bed upset."

He didn't ever want to be the reason Hadley was upset. They'd been friends through so many things, it wasn't right that deepening their relationship put stress on it. That wasn't the way it was supposed to be.

A night bird sang in the trees behind the house and lights in the downtown area came on. A boat horn sounded. "She'll be home soon," Mike assured Betty, even though he was really reassuring himself. It was almost completely dark now, and the island roads were narrow and twisty. But Wendy's house was only a mile away. He pulled his phone from his pocket and considered calling Hadley, but he didn't want to bother her if she was driving.

Mercifully, a set of headlights left downtown and headed his way, and Mike soon recognized the shape of Hadley's car in the darkness. She pulled into the driveway next to Mike's truck, which he'd parked off to the side. Hadley got out of her car and approached the porch.

"Thanks for letting Betty out," she said. "I was starting to worry about her."

"My pleasure," he said. "She's been keeping me company."

"You could have gone inside."

"I didn't want to make assumptions."

Hadley climbed the three steps to the porch. "You'll be eaten alive. Mosquitoes love you."

Mike laughed. "It keeps all my friends safe because those bloodsuckers will choose me over anyone else all the time."

"That's what makes you such a nice guy," Hadley said.

"It's not the only thing," he said softly.

"I know. Come in before you get any more bit up."

Hadley pushed open her door, waited for Mike and Betty to come inside and then turned on the lights. She kicked off her shoes and toed them into their spot on the rug.

"Go ahead," she said, pointing to Mike's shoes.

It was an invitation to stay a while. If Hadley had wanted to say a quick good-night at the door, she would have let him leave his shoes on.

Betty followed them to the living room

where they took the spots on the couch they always claimed when they watched television during the winter or sometimes lived it up and ate take-out food in the living room in front of the fireplace.

"I'm sorry about that kiss," Hadley said.

Mike was relieved she brought it up, because he didn't think he had the ability to skirt around it for more than two minutes, and he wanted to stay longer than two minutes.

"I'm not sorry," he said. "Although it did end the party early for both of us."

Hadley looked down at her hands. "I feel bad about leaving the reception without saying anything to the bride and groom."

"I think people understood."

"And you left early, too?"

Mike nodded. "Not long after you. I didn't have answers to the questions on people's minds, and I didn't think I owed them an explanation, anyway."

"But I owe you one," Hadley said.

Mike leaned into the couch and crossed one leg over the other. "Okay," he said. "I'm all ears."

"It was a…um…test."

"You were testing me?" he blurted out.

"No. I was testing myself. I wanted to see if there was any, you know, attraction or feeling between us. Anything that might cause problems later."

"Problems?"

"Complications," she said. "We're going to co-parent, so I wanted to tidy away any doubts. Clear my head. That kind of thing."

Mike scratched at a mosquito bite on his knee. "That seems very logical," he said.

"Yes. Exactly," Hadley said, enthusiasm entering her voice for the first time since she'd arrived home.

Mike almost laughed. Of course, Hadley would run home to her comfort zone of logic and planning. But she was clearly nervous. Her hands were fidgety, and one of her knees bobbed back and forth. She looked at his face but not quite in his eyes. Even Betty sensed there was something off. The dog stood next to Hadley instead of flopping down comfortably on the rug.

"Well," Mike said, keeping his tone serious despite how difficult it was. This was unexpected and amazing. The fact that Hadley was making up a story and denying her feelings were any deeper than a puddle told him that the opposite was true. "What did you discover when you surprised me with that kiss?"

While he would like to hear she'd discovered her deep and world-shattering love for him and rediscovered the fact that he was an especially adept kisser, he knew Hadley well enough to know that was not on her pre-planned dialogue. She'd thought about this, considered exactly what words would be her escape route. And he'd played right into her hands by waiting on her porch.

She didn't have to sleep on it. She didn't have to wonder when she'd see him next. He'd placed himself right there for her to give him the dismissal speech.

"Nothing," she said. "Nothing happened. Which is good," she added quickly. "That would be weird, right? And awkward. Uncomfortable. I mean, we wouldn't want to feel like there was something unsaid between us."

"Like we were cheating ourselves of true love," Mike said, nodding and smiling as if he were in total compliance, encouraging her to go on.

Hadley drew her brows together. "I didn't say that."

"Oh," Mike said. "So the co-parenting, di-aper-buddies relationship is what you meant."

"Right? I knew you'd see exactly where I was going with that. And I love that you played along with the kiss. It must have really put your mind at rest, too, right? After Christmas and what happened there, you might have thought…might have been wondering…maybe you even considered testing the air between us in the area of…"

Mike smiled. "What area is that?" This was too good. He'd camped out on her porch because he wanted to be sure she wasn't going to bed upset about what had clearly been an impulsive kiss. His plan was a failure, though, because Hadley was rattled. Delightfully rattled. He doubted she'd sleep a wink that night, and he almost didn't feel bad about it.

She could tell him six ways to Sunday how much that kiss had *not* meant to her, but every word she uttered gave her away. That kiss had been the chink in the armor. She had relinquished some of her tightly held control, and she didn't like it. What was between them was far more than any kind of teammate, co-parenting, just friends navigating the baby aisle business. And there was no way he was letting that opportunity slip away.

He didn't wait for her to fabricate an answer to his question and fumble through an explanation any further. It was better to leave the field with his head high and be ready to fight another day.

He stood. "Tomorrow is that event at the Great Island Hotel," Mike said. "I already told your grandmother about it, so there's no backing out now."

Hadley lifted her chin and gave him a bright smile. "I'm looking forward to it."

"I'm sure," Mike said. "Good night, Hadley. I'll let myself out."

Betty followed him to the door and waited patiently while he donned his shoes, and then he slipped out and sauntered to his truck, feeling as if he'd lifted a weight from his shoulders. That squeezing sensation in his chest might just have a companion in his old friend Hadley's heart. The question was what was he going to do about it?

CHAPTER NINETEEN

HADLEY WAS A third wheel. Ahead of her, Mike and Grandma Penny walked, arm in arm, through the convention area of the Great Island Hotel. They stopped in front of a massive display of handmade quilts. With their heads close together, they appeared to be admiring the artistry and sharing a laugh.

As if they were on a date and she was there on her own. "That one is really pretty," she said as she leaned in close behind them. "The blue one."

Her grandmother and Mike exchanged a grin. "We were just saying how its pattern is actually better if you close one eye."

Hadley closed one eye and considered the combination of triangles and squares making up the bed-sized quilt hanging in front of them. As much as she liked order instead of chaos, it was a lot more interesting with one eye closed, making the triangles and squares swirl off-kilter.

"I'm ready to see the yarn," Grandma Penny said. "It was the real reason I agreed to let you wine and dine me today."

"Are they serving wine at the luncheon?" Mike asked. He affected an innocent look. "I had no idea."

"You're so funny." The older woman turned herself and Mike toward the walkway that wound through the convention center. Hadley had been to this show only once before, even though it was one of the many organizations that held its annual convention at the Great Island Hotel. Throughout the year, the large meeting and conference space hosted bankers, golfers, politicians, entrepreneurs, chefs, musicians and people who loved textiles. Tickets for the accompanying yarn and fabric exhibition were expensive, and her grandmother only went every few years.

"I shouldn't have let you splurge on these tickets," Grandma Penny said.

Mike laughed. "They were free because I did the hotel manager a huge favor. When he offered me a ticket to the hotel luncheon and an event of my choice, I knew it was my chance for a day out with my favorite ladies."

"What kind of favor?" Hadley asked. She walked on his other side because their group seemed off-balance if she walked behind them. She needed balance. She took Mike's other arm.

"The only thing I'm good at," Mike admitted.

"You're good at plenty of things," Grandma Penny said.

While Hadley knew that was true, she wondered if her grandmother could draw up a list if she needed to. How well did Grandma Penny know Mike, or did she just know him as the island Good Guy?

"The mechanic who had been maintaining the small fleet of loaner bikes for the hotel suddenly took a job on the mainland, and someone needed to get the bikes out of storage, grease the chains, pump up the tires and generally knock off the rust from a long winter."

"Mike to the rescue," Grandma Penny said.

Mike laughed and flashed a grin at Hadley, but Hadley was forced to relinquish his arm when the walkway narrowed, and they met an oncoming group. As she walked behind them, she tried to ignore their laughing and chatting. She knew what Mike was doing. He was getting her back for kissing him in front of all their friends and then telling him the kiss meant nothing. He'd gone home covered in mosquito bites and probably feeling as if he'd been misled.

They entered another section of the large conference center, and Grandma Penny paused and put a hand on her heart. "Look at all that beautiful yarn," she said. She dropped Mike's arm and walked purposefully toward a display of skeins dyed exquisite colors.

Mike turned to Hadley. "I've been dumped for yarn."

"It could get worse," she said. "She could buy enough yarn to get through the next two winters and you'll have to haul it all to the car."

"I'm glad we brought your car instead of my pickup," Mike said. "Maybe I should get something different to drive. A car seat will take up half the seat in the pickup and I don't want Betty to have to ride in the bed."

"What about me?" Hadley asked.

"You're not riding in the bed of the truck."

She shouldn't read too much into his firm statement. He wouldn't let anyone, even her dog, ride where it wasn't safe. Mike was nice to everyone and took care of people he only casually knew. It wasn't his words; it was more the intensity and the way he looked at her.

She should never have kissed him. Before that reckless move at the wedding reception, she'd persuaded herself she could forget the physical and emotional parts of their relationship and that she could view him as her friend, partner and a reliable co-parent of her daughter. They already shared a past, so they could share a future without getting all emotional and melty when she thought about his arms around her and the way he lowered his voice to talk to her because he only wanted her to hear him. The way they shared jokes and knew each other inside and out.

She could have squelched it a lot easier without that clanging reminder bell of a kiss the day before. Her fingers went to the necklace Mike had given her that morning. It was a simple white daisy on a chain, five petals to symbolize five days until their birthday.

She cleared her throat. "We can always use my car if we're going somewhere as a…"

"Family," Mike supplied.

"As a group," she said, nodding vehemently as if she'd just declared something very important. "A nice friendly group."

Mike didn't smile. "Call it what you want," he said.

At that moment, Hadley realized something about that impulsive kiss. It had affected Mike. It had shaken him as much as it had taken the ground out from underneath her.

He'd waited in the dark with her dog despite the night insects not just to check on her but because he was too impacted by that kiss to stay at the party or go home to his empty house.

The kiss had rocked his world… But what did it mean? Was he attracted to her? Confused? Questioning what they were to each other?

Maybe he had a squeezing feeling around his heart when he saw her or thought of her, and maybe he even recognized that feeling as love. She'd known she loved him since Christmas, so perhaps he'd come to that realization, too.

If he loved her, it would change everything. But if it were true, why hadn't he said so when he proposed?

"I think I can guess from your expression of deep thought and longing what you're thinking," Mike said. "And I'm right there with you, but I don't want to rush your grandmother while she looks at yarn."

Hadley held her breath. Mike said he could guess her thoughts—something she readily believed because of their long friendship where they often didn't need words to communicate—so he must know she was thinking about the fact that she loved him and was scared to death he might feel the same way—no matter how nice it would be. But… wait…what did that have to do with rushing Grandma Penny through the textile display?

"What are you saying?" Hadley asked. She was tired of the verbal repartee. No more games. It was time to come out and say what he was thinking, or maybe she'd better be the one to break the seal and open the jar, even knowing there was no way to put it back.

"I'm saying," Mike said, leaning close and putting a light hand on her shoulder, "That you must be just as hungry as I am and the luncheon ticket that came with our admittance is burning a hole in my pocket. Maybe I should go offer Grandma Penny an arm so she can get through the displays more efficiently."

"Don't," Hadley said. She meant *don't play with my feelings*.

Mike smiled. "You know I won't, even though I'm starting to learn that the only way to get what you really want is to be direct about it. Come right out and declare it."

If he was daring her to come out and say how she felt about him, she wasn't feeling up to the challenge. Not in a stuffy convention center with too many people around and colorful yarn swirling everywhere in her periphery, and certainly not on an empty stomach. She took a deep breath.

"Right now, I want to go sit down outside and wait for lunch while you entertain your date for the day."

She turned and took two steps before Mike stepped in front of her. "Are you okay?"

Hadley nodded. "I'm fine. I just need fresh air and a seat until lunch."

Mike scrutinized her face for a moment and finally nodded. "Good. I couldn't enjoy yarn gazing with your grandmother if everything wasn't okay with you."

"Everything's fine," Hadley said.

Mike reached for her hand. "Actually, it isn't."

"I'm just hot. It's hot in here and there are a lot of people."

"What I mean is that I want to talk about that kiss last night."

Hadley tugged her hand loose from his. "We already did."

"We were lying to each other and maybe ourselves," Mike said. "You claimed it meant nothing to you, and I sure hope that isn't true. Because it meant something very important to me. It made me realize it's time to tell you I love you, Hadley. Whether you want to hear it or not, whether or not you feel the same way about me."

It was everything she'd hoped for but also a complete source of panic, like a dream home built on the edge of a steep cliff. If Mike loved her so much that he lost control and blurted it out at a textile convention surrounded by knitters and old ladies, then they were in real trouble. First of all, there was no way to be sure Mike was right about his feelings. Secondly, one of them had to remain in control or their lives would speed out of control. Again.

"No, you don't," Hadley said. "You don't love me. You're just swept up in the emotions of having a baby."

"I love you, Hadley. It came out of nowhere, but it's not going anywhere."

Hadley held up a hand as if she were stopping traffic. "You need to keep your feelings under control."

"Do I?" Mike asked. "How about you?"

"Me? I'm not the one acting like one little kiss changed my life."

"Oh, please," Grandma Penny said. Hadley wondered how much of the conversation her grandma had heard. Wasn't she looking at yarn? "Don't you know a good thing when you see it?" Grandma Penny demanded.

Hadley mustered all her logic and courage and strength and looked from her grandmother to Mike. "We have a plan. Friendly cooperation as we raise a daughter together.

Kissing and declarations of love weren't part of our relationship before we got pregnant, and there's no reason they should be now."

She started to walk away, but then she stopped and turned. "Don't keep Grandma Penny on her feet too long. Her ankles will swell."

With that last bit of practicality, Hadley swept out of the convention hall and called her sister for a ride.

CHAPTER TWENTY

MIKE DIDN'T CALL Hadley after the yarn event. He let an entire day go by without making an attempt to see her, even though he couldn't stop replaying their conversation in the Great Island Hotel's convention center. He'd told her he loved her and she told him he was wrong. He'd taken the ultimate risk and bared his heart to her.

She walked away.

But she hadn't said she didn't love him. And that fact kept him on the practical plan he'd begun weeks earlier.

When he advertised his boat in the online marketplace, absolutely nothing had happened for three days. He'd almost given up, certain that the picture he'd taken of the boat wasn't a flattering one. And then the phone calls had started. Two sent up red flags that said *SCAMMER* in flashing letters, one guy offered to trade him a used dump truck and one person would only buy if he could deliver the boat to Texas. *Texas*. He'd pulled the ad after a few more days, but then gotten a surprise phone call from someone who seemed like a real person and legitimate buyer. All he had to do was get *Flounder* across to the mainland after six o'clock when the buyer could meet him at the dock for a test drive, and then finalize the deal and grab a ferry back to Christmas Island.

Timing was going to be everything, but the buyer hadn't tried to haggle and offered cash. Mike left his bike shop, skipped dinner and jogged to the marina. He turned on the bilge fan, spent five minutes untying the lines and bringing in the fenders, and then turned the key.

Nothing but a clicking sound.

"No, no, no," he said. "This is the last thing I'm ever going to ask of you."

He tried again. Opened the engine hatch. Kicked it closed. Ran his hands through his hair as he looked at the evening sky and then tried the key again.

"Sounds like you've got a dead battery."

Mike glanced up and found Bertie the postmaster watching him from two boats down.

Bertie was an avid fisherman, one of the reasons his friends on the island were happy for him that he'd finally reached retirement age.

"Afraid you're right," Mike said. He sat on the sidewall of his boat. His evening was not going as planned, and it was obvious that *Flounder* would remain in his possession for at least another day.

"I have a battery jumper box," Bertie said.

Mike felt tension slide off his shoulders. "Really?"

Bertie nodded. "I have a short somewhere in my wiring, and sometimes it drains the battery. I don't want to be out there on the lake and get caught, so I keep a jumper box charged. Used it twice last season. I'll bring it over."

"Thank you," Mike said.

Bertie opened a hatch on his boat that was considerably nicer than Mike's. He'd suspected the postmaster job was a better financial gig than a summer bicycle rental. Looking at Bertie's boat reminded him that there were trade-offs. Spending the day sorting mail and packages wasn't as fun as renting bikes and being the master of your own time schedule, but it clearly had its perks.

"My grandkids are coming in a few minutes for a sunset cruise," Bertie said as he carried his jumper box onto Mike's boat. "So you're in luck. Where are you headed this evening?"

"Mainland," Mike said. "I'm meeting a buyer interested in my boat."

"You're parting with *Flounder*?"

Mike nodded. "It's time."

Bertie paused and gave Mike a serious look. "I see." He hooked up the jumper box to Mike's battery and gave Mike the thumbs-up to try starting the boat. Mike turned the key, and the engine turned over and came to life.

"Never fails," Bertie said.

"Thanks. You're a lifesaver," Mike said.

"You've helped me out plenty of times. Remember when you dug the mail truck out of a ditch?" Bertie asked.

Mike laughed. "Was it only once?"

"I think it was three times, at least it seems like it. I sure won't miss trying to haul mail on snowy island roads even though, of course, I'm in the office most of the time." Bertie wound up the cables on his jumper box and tucked it under his arm. "Have you given the job any more thought?"

"Plenty," Mike said.

"It comes with health care and the wonderful smell of cardboard and envelope glue. Best job in the world."

"Except for retirement, maybe," Mike said with a grin. "That looks like a great gig."

"I'm just about to test that theory. You should know that the job is yours for the asking. The boss from the mainland liked you when we met up last week, and you're our only applicant still in the running. You let me know what you decide."

Mike nodded. "I will. And I appreciate the offer, but there's someone else I have to include in the decision."

"You wouldn't happen to be buying an engagement ring with your boat money, would you?" Bertie asked.

Mike cocked his head. "What makes you guess that?"

Of course, the idea was part of his plan from the first day he'd advertised his boat. Back then, he'd thought it was the missing link, the reason Hadley had said no to his empty-handed proposals.

He knew better now. At least he hoped so. He'd given her plenty to think about when he'd told her he loved her. She'd run away, but he hoped when she went home and drew up a neat list of pros and cons to letting Mike love her, she'd find a lot more items in the pro column.

Bertie laughed and shook his head. "It's none of my business, but I've seen a lot of advertisements in the mail for Gilbert's Jewelers on the mainland. They send out glossy flyers, and I've often thought I'd shop there if I had something really special to buy."

"Thanks," Mike said. "For everything."

He took out his phone and made a note of the store Bertie had recommended, and then he backed *Flounder* out of its slip for the last time. If things went according to plan, he'd be coming home on the Christmas Island ferry in a few hours with money in his pocket. He had only four days left until he and Hadley turned thirty, and he still had a lot to figure out.

HADLEY SAT ON a velvet loveseat in the Victorian parlor of the island mansion everyone affectionately called The Winter Palace. She had a bridal magazine open in her lap and a virgin cocktail in one hand. Camille sat in a floral damask covered recliner across from her with her feet up and her eyes closed.

"I'm trying to picture the whole thing," Camille said, "and then I'm going to decide which elements I'll copy for my wedding."

"You don't want to copy your sister's wedding?" Hadley asked. "I thought it was beautiful the way Chloe had a Christmas wedding with all the red and green touches."

Camille grinned but kept her eyes closed. "Maybe a bit cliché for someone who grew up on Christmas Island."

"Or maybe it's perfect," Hadley said. "Do you think you should just give in to it and go with what feels right?"

Camille opened her eyes. "Is there something you're not telling me?"

Hadley flipped the bridal magazine closed and took a long sip of her fruity drink. "I have hormones swirling everywhere, so talking about Christmas and weddings and flowers and music is playing with fire. I could start laughing or weeping at pretty much any moment."

Camille laughed. "I grew up with Chloe, so I'm immune to big emotional displays. Not as immune as Cara, but close."

"Chloe is sweet and happy," Hadley said. "She snagged a handsome doctor who hates boats but somehow ended up at the island clinic, anyway. You don't even have to be a fairy-tale romantic to see that was fate."

Rebecca came into the room with a tray of cheese, crackers and cookies. "You want to talk about a twist of fate? A girl like me who grew up homeless gets to live in this fabulous house."

"You deserve it. You helped Flora Winter save her fortune."

Rebecca put the tray of food on a low table and sat on the loveseat next to Hadley. "Sometimes I wake up in the middle of the night with that old familiar fear that I don't know where I am or where I'm going next."

"And then you turn on the light in your gorgeous bedroom and think, oh, wait, I'm Christmas Island royalty now," Camille said.

Rebecca laughed and made a little stack of cheese and crackers. "You Candy Girls are royalty. I'm just marrying into the title."

Hadley tilted her head to the side. "Maybe I should have grabbed one of the May brothers when I had the chance. If I'd known they were going to be millionaires and inherit the

Winter Palace, I would have at least gotten my sister to try to marry one of them."

"They're taken," Camille said with a smile. "And what are you complaining about? You're having a baby with a man who would jump in front of a speeding train for you."

"Or run barefoot over hot coals," Rebecca added.

"Give you his last dollar and plunge your toilet if necessary," Camille said.

Rebecca shook her head. "Those examples went in a different direction."

"Fine," Camille said on a long exhale. "Mike's a nice guy, which we all know, but the point we were trying to make is that—"

"Is that we're here to talk about Rebecca and Griffin's wedding and nail down the details," Hadley said. She picked up a tablet and swiped it to bring the screen to life. "I downloaded a template to keep track of wedding details, and there's also a handy checklist of frequently overlooked things. Maybe we should start with that just to make sure we're not forgetting anything and then we'll go systematically through the timetable and spreadsheet."

If she didn't start talking about practical

and logistical matters pertaining to the wedding of her friend and her boss, Hadley was afraid she was going to dwell on the fact that Mike had told her he loved her and she had told him he was mistaken. Not only would she dwell on it, but she might say the words aloud and that would ruin the girls' night of planning.

He'd let day four slip past without sending four flowers or four doughnuts or hiring a barbershop quartet or anything. She'd waited all day and finally concluded that he'd backed away after his failed declaration of love. Her pillow was still damp from her tears the next morning when she'd dragged herself out of bed. Driving him away was the last thing she wanted. Telling him they weren't in love was the safest way to save their relationship and manage all the changes coming at them like a speedboat.

When he'd texted to ask her to dinner, she'd almost ignored his message in favor of time and space, but she had plans with Rebecca and Camille and, therefore, a solid and logical reason to turn down the man she'd walked away from two days earlier.

"Every girl loves a timetable and spreadsheet," Camille said as she reached for the bridal magazine in Hadley's lap. "But first, can we gush over wedding cakes for a few minutes? There's a big section in here that's all about fondant and gum-paste flowers, and it's calling my name."

The doorbell rang, and Rebecca hopped up. "I hope it's not a tourist thinking this is a bed-and-breakfast. That's happened twice so far this summer, and Griffin is thinking of putting up a sign directing everyone to the Holiday Hotel."

She left and came back in just a moment with Mike who carried three white boxes.

"I have three different kinds of cookies for three of my favorite ladies," he announced cheerfully. Hadley sucked in a breath. Had Mike decided to forget about telling her he loved her? Just push it aside? Of course, that was what she wanted, but part of her wondered how he could be so casual about it. He was making it look easy to pretend they were just friends and would-be parents. Did that mean he didn't care? Maybe she was the fool, not him. And she was right in telling him he didn't love her.

"How did you know we were having a party?" Camille asked.

"Hadley turned me down for a dinner date tonight and Maddox told me you were having a wedding-planning meeting. I thought you could use a treat."

"We could have rescheduled if you had a date," Rebecca said, her expression serious as she glanced from Hadley to Mike. Hadley gave her a tiny headshake.

"Not an actual date," Hadley said. "More a mile marker on the way to the fantastic age of thirty."

"Three more days," Mike said. "Which calls for a celebration."

"I hope you'll remember this in a few years when we turn thirty," Camille said, gesturing between herself and Rebecca.

Mike shook his head. "Sorry, this is a private countdown with Hadley because we share a birthday."

And a pact, Hadley thought. If he invoked the pact again, it would be ridiculous but almost welcome. Agreeing to marry him for a practical reason—before he'd somehow fallen into the belief he loved her—would have been easier to navigate and manage. Maybe she should have said yes back then, and she wouldn't be in this situation now.

"Want to stay and snack with us?" Hadley offered.

"I'm not here to intrude on your girl time," he said. "I just wanted to let Hadley know I was thinking of her as always."

With a smile aimed straight at Hadley, Mike put the boxes on the coffee table and then showed himself out.

"It's statistically unlikely for two people living on an island with a very low population to have exactly the same birthday," Rebecca said thoughtfully as she opened one of the boxes. Inside was a big round cookie, and she broke a piece off. "You two are something special."

"We're not," Hadley said. "We're two people tied together by a birthday, a baby and the fact that my grandmother is in love with him."

"Those are compelling reasons," Camille said. "You should be glad Mike commemorated the three day mark with cookies instead of a third proposal."

"I am glad," Hadley said. But then she pictured Mike driving back to his lonely apartment over the bike rental. Was that really going to be the way they lived? Her staining her pillowcase with tears and Mike trying to prove his love with flowers and yarn conventions and daisy necklaces and oversized cookies? Would she and Mike dance at Rebecca and Griffin's wedding and then go to their separate houses without even a goodnight kiss?

CHAPTER TWENTY-ONE

THE MAY BROTHERS had offered Hadley the day off in honor of her birthday, but she'd declined. If she had all day to herself, she'd spend it thinking about how to *not* think about how she was entering her thirties with a baby on board and a life that was changing every day. Those thoughts made her world feel out of control, but managing the front desk at the Holiday Hotel made her feel more like her organized self.

She needed that more than she cared to admit. Ever since Mike's admission he loved her, nothing had been under her control.

Including her calendar. She'd agreed to a birthday dinner with Mike in the hotel restaurant where everything was familiar and orderly. She knew how many tables and chairs were arranged in the room and the location of every light switch and fire extinguisher. She could get through a birthday dinner, even if it was a milestone.

An hour into Hadley's shift at the front desk, Wendy stopped by with her three kids and Grandma Penny to bring birthday cupcakes and a gift. Hadley got hugs from her nieces and nephew, ate a cupcake and opened the package from her sister, which contained a book from her favorite mystery author, a new tube of lipstick in her favorite shade, lavender bath bombs and a box of truffles.

Macey told her the contents of the package before she opened it, but Hadley was at least surprised by the color of the bath bombs. It was a nice present.

"I made something special for you," Grandma Penny said. She held out a gift bag with tissue paper artfully sticking out the top.

Hadley pulled away the paper and found an elegant lacy wrap made from ivory yarn with a hint of glitter. "Wow," she said. "It's beautiful. Thank you."

"It'll dress up any outfit," her grandmother said. "And it's light enough for summer nights when you need to keep off the chill and look pretty."

"I'll wear it to dinner with Mike tonight," she said. "We're celebrating our birthdays together."

"You two are going to have lots of things

to celebrate together," Grandma Penny said. Hadley knew it wasn't just the wisdom of age talking. She and Mike would have every one of their daughter's birthdays to celebrate in addition to all the other milestones. First lost tooth, first day of school, holidays, driver's license, graduation, her wedding someday and then…grandchildren?

This child would tie her life to Mike's in too many ways to count.

A family came through the front doors with luggage, and Hadley's visitors left. As she checked in the hotel guests, she noticed the doors of the dining room closing. The restaurant almost never closed during tourist season. She could only remember one or two times when the cook was sick and their usual part-time help couldn't come in. Maddox came down the hotel stairs as she was handing over keys and giving the guests their welcome packet.

"Is the restaurant closing?" she asked Maddox. "I should let our guests know if dinner there isn't an option."

"It will be open for dinner as usual at six," Maddox said. He smiled affably at the guests as they took their keys and headed down the hall to their rooms.

"So what's up?" Hadley asked.

"We're stripping and waxing the floor," Maddox said. "Nasty stuff, that stripper. I didn't want the fumes getting out here in the lobby where you and guests would have to smell them."

"We're stripping and waxing during tourist season?" Hadley asked.

Maddox looked away for a moment and then focused back on Hadley. "I didn't want to bother you with this, but our new server tried to help clean yesterday and she used the wrong cleaning fluid. You should see the mess it made of the floors. Griffin thought the only way to fix it was to start over. It'll only take a few hours, and no one will even know it happened."

Hadley's shoulders sank. If she'd been at her usual job in the restaurant or paying closer attention to the summer help, this wouldn't have happened.

"Don't worry about it," Maddox said. "No harm done. Just make sure those doors stay closed." He walked over and locked the doors for good measure.

Throughout the day, Hadley heard tables being moved and voices in the restaurant beyond the locked doors, and each scrape or bit of conversation reminded her of the ripple effects of her pregnancy and the changes it brought. She was only on phase one of that series of events.

When the last guest checked in and she closed the drawer at the front desk, Hadley ducked into the small lobby restroom to change into one of the maternity dresses she'd borrowed from her sister. She hadn't worn it yet because it was too fancy for every day. Her thirtieth birthday seemed to warrant a floral dress with a flattering square neck and a mid-calf length skirt with a flounce. With a pair of sandals, the dress was perfect for a summer night.

Hadley took the ivory shawl with its woven-in sparkle and draped it over her shoulders.

When she emerged from the restroom, Mike was sitting in a lobby chair, one leg crossed over the other. He wore a collared shirt and a dark blue jacket, and he held a bouquet of pink roses. He stood as soon as he saw her.

"Happy birthday," he said as he crossed the lobby. He handed her the flowers and kissed her cheek.

"Don't tell me there are thirty flowers in that bouquet," Hadley said.

Mike shook his head. "I have no idea how many there are. There's no reason to continue the countdown because…we're here."

Hadley let out a long breath. "We made it to thirty."

"Do you think it's old age causing this uncomfortable feeling in my stomach?"

Hadley laughed. "I feel the same way, but maybe we're both just hungry."

Mike studied her for a moment and she realized his familiar face wasn't just the boy she'd grown up with. He was the man she wanted to spend the rest of her life with.

The restaurant doors opened from the other side and Mike took her hand. "Are we ready to do this thirtieth birthday thing?"

"Mike, I…"

"Yes?"

"I'm just glad we're doing it together."

He smiled. "That was the plan all along."

They walked into the restaurant and Hadley gasped. Streamers dangled from the ceiling and draped across the windows. Balloons floated in bunches and bounced across the floor. A massive Happy 30th Birthday sign hung in front of the bar, and there were dozens of family and friends waiting with big goofy grins on their faces.

"One. Two. Three. Happy birthday, Hadley and Mike!" everyone shouted.

Grandma Penny added, "And many more," and everyone laughed.

Hadley took a deep breath and smiled. So the room was closed not for a waxing but to prepare for a party.

"Did you know about this?" she whispered to Mike.

He shook his head and his expression told her he was as surprised as she was. Her sister came up to her and wrapped an arm around her shoulders. "I'm sorry," she said, "I know you hate surprise parties, but I got outvoted by at least half of the island. Having two of the most-liked islanders turning thirty on the same day was too much to resist."

"Everyone loves Mike because he takes care of people," Hadley said.

"That's not why everyone loves him," Wendy said. "There's a lot more to it as you well know."

Something shifted in the air and a streamer brushed Hadley's cheek. She loved Mike be-cause…because he was sweet and funny and he accepted people exactly as they were. He hadn't minded when she'd rearranged all his bins of spare parts in his bike shop, even though he'd confessed later that it took him a year to get used to it. He sent her flowers on her mother's birthday because he knew she'd be missing her. He took his shoes off without being asked and always paused whatever show they were streaming when she opened her mouth to say anything.

He knew what she liked and disliked. Bought her a new calendar with a matching daybook every year for Christmas. Rode first down muddy hills or walked through spiderwebs and knocked them down for her. Showed her he cared about her in large and small ways.

She turned to him and smiled. "Happy birthday."

Mike leaned in and his lips brushed her ear. "Now I'm really glad we're suffering through surprise balloons and cake together."

"There's no one else I'd rather tough it out with," she said.

"Same." Mike gripped her hand. "Let's make a circuit of the room and then sit down and order food before we both get too hungry and just dive into the cake."

Hand in hand, they walked around the room where they greeted Camille and Cara Peterson and their parents; Shirley from the chamber of commerce and her husband; the author Miranda Mitchell; Violet Brookstone and her brother, Ryan, who happened to be visiting; Jordan Frome who worked at the Great Island Hotel; Bertie the postmaster; the May brothers; Grandma Penny and her friend Mary-Anna; the nurse from the island clinic; and at least a dozen more locals. As they walked from table to table, Hadley realized that she and Mike were a pair. Not just because of their longstanding friendship, their shared birthday or even their baby. They belonged together. She loved him. His hand gripped hers and never let up. Was he drawing support from her as well? Did he need her like she needed him?

Did he love her as much as she loved him? She glanced over and caught him looking at her and there was no mistaking the expression in his eyes.

It was time to take a chance.

MIKE DIDN'T KNOW what was happening, but Hadley was pulling him to the center of the room where she held up a hand, signaling for attention. It was the most un-Hadley thing to do. She didn't like the limelight, but whatever she planned to say, she was dragging him along for the ride.

Not that he objected. He'd go anywhere she was going. They were on the same journey and always had been.

"Thank you," Hadley said when the entire crowd had quieted down to focus on her. Mike was certainly focused. Hadley didn't do spontaneous or off the cuff, but she appeared to be about to.

"Mike and I truly appreciate all of you being here to celebrate our thirtieth birthdays, and I want you all to know I'll be returning the favor because you know I have a spreadsheet that includes nearly every one of your birthdays."

People in the crowd laughed, but Mike could barely manage a smile. There was something huge going on here. He felt as if he'd parted his bedroom curtains just before dawn and at any moment the sun would flood the room with light.

"In all seriousness, I really appreciate having this chance to be with all my friends and family and have you all here for me to say something that's been on my mind for a long time. Growing up and living on an island, you get to know a lot about your fellow residents, sometimes more than you want to."

Mike felt the dawn spreading in his chest, but he could barely breathe. Hadley still held his hand and she stood in the middle of the familiar restaurant in her pretty flowered dress cascading over her baby bump. His baby. He wanted to fold her into his arms and have her all to himself, pretending there weren't dozens of other people in the room. Hadley was his. She'd always been.

"And sometimes, you think you know everything about a person but then you find out you've been missing something." She turned to Mike and paused, and he felt the weight of dozens of eyes on him.

"If this is about the post-office-job thing," he said, "I thought we could figure out finances and schedules together somehow without changing everything. So I withdrew my application."

"I know." Hadley smiled.

"How?"

"Bertie told me when I picked up a package yesterday. But it's not about that. Or the fact that you sold your boat without telling me. I don't have to know everything or be in charge of everything."

"You don't?"

She shook her head.

"Did this new wisdom come with your thirtieth birthday?" Mike asked.

Hadley laughed. "I think it comes from learning something about myself. And about us."

Mike wanted to take a moment to savor that unexpected announcement, but instead he put his left hand in his pocket and felt for the ring that was wrapped in a pink velvet pouch. Was this the time? Should he?

Hadley turned back to the birthday crowd. "I thought I knew all about Mike Martin right down to the brand of his favorite socks, but I didn't know the most important thing. That I was in love with him and have been for a long time."

Mike's jaw dropped. His eyes burned. His throat thickened. His heart pounded.

Someone in the crowd said woo-hoo and there was a lot of applause, but he could barely form the question he thirsted to ask.

"You love me?"

"Yes," Hadley said. "And telling you right now in front of everyone I know is the scariest thing I've ever done, but I don't want to wait any longer."

"You're not getting any younger," Shirley called from her table and a lot of people laughed.

"She's right," Hadley said. "You've asked me to marry you twice, so—"

"Twice?" someone in the crowd repeated.

"So I think you obviously don't hate the idea of being married to me," she said.

"Hadley, what are you saying?"

"I'm asking you to—"

"I love you," Mike blurted out. "I'm so in love with you I can't breathe right now, and you might have to kiss me to bring me back to life."

"Is that what you want?"

"After you finish what you were asking me," he said.

She turned to him and took both his hands. "Mike Martin, will you marry me?"

In answer, Mike fumbled in his pocket, pulled out the ring and got down on one knee.

"Third time's a charm," Grandma Penny said. "And I've got your honeymoon tickets to the Bahamas ready to go."

He took Hadley's ring finger and slid the small diamond onto it. "Technically, I asked you first, twice, but the answer is still yes."

Hadley pulled him to his feet and kissed

him while applause erupted around them and a very cheerful medley combining "Happy Birthday" and the "Wedding March" came from the piano. Mike glanced over and saw Rebecca Browne at the keyboard, his friends Griffin and Maddox, Hadley's family that would now officially be his, too, and all their island friends. His heart still raced, but the weight was lifted, and he took a huge breath for what felt like the first time.

"Happy birthday," Hadley said as she let tears stream down her face. "I never would have thought we'd honor the birthday pact like this, but here we are."

"You didn't expect to be five months pregnant and crazy in love with me?" Mike asked. "I totally predicted that."

"And you had a ring in your pocket," Hadley said. "Were you going to ask me again tonight?"

"No," Mike said. His smile was so broad it almost hurt. "I was going to beg you, and I was going to get it right this time by saying the most important thing first."

"Please?"

He shook his head, laughing. Then he sobered and said, "I love you. I love you, Hadley, and I can't wait to spend the rest of my life with you."

"And our baby."

"And the rest of our children," he said. "I've got a huge fleet of bikes just waiting for riders."

Hadley laughed. "Let's start with one and see where life takes us."

Mike kissed her hand. "As long as I'm with you."

* * * * *

Don't miss the next book in Amie Denman's Return To Christmas Island miniseries, coming August 2023 from Harlequin Heartwarming.

Get 4 FREE REWARDS!

We'll send you 2 FREE Books plus 2 FREE Mystery Gifts.

FREE Value Over **$20**

Both the **Love Inspired®** and **Love Inspired® Suspense** series feature compelling novels filled with inspirational romance, faith, forgiveness and hope.

COUNTRY LEGACY COLLECTION

19 FREE BOOKS IN ALL!

Cowboys, adventure and romance await you in this new collection! Enjoy superb reading all year long with books by bestselling authors like Diana Palmer, Sasha Summers and Marie Ferrarella!

COMING NEXT MONTH FROM

HARLEQUIN
HEARTWARMING

#459 THE COWBOY NEXT DOOR
The Fortunes of Prospect • by Cheryl Harper

Sarah Hearst isn't sure what to think of her inherited fishing lodge in Colorado, but it's important to Wes Armstrong and his family's ranch. Will he convince her to sell or lose his heart in the process?

#460 HER SURPRISE HOMETOWN MATCH
The Golden Matchmakers Club • by Tara Randel

Town darling Juliette Bishop feels like a fraud after a good deed is misinterpreted—and she can't let anyone find out the truth. But volunteering with Ty Pendergrass teaches her a few things about letting her guard down...

#461 THE NAVY DAD'S RETURN
Big Sky Navy Heroes • by Julianna Morris

When widower Wyatt returns home with his young daughter, he hires Katrina, his former schoolmate, as a nanny. Working on a ranch isn't without its challenges—but it's his growing feelings for Katrina that are the biggest challenge of all.

#462 HIS WYOMING REDEMPTION
by Trish Milburn

Sheriff Angie Lee believes that people should be judged on what they do in the present—not the past. But when former bad boy Eric Novak returns to Jade Valley, he has her thinking about the future...

YOU CAN FIND MORE INFORMATION ON UPCOMING HARLEQUIN TITLES,
FREE EXCERPTS AND MORE AT HARLEQUIN.COM.

HWCNM0123

HARLEQUIN
PLUS

Try the best multimedia
subscription service for romance
readers like you!

Read, Watch and Play.

Experience the easiest way to get
the romance content you crave.

Start your **FREE TRIAL** at
<u>www.harlequinplus.com/freetrial</u>.